THIEF OF HEARTS

"Are you a thief, Crystal Braden? And if so, are you after my cash or my heart?"

"I'm not—"

"No matter. They both are yours."

His hands grasped her narrow waist and before she could protest, he swung her out of the saddle and eased her to the ground. Light as the air, she fairly floated to a stand in front of him.

The roan shifted nervously. Not Conn and, to his great pleasure, not Crystal.

Her hands rested on his shirt. She lifted thick black lashes and looked at him with eyes as deep as the world. He pulled her close and kissed her. Soft and sweet he made it, tempting them both, and then he smiled.

"You've caught me, lass. It's a scandalous thing you've done, lassoing a man like that. There's no way out for either of us. We'll have to be wed."

Other *Leisure* books by Evelyn Rogers:
THE FOREVER BRIDE
WICKED

BETRAYAL

Evelyn Rogers

LEISURE BOOKS  NEW YORK CITY

To the best RWA chapter
a writer could have:
San Antonio Romance Authors.
Thanks, SARA, for keeping writing fun.

A LEISURE BOOK®

June 1997

Published by

Dorchester Publishing Co., Inc.
276 Fifth Avenue
New York, NY 10001

Printed in the United States of America.

BETRAYAL

Prologue

Bushwhack Ranch
Kerr County, Texas
April 11, 1869

The old man had to die faster. Maybe what he needed was some help.

Royce grinned to himself. At twenty-six, he'd never killed a man before. In some parts of Texas that was a real shortcoming. Besides, killing was an experience he might enjoy.

And once Papa got over his grumbling, he would be pleased.

If Royce decided to tell him.

The woman stirred in his arms. She stood pressed against him in the darkened room, her skirts bunched around her waist, her naked hips and thighs pressed against his trousers.

Absentmindedly he stroked her buttocks and made his plans. The intended victim lay sleeping peacefully in another part of the ranch house. There was no one else about—just him, the old man, and the woman. All Royce had to do was go to his room, tiptoe beside the bed and . . . and what? Shoot him? Too loud, too messy, and besides, he'd left his gun outside.

This took some thought, but the woman wouldn't let him be.

"*Escarcho,*" she whispered against his neck. "Do you not want your Graciela tonight?"

He pinched her bottom. "Hush, Graceless. I'm thinking."

"With the mind?" She reached between his legs and put her expert fingers to work. "Or with *sus cojones*?"

He squeezed her bottom and pictured his hands around the old man's neck.

"You hurt me tonight," she said.

He'd hurt her on other nights, too; he paid her protest no mind except to keep squeezing. He grew hard from the images of what he must do. And from the workings of her fingers. Should he give it to her now? Or afterwards?

Afterwards. When he could concentrate.

Graceless was a woman who took his full attention. The name didn't suit. She wasn't graceless, but he liked calling her so. It put her in her place. And it bothered her. Got her aroused, which was the way he liked her.

Escarcho, she called him—Mexican sweet talk for something good, something she liked. Something she couldn't get enough of. Someday he'd ask her exactly what it meant.

Graciela was a hot one, dark-skinned with high cheekbones that showed the Indian blood in her. She liked him crossing the creek at night and slipping into the ranch house when no one was watching. He liked it, too. No need for the whole county to know he was poking his neighbor's serving woman.

Trouble was, right now all he could think of was a gray, scrawny neck and an old man who needed to die. He'd come here tonight hoping to hear the fool had breathed his last. Instead, Graceless said he grew stronger, his sleep less troubled, and all because of a letter his lawyer had brought today from town. She claimed not to know who wrote it or what it said, but she probably lied.

The woman nibbled at his lips. Royce shifted a hand between her legs and gave her something to think about. She moaned. He pulled away.

"Stay here. I'll be back."

"No," she whined.

"Don't be fretting. I said I'd be back."

"But the señor—"

"He won't know I'm around. Now you strip naked and get on the bed. I won't be long."

He left her room, closing the door firmly behind him, eased through the kitchen and made his way down the long hallway that led to the old man's room. He had a bigger room upstairs on the second floor, but since taking ill, he'd moved down to make it easier on Graceless.

The old man's raspy breathing could be heard all the way out in the hall. Royce moved cautiously into the room. A guttering bedside oil lamp cast ghostly shadows across the old man's face, white as the pillow beneath him, yet there seemed to be a trace of color to his cheeks.

Royce moved closer. Graciela had spoken the truth. Damned if he didn't look better, like he might not give in to the weak heart that had him at death's door. Even his breathing, raspy though it was, sounded stronger. His gnarled hand gripped the letter against the covers. Royce pulled it free and read it fast.

He felt a rush of anger, of panic, and then a surprising sense of exultation. Good thing he'd crossed the creek this moonless night. He'd been right. The old man had to die right away. He'd got himself into this predicament, stirring things up with a letter of his own. He deserved what he would get.

The fool stirred. "Who's there? That you, boy? Home already?"

Royce smiled down into a pair of pale gray eyes, fluttering and blinking, adjusting to the light.

"No, sir," he said, being polite the way he'd been raised. "You're dreaming. It's just me. Come to make sure you're all right." He waved the letter. "Looks like you got some good news."

The old man settled back against the bed. "Seems like it." He grabbed for the letter. Royce dropped it on the covers out of reach.

An idea occurred to him. "Let me get the pillow for you first. Make you comfortable so you can read better."

"You're a good man, Royce."

"The Lord knows I try to be."

He took the pillow from under the old man's head, then lowered it, watching the pale gray eyes, the trust and then the puzzlement in their depths, and last of all the fear. Fear satisfied him the most. He did the deed fast, the way he'd scanned the letter, holding the pillow tight against the tired face, enjoying the exultation, thinking that for a sick old buzzard, the man sure could put up a powerful fight.

But not for long. At last he lay still, the struggle gone out of him, along with the breath.

Royce's blood pounded, and the taste of death lay sweet on his tongue. Damn, but this was better than sex. Slowly, almost lovingly, he put the pillow back in place beneath the lax head, then turned. Graciela stood in the door, naked the way he'd told her, a blanket pressed against brown skin, hiding her dark-tipped breasts, covering her woman's hair.

Killing might be better than sex, Royce thought with a grin, but sex was a close second.

"Does the señor rest?" she asked.

"He'll be doing just that for a long time." Glancing at the letter on the bed, Royce unbuckled his belt. "A long, long time."

She came deeper into the room, her black eyes

round, her thick lips parted. She stood beside him close to the bed and stared down at the still figure.

"No," she whispered. "No." Her eyes cut to Royce. "What have you done?"

"I found him like this."

Her gaze narrowed, sharp as a Mexican blade. She didn't believe him. Little he cared.

"His time was overdue," Royce said, knowing he needed to leave, to report the letter to Papa as soon as he could.

But there was still Graciela. With all the hell that would break loose around here when day came, there was no telling when he could poke her again.

He jerked the blanket from her hands and tossed it on the rug. "Get down," he ordered. "On your knees."

"Madre de Dios."

"We can do it on the bed, if you'd like. There's room."

She gasped and made the sign of the cross. He grabbed her wrist and twisted until she fell to her knees. His trousers dropped. "Get that sweet little tongue of yours to working, Graceless. I'm ready to celebrate."

Chapter One

San Antonio
April 14, 1869

Conn O'Brien fell in love the moment he saw the woman across the saloon. He'd never seen her before, had no idea who she was, but that one look had a kick stronger than the whiskey he'd been drinking.

He grinned. The odds were better than even that he'd found the woman of his dreams.

Pretty and fair she was in a simple green dress, nothing like the gaudy would-be finery of the other women who walked around the tables. She sat against the wall, looking bold and fragile at the same time, and very much alone. When their eyes met, bells rang. She glanced away, but something about her expression said she heard them, too.

He upped the odds. She was the one, a sure thing. For the first time in years peace settled in his heart. For all his gambling ways, he was not a totally impulsive man. He'd best introduce himself before asking for her hand.

He'd barely cleared the chair when a beer bottle came out of nowhere aimed straight for his head.

"Damnation," he muttered.

Much as he wanted to get to the woman, the bottle took precedence. He ducked and heard a crash somewhere behind him. Nearby a table upended, cards and coins flying.

Again he let loose with a curse. He must be slipping. For the past half hour he'd been passing time in what used to be his favorite watering hole, solemnly minding his own business, thinking through the strange twists his life had taken and pondering the days ahead, and suddenly all hell erupted.

Worse, a golden-haired beauty stole unnoticed into the Alamo Arms. He might miss an occasional fight, but he usually noticed blondes.

With bottles and bodies filling the air, he grabbed his hat and made once again for the corner where she'd been sitting. He lost her for a minute, then saw that she'd tucked herself beneath her table clear of the combatants. Smart woman, as well as comely.

He dropped crosslegged on the floor beside her and tipped his hat. "Good evening," he said.

She jumped, as if a two-headed dog had settled

at her side and not the man she'd been waiting for all her life.

"Oh, my," she said, but she didn't scream or smack him or even edge away. He took it as a good sign.

Beneath him he felt the vibrations of the fray, but he was too lost in the presence of femininity to pay anything else much mind, too glad to be thinking about someone other than his own troubled self.

Brown eyes deep enough to swim in stared at him. He stared right back. Up close, she looked even better than at a distance. Honey-blond hair framed a delicate face, then curled softly against slender shoulders. Her skin had a tawny, healthy glow; her lips were full, her eyes thick-lashed. Best he could tell from the way her muslin gown fit, she was slender all the way down, but not necessarily in every place.

Conn knew horses and women. He was looking at prime stock. In truth, she looked as out of place as a thoroughbred in a pack of plugs. But she didn't look skittish; she didn't look afraid, just kind of lost and stunned by what was happening to her.

Better and better, he thought. A woman to take for a wife.

His late mother had always sworn by the power of fate. And a man must never dispute a mother's belief.

"Are you all right?" he shouted over the rising din.

She opened her mouth to speak, then snapped it closed, settling for a mute nod.

A chair flew over the table and splintered against the wall behind them. Both ducked. During his years in New York, he'd enjoyed attending an occasional bout of professional fisticuffs. The Arms, having lost the elegance he remembered from before the war, was offering a brawl.

The floor shook ever harder, and the sound of breaking glass increased. Conn glanced at his damsel in distress. Their eyes met, and once again he heard bells. For all his worry about this long-delayed return, it was good to be back in Texas.

Good? No, it was splendid. The shadows that had darkened his thoughts for so long began to lighten.

"She's my woman," a coarse voice yelled from somewhere in the melee. "I'll do with her what I damned well please."

"You sorry son of a—"

The reply was lost in another crash. A body flew over the table protecting Conn and his companion, landing with a thud on the floor close by. There were clouds of dust and cursing the like of which he hadn't heard since his army days.

The woman took it the way she'd taken everything else. Oh, he could see a trace of concern in her big brown eyes—she was sensible, after all—but he also saw a flash of anger, as if she'd like to swab the culprit's mouth with a handful of her strongest lye soap.

Prime, Conn thought again. He'd definitely fallen in love.

"Had enough?" he asked, gesturing toward the pair of swinging doors and the silvered darkness that lay beyond.

He didn't have to do a lot of explaining. What he had to do was scramble to his feet to keep up as she dashed into the moonlit night. Graceful, he added to her other charms, sprinting like that when she was still in a crouch.

Outside, she straightened but didn't slow up until she was half a block from the saloon, standing on the wooden walkway that lined Houston Street, staring out at the mud-and-manure avenue that was the heart of the town.

"You followed me," she said without looking at him. Her voice was soft and sweet on the damp evening air.

"If you'd walked into the fires of hell, I'd have followed."

She smoothed a stray curl away from her cheek. "Don't be ridiculous."

He stifled disappointment at her brusqueness. "The truth is oftentimes just that," he said.

She kept staring at the street.

He offered the ultimate sacrifice. "Would you like me to go away?" he asked.

"Oh, no," she said hastily, then broke off as if she'd said too much. "That is—"

She settled for a shrug, as if what he did made no difference. Still, with the stiff way she was holding herself, he didn't feel she was totally unconcerned. And there was that hasty *oh, no* that whispered in his ears.

Natural moonlight blended with the yellow glow from a half dozen windows along the way, giving him a good look at her. She was taller than he'd thought, but just as slender and just as filled out in the right places as he'd been hoping.

Not that she was perfect. Her dress didn't fit exactly right, tight across the bosom, short in the waist and hem, showing a pair of sturdy calfskin boots that didn't go with the delicacy of the fern-green muslin.

It almost looked as if the dress belonged to someone else. He wasn't surprised. Times were hard in this part of the world.

A contradictory miss, full of secrets for a man to explore. Complicated. Comely. Oh yes, he was definitely in love.

Ah, did he never learn? Once before in a matter of great importance he'd spoken his feelings rashly and had let his actions echo those words. He'd been paying ever since.

But this was different. This was fate. And he'd never been in love before.

He stepped close, caution tempering his usual confidence around the fairer sex.

"Let's start over," he said, extending his hand. "Good evening again. The name's Conn O'Brien."

She stared down as if she'd never seen a man's hand before. Squaring her shoulders, clearly coming to some kind of decision, she extended her own. The shake was firm, her palm bearing calluses that said she was not a stranger to work. Having had his fill of pampered women, he admired her all the more.

"Crystal Braden," she said. "Thanks for helping me back there."

"Can't see that I did much, Mrs. Braden."

"Miss Braden," she corrected.

He smiled. "I'm a single man myself. Crystal, is it? I've heard of the Irish brand, but I'd no idea Texas offered anything of such quality."

She tried to return his smile, but didn't meet with much success.

"Could there be a young swain hoping to claim you as his?"

"Whyever should you care?"

"Ah, then, there is—one or a dozen, if there's justice in the world."

She shuddered and hugged herself. "There's no justice, at least around here, and there's no swain."

"Have the men of Texas lost their senses?"

"Please," she said, looking up at him with eyes as deep and dark as the night. "I'd rather you not be so nice."

Now that didn't make a whole lot of sense. Maybe she was more shaken than he'd thought.

She shifted about in place, as if poised for flight and at the same time tethered in place. She looked trapped. So were they both. Trapped by fate.

"Don't think you did little to help me," she continued. "You made me feel not so alone."

Again she tried the smile. Her right cheek dimpled for a second, and a soft warmth stroked Conn's heart.

"Alone, are you?" he said, inspired to throw caution to the wind. "That makes a pair of us. Could it be we're destined for one another?"

"Destined?"

"Aye. As in man and wife."

She stared at him as though he had indeed sprouted a second head. At least, he thought, he had her full attention.

"How long have you been in that saloon?" she asked. "The smoke and whiskey have addled your brain."

It was not the reaction he would have chosen.

Before he could continue his suit, from the corner of his eye he saw a body come flying through the swinging doors of the saloon. From half a block away they heard the thud as it landed in the street. A dozen combatants joined the hapless man, and the fight spilled out of doors.

She shuddered. He took her by the arm. "Let's go where it's quieter. My hotel." The last words he said under his breath, lest she misconstrue his meaning and think he was up to no good.

Which under other circumstances he might have been. He wasn't a gentleman all the time. Women seemed to take to him, especially the society women back in Saratoga Springs. Miss Crystal Braden was not of the same breed.

And he had far more important plans for her than a brief evening of delight, tempting though the prospect was.

An angry roar sounded above the fight noise.

"Let go of 'er, you woman-stealing bastard. I got first claim."

He felt her stiffen. They both turned to see a burly, grizzled brawler lumbering down the street toward them.

"Are you talking to me, sir?" Conn called out.

The brawler kept lumbering on, and Conn saw no escape. With a sigh of resignation, he eased Crystal aside, stepped into a muddy rut by the side of the wooden walkway, and tugged at the sleeves of his coat. His duds were a little fancy for a San Antonio street fight, but he doubted the stranger would give him time to change.

He'd been expecting trouble since returning from the north, ready to take on whatever came along, but nothing like this.

The man halted an arm's length away, looked him over, and broke into a black-toothed grin. "I said let 'er go," he growled, more determination than humor in his small dark eyes. He looked Conn up and down. "I'll squash you flatter'n a bug iffen you don't."

He shot a fist in Conn's direction. Conn shifted just in time. A right to the nose and a left to the solar plexus bent his opponent double. Receiving a final chop on his log-hard neck, the brute dropped like an anvil into a pile of manure and lay still.

Conn shook his stinging hand. Wiping the soles of his Wellingtons against the edge of the walkway, he returned to Crystal's side.

"Sorry," he said, "but I couldn't see any way around a fight."

She shuddered, stared at the fallen man, and then back at Conn.

"Fight? He looks like he walked into a wall."

Conn couldn't tell if she sounded admiring or critical. All things considered, she was amazingly calm. She must have seen major troubles in her time.

If so, it would give them something in common.

The sounds of the brawl faded in the background. He stretched his shoulders, trying to work out the tightness of a coat that had been tailored for more passive pursuits. Straightening his homberg, thinking he must look like the dandy he'd almost become, he led her down the walkway, turned right down Alamo Plaza in front of the famous old mission that gave its name to half the establishments in town, and through the front door of the nearby Menger Hotel.

A narrow, uneven stone passageway greeted them, and then an open courtyard resplendent with April flowers, in the center of which rose a massive mulberry tree. Beneath its spreading branches, she dug in her heels, ignoring the gracious charm surrounding her.

"We're far enough from the saloon now," she said, twisting her hands in front of her and showing more distress than she had when the chair crashed close to her head.

"You don't look especially at ease. Don't fret. I'm not expecting a confession right away."

She looked startled enough to jump out of her dress, but not, unfortunately, from uncontrollable lust.

"What confession?"

"Why, that you share my feeling of devotion."

"Oh, that," she said, looking decidedly relieved. "I wish you'd quit teasing."

"I've been known to do such, but in this I'm dead serious, love."

Her fine brown eyes made a thorough study of his face, as if she would see past his exterior and peer into his heart.

With a sigh, she looked away. "You're hopeless."

Perhaps, Conn thought, being direct was not the best wooing tactic just yet.

"Hopeless?" He tried humility. "Aye, I've thought so a time or two myself."

She looked as though she might respond. Instead, she stared past him to the tree. To his surprise, an expression of desolation washed across her face. Of course she would break down now, when all the danger was past.

He longed to hold her and whisper words of reassurance. In time, he told himself, in time.

"Is there someone who should know that you're here?" he asked. "Someone who was supposed to meet you at the Arms?"

She shook her head but seemed little inclined to elaborate.

"Anyone at all in town?"

Again she shook her head. Conn's curiosity ate at him. She didn't look like someone who'd seek a stranger's companionship in a saloon, or someone who was looking for a drink. She was, in fact, the most innocent, vulnerable, lovely woman he'd ever met. Yet she gave hints of a backbone made of steel.

He tried to pick up clues about her from her voice. Gently spoken but direct, her accent held the definite influence of Texas but with an underlying softness that spoke of other places in the South.

"Virginia," he said.

She started. "What?"

"You haven't always lived here. I'd say your place of birth was far away. I'm guessing Virginia."

She studied the tree all the harder.

"South of Richmond. But I've been gone for almost ten years."

"The same time I've been gone from Texas."

"You left before the war."

She said it as a statement of fact, without a hint of surprise, as if she already knew something about him. Was that a trace of censure that he heard? Considering the way he'd spent the war, he'd been expecting it and worse, but still it took him unawares.

"I left, but I'm still a Texan. Born on an Indianola beach the day my parents got off the boat from Ireland, wet-nursed by a Karankawa Indian, raised to farm and ranch. That's about as Texan as you can get."

He hesitated. "I've got a confession, though."

He reached inside his coat, thinking he might as well get the truth out in the open, where he could see how she would handle it.

"I fought for the Yankees. Here's a pistol if you'd care to shoot me."

He'd meant the offer as another jest, though his words held a world of pain.

She hugged herself, and he could have sworn her eyes grew damp.

"I don't want to shoot you," she said.

"That comes as good news, though there are others who would gladly take up the offer. I've had some bad times in my life, Miss Crystal Braden, but getting a bullet in my chest would definitely be one of the worst."

This time the jest brought a tiny smile. To his tired eyes, it was like fireworks lighting the sky. As long as he was looking for portents, he took it as another good sign.

"Funny thing," he said, letting his instincts guide him, "for the first time in a long while I've got a feeling things are going to work out all right."

She stifled a cry.

Something was wrong here besides his bad jokes. It took all of his self-control to keep from taking her in his arms. "I'm not going to hurt you. You have my word, love. I just don't know what to do with you right now except make sure you're safe. It would help if I knew what was going on."

A silence descended between them. She was the first to speak. "My brother left me here. And if I ever find him, he'd better watch out. I declined to shoot you, Mister O'Brien, but I'd consider putting a bullet where it might teach him a lesson. And I'm better with a gun than he is, which he knows."

A woman with spirit. Prime. Conn's hands itched to touch her, to search for flaws. Right now he couldn't see a single one. Even the ill-fitting gown was growing on him, giving her an added vulnerability.

"Have you got any other kin close to San Antonio?"

She shook her head. "We were just traveling through—" She broke off and clenched her hands. "Don't make me tell you any more." Desperation edged her words.

He let the questions go. If talking about herself distressed her more than being in the midst of a brawl, sooner or later he would find out why.

"You might mention when you last had a good meal."

"I'm not hungry."

He looked her over. "Wish I could say the same."

She bristled. "Don't start getting ideas. I'm a virtuous woman, despite what you must think."

He liked the anger more than the distress, liked the quickness of her mind as well as of her tongue.

"Crystal, your virtue is safe with me. I was considering ripping into a thick steak. Haven't had a decent one since I went East. Will you join me?"

"I don't have any money."

"I do."

Lots of it, as a matter of fact. He hadn't returned home looking for charity. But he decided that even with hard times choking Reconstruction Texas, she wouldn't be impressed.

Standing so close beside him, eyes flicking nervously around her, she looked as skittish as an unbroken filly, ready to bolt at a sign of danger.

"I truly mean you no harm, lass," he said, stepping away to give her breathing room. "Since you've not yet given me your hand, all I want for now is a dinner companion, seeing that this is my first night close to home in a long, long while."

Her eyes barely flickered at the reference to their betrothal. Could she be getting used to the idea?

"I won't be very good company," she said.

"I'll be the judge of that," he said.

With no more protests forthcoming, he guided her through the courtyard into the hotel lobby, ordered her a room close to his, instructed that hot baths be drawn right away and steaks for two be delivered within the hour; then he took her to the second floor and left her to bathe herself.

Leaving her was the hardest to do.

While she saw to her ablutions, he did a little shopping through the hotel's officious desk clerk, saying he didn't care what storekeeper had to be disturbed this late in the evening as long as the order was filled. He laid a generous wad of bills on the counter, then went up to prepare for dinner, whistling all the way.

In the ten years he'd been gone from home, a day hadn't gone by that he didn't want to return. After all that time, waiting and hoping, feeling regrets and a heart full of doubt, grieving when the times for grief came, burying the sorrows in his heart, he'd at last been made to feel welcome.

Or at least hope that a welcome might be forthcoming. A curt letter received a month ago had done the trick. He'd cleared his business dealings, made a few arrangements that he'd been planning for years, then booked passage on the next Galveston-bound ship leaving New York.

If he'd learned anything over the past years, it was that money didn't bring a man much comfort, and casual affairs, pleasurable though they were, did little but pass the time. Having someone close by to care for was what gave life meaning. And having that someone care in return.

One of those someones awaited him at the ranch. He would be there in no more than two days, ready to heal old wounds and, if all went well, to pursue the realization of his dreams: the establishment of a Texas horse ranch and the start of a family of his own.

He had money enough for the first, along with breeding stock and knowledge he'd been gaining all his life.

For the second, he needed a loving woman, but he'd thought a wait would be in order before he found her. Had the search truly ended so soon?

Remembering the way he'd felt the first time he saw her, he knew it had. Love at first sight was more than just a myth.

All over the country lives had been upended by the war, and the effects lingered through the years. For him they certainly had, and perhaps as well for Crystal Braden. She needed help, for sure, and she needed to unburden herself of a few secrets. That's why he was there.

When the hot bath had been sent up by the hotel staff, he stripped and settled in the tub for a thorough scrub. He must look and smell his absolute best if his Texas Crystal was to fall in love.

Chapter Two

This was proving much easier than she'd thought.

Crystal stared at the dress spread out on the bed, pink silk with lace trim around the neck and wrists, soft and slippery and delicate as an evening cloud.

Too easy, and at the same time much, much too hard.

Her gaze moved on to the soft-soled slippers, the hosiery, the petticoats. The finery had been delivered just a few minutes ago, right after she'd bathed and donned once again the ill-fitting muslin.

The new clothes were everything a girl could want, right down to a pair of lace garters.

Most girls, that was. Not Crystal. She wasn't made for such feminine things, no more than she was made for subterfuge.

"I'm not putting a stitch of it on," she said to the wall between her room and Conn O'Brien's.

She paced the floor.

"I didn't ask for presents."

No, but she'd gotten them, much as she'd gotten the current mess in which she found herself. If she denied his gift, he might grow suspicious of her strange behavior, more than he already was.

And suspicious he must not be.

Stopping again by the bed, she thought of how he'd stared at her across the saloon, the two of them sitting alone and, to all appearances, equally lonely. She'd actually thought she heard bells. That must have been because she'd been so terrified.

Forget the bells. She'd been told he was a villain, and she had to keep on believing it. He'd abandoned his family when he saw the war coming, had fought for the enemy and then stayed away, getting rich during the hard years of Reconstruction.

A villain, for sure. Unfortunately, she kept picturing a pair of smiling eyes, as blue as a noonday sky, and a shock of midnight-black hair falling beneath the brim of a city man's hat. She pictured, too, a lean face brushed with faint stubble, skin brown from the sun and wrinkled around the eyes, brows as dark as the shock of hair above them, a strong nose broken more than once, a mouth quick to smile.

The memory of that mouth and of that smile brought a shiver to her spine. She had a task before her, and promises to keep. A man's smile must not deter her, no matter how quickly it could light up a room.

Get him interested.

Such had been her first instruction and she'd done just that, with the help of some luck and a riot in the saloon. Why had he really talked to her in the first place, pursued her, brought her back here? She wasn't the only woman in the only saloon in town. And her conversation had been about as scintillating as that of her horse.

Conn O'Brien must be desperate for female companionship, or else he was easily pleased.

And she must look like very easy prey.

Keep him occupied.

Here was the tough part.

Do whatever you have to do.

Panic tore at her stomach. It was the *whatever* that had her in such an agitated state. She felt betrayed at the same time she was betraying someone else, ordered to do something that was alien to her, something she knew pitifully little about.

All she truly wanted to do was what she saw as right, to follow the promise she'd made so long ago and so far away, to keep her privacy as best she could.

Did Conn really think she was pining for a husband? She wasn't, not anymore. And he wasn't pining for a wife, not a man who looked like him. When he left New York, he must have left behind a trail of broken hearts.

All that talk of his about love and marriage and

their being destined for one another didn't fool her. She ran a hand over one of the garters. Oh, no, she wasn't fooled one bit. She might not be widely experienced concerning men, but going by a few Braden examples, she knew they weren't particularly truthful. And they liked to get their way.

It was her own foolishness that made her tingle when he looked at her and even more when he called her *love.* When he came to her room tonight, she had best not start tingling again, although how she was to manage that she didn't know.

Reluctantly, accepting the inevitable, she changed clothes. Each new item eased onto her body as if it had been made for her. The silk felt incredibly soft against her skin. It truly felt as if she were wearing a cloud.

Don't get used to it, she warned herself. *It wouldn't suit the kind of life you lead.*

Forget the dress. She needed to concentrate on Mama and Judge. They were the reasons she was here, doing something as unnatural to her as flying from tree to tree.

Viciously she attacked her hair with a brush. A knock came before she had time to twist it into its usual braid.

Crystal Emmeline Braden, do your job.

She'd rather wrestle a bull in heat than open the door, but she did so and bade Conn enter. Or at least she started to, but when she got a good look at him, her new slippers might as well have been nailed to the floor.

He'd changed into Texas wear, a dark blue shirt and fitted brown trousers, a leather vest, boots, and a broad-brimmed Stetson resting at the back of his head. He'd shaved and she caught the fresh scent of soap and a hint of bay rum, along with the scent of leather. She'd never liked bay rum. She liked it on him.

He wasn't overly tall, though he topped her by several inches. But he was well muscled; she could tell by the fit of his clothes. The details of his body, fascinating though they were, also proved too disconcerting to consider for long.

He'd nicked himself at a corner of his jaw. The tiny drop of dried blood looked endearingly human.

Endearing indeed! What was she thinking of? For all his Irish charm, he was a greedy, self-serving bastard—her brother's term—and he deserved what he was going to get.

He tipped his hat, then took it off altogether.

"I wanted you to see the whole ensemble, in case you had suggestions," he said with that devastating grin of his. He looked her over, and she could feel a few places inside her begin to burn.

"No suggestions," she said in what was alarmingly close to a squeak. "You look different," she managed in a stronger voice.

"I don't clean up badly," he said. "Or maybe you didn't mean it as a compliment."

"Just noticing, that's all."

"I can take off what you don't like."

"No!"

"In good time, then." He gave her another thorough study. "I see the clerk chose right for you," he said.

She felt an irrational regret that he hadn't picked out the clothes himself.

Stepping aside, she gestured for him to enter. An awkward silence descended, broken by the arrival of the food. The waiter set up two places on a table at the far end of her suite, far away from the bed. She hadn't meant to eat anything, just the way she hadn't wanted to wear his clothes or accept the hospitality of the room, but in lieu of talking it seemed appropriate to concentrate on meat and potatoes, ignoring his strong brown hands as they wielded the utensils, ignoring, too, the way he watched her from the corner of his eye.

When he was done, he folded his napkin neatly beside his plate and waited for her. Deciding she'd had enough, she did the same.

She thought of bolting for the door. She sighed. Running wasn't an option. It never had been and it never would.

"You shouldn't have bought me clothes," she said.

"Is that what's bothering you?"

"I insist on repaying you."

"All right."

Her eyes darted to his. Mistake. His look could melt her garters. "I mean with money."

"I thought you didn't have any."

"Not with me."

"Then we'll go get it. To set your conscience clear."

She swallowed. "We can't."

"Why? Where is it?"

"It's—" Her mind floundered. She was better with a rope and gun than she was with lies. "Someone's sending it by mail."

"You came into town with your brother from God knows where to collect a letter containing cash."

"I know it sounds strange, but it's true."

"Was he at the saloon?"

"For a while." She closed her eyes to hide the shame they must reveal. "Until he sold me to that man you fought on the street. I went for the price of his mule."

"Which is why he thought you were his."

She dared look at him again. Conn's stare had turned to such warm sympathy that she almost burst into tears. She'd never met a less villainous man. Her heart shriveled into a hard, pulsing knot.

"You've more problems, love, than I've been thinking."

More than you can possibly realize.

Conn did not let up. "Your brother sold you to Mister Mule and departed."

"He swore he was leaving Texas forever," she said, elaborating on her tale with a lie.

"Too bad he couldn't wait another day."

"For what?"

"The letter with the money."

"You don't believe me."

"No."

She sat straight in righteous anger, trying to forget the fact that she lied. "Well, that's your loss. It should be here in a couple of days."

"Much as I'd like to hang around, I can't, Crystal. I'm expected elsewhere."

For the first time since he'd joined her beneath the saloon table, she heard an urgency in his voice. She turned icy inside. He sounded determined to leave, and her sworn mission was to keep him in town.

She stood to smooth the skirt of the unfamiliar gown, then walked away from the table. To her distress, he followed. He caught her by the wrist halfway across the room, his fingers warm and firm against her skin.

"That doesn't mean I'm abandoning you. Come with me. That way I know you'll be all right."

Oh, dear, she thought as she shifted to face him. This was getting worse and worse. She shook her head when the words of denial would not come.

"Tell you what," he said, all solemn except for the wicked glint in his eye. "We'll talk about traveling later. If you want things even between us, you can pay me now." He paused a moment. "Then we'll both be satisfied."

Her heart thundered, and the tingling she'd been so afraid of skittered across the surface of her skin. She ought to be terrified, but it wasn't terror that made her breath catch and her knees grow weak. She'd never been in such private quarters with a man who wasn't kin. She was twenty-four, a spinster, past her prime and long past her dreams, but at the moment she didn't feel past anything except restraint.

She looked away. Conn was a villain, she reminded herself, a bad guy, a charmer with a heart of stone. But he certainly did have warm eyes and hands.

He loosened his hold on her wrist. She backed away, step by unsteady step. He took her hands to stop her, and his fingers worked their determined way up her arms, each touch burning through the silk sleeves of her gown. He held her loosely by the shoulders, and she forgot to breathe.

"Crystal, my love, a man can be only so strong."

As if he willed it, she lifted her gaze to meet his. "You promised," she managed and took a step backwards.

He kept pace. "One kiss," he said as his mouth descended toward hers. She couldn't pull away.

He moved so close that she could see flecks of darkness in his eyes, could count the small furrows across his forehead beneath the shock of black hair, could see just how bronzed his skin really was.

She closed her eyes. He kissed her. His lips were the sweetest things she'd ever felt, soft and probing, and asking without words for whatever she wanted to give. Instead of fighting as any decent girl should, she found her arms creeping around his neck and in her ignorance offering everything she could.

She heard a growl from somewhere deep inside him, and from inside her a soft groan escaped.

She felt the mattress at the back of her legs. How had they ended so close to the bed? She pulled from his embrace, her eyes avoiding his as she edged sideways, feeling more and more like a rabbit caught in a trap.

He backed her against the door, his body pressed to hers, as hard and hot as she had imagined it would be, and a thousand times more arousing. She burned—oh, how she burned—the aching void within her filling fast with fire. All thought except of him turned to ashes. Somehow he made her feel protected from the ugliness of her world.

He kissed her again. She could not deny him. Her lips parted, and his tongue touched hers.

It was a moment of great intimacy. She would have thought such an act repulsive . . . until she tasted Conn. She groaned again and let the kiss deepen. The room whirled. She clung to him. Her heart pounded as it had never done before.

He stroked her upper arm and down her side, brushing his fingers along the side of her breast. Without shame, without purpose except relief for a raging need, she pressed herself into his hard heat.

She little thought about what she was doing, unexpected instincts guiding her for the first time in her life. How wonderful it was not to calculate what she did, but simply to feel, and wonderful feelings they were, foreign and yet right.

She trembled, she soared, she hungered. . . .

And suddenly she felt him pull away.

He stared down at her, hands at his sides. The trembles were slow to subside. She studied the edge of his collar where it met the tight, tanned skin of his throat. Her burning turned from hunger to humiliation. How could she feel both hot and cold?

He brushed a strand of hair from her face. "I forgot myself."

She took little pleasure in the huskiness of his voice. At least he could speak. If she tried to do so, her words would have come out a whimper or, worse, a whine.

"You deserve better, lass. Forgive me."

He sounded far too much in control. Her humiliation knew no bounds. She wanted to slap him, but she couldn't. Liar and deceiver she might be, certainly of late, but she wasn't a total hypocrite. If she slapped anyone, it should be herself.

He stepped backward, and she eased past him into the room. She heard the door open behind her. Her mind reeled with too many thoughts and too little purpose. Here was where she ought to ask him to stay, to plunge into the *whatever* of her command.

The words wouldn't come.

"I'd best leave or we'll both hate me in the morning."

She nodded. *Yes, leave,* she wanted to cry, and even more urgently, *no, stay*.

"Are you all right?" he asked.

She managed a soft, "Yes."

"Sleep, then. It's what we both need. We'll talk again in the morning." She heard him take a few deep and not altogether steady breaths. "We've a shared destiny to discuss. I know it more than ever, and I'm thinking that now so do you."

The door closed gently and he was gone.

A few hours later, Crystal kneed her leggy roan gelding into a gallop along the road leading north-west from San Antonio, away from the breaking dawn, away from the Menger Hotel. With the skirt of her mother's green muslin gown tucked between her legs, she sat astride as was her habit, a single thick braid of hair bouncing against her back. She should have felt exhilarated, also her habit when she was riding like this, all-out and alone.

Instead, she felt awkward and cold, embarrassed, angry and scared. Mostly she felt Conn O'Brien's lips on hers. And the kiss had been an eternity ago.

A love-starved spinster, that's what she was, going crazy with her first real kiss, forgetting promises, forgetting the troubles she would be causing, forgetting what a cad the man was supposed to be. She'd snuggled in his arms like a loose woman who couldn't wait to get out of her clothes.

She was afraid, all right, but not of the dark that surrounded her on the pre-dawn ride, certainly not of her solitude, not even of the anger she would soon face. She feared Conn O'Brien and the wild emotions he had aroused. Her cheeks burned from the memory and she forgot the cold morning air.

The worst part of all was that he was the one who pulled away, in control where she was not, remembering the promise he'd given her while she forgot about the vows she'd made. In control, that was the hard part to recall, as if he'd got all he wanted from her, as if he wanted no more. Oh, he'd renewed the foolish talk about their destiny, but it had to be the Irish in him that made the comforting lie slip out so easily.

No matter the reason, he'd been a gentleman, while she'd been far from a lady. And he hadn't seemed villainous at all.

All the while she was reliving her shame, the roan was moving fast through the early light, lapping up miles along the ribbon of road. What she ought to be doing during the ride was to plan on what she would say when she got to her destination. And she had plenty to say. She was working on the particulars when she spied the cutoff that led to the camp.

Reining to the side of the road, she listened for the sound of horses. A mockingbird sang somewhere in the shadowy trees and the wind soughed through the leaves, but except for her pounding heart all else was silent.

The roan snorted in impatience at the break in the ride, and his muscles bunched beneath her knees. She stroked his damp neck. "Okay, Trouble, we'll be on our way in a second. Wouldn't want any unwelcome visitors, would we?"

The roan snorted again, unimpressed. He had a way of favoring one of his hoofs that left a trail easy to spot for a good tracking man. She doubted Conn O'Brien was such a one, having lived the past ten years with Yankees. She doubted, too, that he would make the effort to follow her, but she'd learned long ago to be cautious.

Riding on, backtracking, riding, backtracking, at last she cut out through a stand of thick brush, taking it slow, finally breaking into a small clearing surrounded by scrub oak and wild pecan. The first hints of sun added to the light from a low fire at the center of the camp. A lone man stood close to the flames sipping coffee, his powerful, blunt hands wrapped tightly around the cup. Shadows played across his craggy features, the wide nose, the full lips almost hidden by a thick gray moustache, the square jaw, the strong neck.

Tossing the coffee aside, he began to pace back and forth along a faint trail he'd worn in the dirt. As always, he wore a black vested suit, white shirt, and string tie, his body as square and strong as his features. In the dim light his limp was barely discernible.

The next minutes, the next few days, were not going to be easy. Crystal urged Trouble closer. The man's head jerked up, and he slapped at a gun holstered beneath his coat.

"It's just me, Father," she said, formal with him as she always was. "Your not-so-dutiful daughter has returned."

Chapter Three

Edgar Braden eased his hand from the holster and blinked in disbelief.

"What are you doing here?" he growled.

The brave greeting Crystal had prepared died on her lips.

Even at his most contented, her father was a brusque man. He was far from contented now. In the flickering light, the stubble graying his cheeks gave him a feral look, and the usually icy blue eyes glared hot with anger and surprise.

Despite his powerful build, she saw for the first time how old he looked, at least a decade past his fifty-one years; the ravages of worry were cut deeply into his leathery face.

He brought the worry on himself. It drove him to a meanness that shaped every Braden's life.

"I came to report," she said, sliding from the

roan, praying she handled things right. She turned from her father and led the horse to the small stream by the campsite, then left him to crop at a stand of grass on the bank. A short distance away, a pair of horses were tethered, along with an all-too-familiar mule. The sight of the mule renewed her resolve.

Edgar ran a hand through his thinning fair hair. "You're supposed to be with O'Brien."

"I—" She searched for the right words. "Things didn't work out." Shaking the wrinkles from her skirt, she thought longingly of her buckskins.

Edgar was having none of it. "We had an agreement. Get on back into town."

Warming her hands at the fire, she started to speak when a sharp-edged, insinuating voice broke into her thoughts.

"Let him get away, I see. Did you smell too much of horse to charm him?"

With a sigh, she forced herself to face her older brother. Tall and lean, almost too much so, fair-haired like their father and brown-eyed like their mother, Royce was the handsomest of the Bradens. Though he had only two years on her, he made her feel like a child.

"Maybe I did," she said. "Could be he took one whiff and sent me on my way."

He assessed her as he might a new hunting dog. Despite her best intentions, she remembered the hotel room—remembered, too, the aroused and yet protected way Conn had made her feel. She didn't feel protected now, not caught as she was between the two men in all the world who should have taken care of her.

"No, siree," Royce said, drawing the words out. "The smell didn't bother him. Not in the least."

Crystal shivered. What a strange person her brother was, for all his pleasant, even features. She decided it was the calculating look in his eyes, the coldness that never went away.

When they first came to Texas, he'd taught her to rope and ride, over their mother's objections and their father's impatience, but when she proved a better shot than he, the lessons had come to an end.

She'd been hurt at first, even knowing he had a streak in him that never let anyone get close. Still, he had a way about him that appealed to women. And women appealed to him. Whores, mostly, according to her younger brother, Judgement. Royce also went for whiskey and cards.

The study he was giving her turned somehow more personal, in a way that didn't seem right for a brother.

"You two sleep together last night?"

Crystal turned away. She had known he would ask, but that didn't make the answering any easier.

Keep him occupied. Do whatever you have to do.

The order had come from Edgar himself, with Royce grinning in approval. Royce always approved of his father, no matter the depth of his cruelty. No wonder Edgar preferred his oldest son above all others and seemed proud of his escapades, though he himself liked to play the part of a gentleman.

He never seemed to know what to do with his only daughter. Until Conn O'Brien returned to Texas.

For his younger son and ailing wife Edgar showed open contempt.

"The way O'Brien was looking at you across that saloon, I thought he might take you on the floor," Royce said. "He practically dragged you down the street toward the Menger. Tell the truth. Did you sleep with him? It's a simple enough question. Yes or no."

"Answer the question, girl," her father ordered.

A green log in the fire snapped like a gunshot and she jumped.

"No," she said, turning back to face the men, "we did not sleep together."

Royce laughed. "Then why are you blushing?"

Because she might have tumbled into bed with Conn O'Brien if he'd asked her—innocent, ignorant Crystal, who'd been carried away by her very first kiss.

Now was not the time for confession, though there were other truths she could impart. All she needed was the backbone.

"I didn't sleep with him, but I liked him. You said he was a greedy bastard come to celebrate the death of his father. I tried to look at him like that, but I couldn't."

"Don't make excuses for him," said Edgar. "He doesn't know his father's dead. The celebrating will come when he finds out."

"Maybe little Crystal told him," Royce put in.

"We didn't mention his father. He'll find out soon enough what's going on."

"And inherit everything," Edgar said.

His voice was roughened with anger and a bitterness she didn't understand. Though he was Southern born and raised, Edgar was not a rabble-rouser, a hanger-on Johnny Reb like a few of their fellow ranchers, hating to see Texas land fall into the hands of a Yankee sympathizer.

He simply wanted Bushwhack Ranch. Not just wanted. He craved it, coveted it, desired it the way she supposed some men desired a woman. In the ten years since buying Shingle Camp Ranch across the creek, he'd stared in open envy at the O'Brien spread, swearing it was superior property—more grazing acreage, richer soil—and he'd let the hunger for it grow.

Conn had already gone north by the time they arrived from Virginia and settled in, gone toward the war that the Bradens had been running from, leaving his father and twin brother James and the beautiful family land.

Crystal barely remembered the brother. He'd been killed long ago in the war.

Daniel O'Brien had died this week owing Edgar money. Bushwhack, collateral for the loan, was practically in Braden hands—unless, that was, Conn showed up before his father was in the ground. The original agreement said he must be allowed to pay the debt, if he could. Word was, he would have no trouble.

The funeral was scheduled for Sunday, three days away. Crystal's task was to keep Conn from attending. Crystal, who had always tried to do the honorable thing. She saw nothing honorable in her agreement or in the way she had behaved last night.

But then, she hadn't been acting for herself.

There was her mother to consider. And there was Judge. She couldn't believe her father would do to them what he threatened, but she hadn't wanted to take the chance. Until Conn took her in his arms.

The injustice of it all got to her, and she turned on Royce.

"You really did sell me to that horrible man."

Royce shrugged. "After he got one look at you, he decided it was a good deal."

"What's she talking about?" Edgar asked, looking from daughter to son. "You were supposed to arrange an accidental meeting with O'Brien, that's all. She was not to get involved with anyone else."

"And that's what I did." Royce strolled to the fire to pour himself a cup of coffee. He offered the cup to Crystal. She shook her head.

"He's stalling. Ask him about the mule," she said to Edgar.

He glanced back at the animals grazing near the stream, then at his son. "She talking about the one you brought back out of town? You swore you found it."

Royce shrugged. "Some fool traded it for Crystal. But don't get in a dander. I followed her into the saloon with him and made sure O'Brien was there. Had to start a little ruckus to get his attention, but things worked out all right. Gentleman Yankee that he's become, he scurried right on over and offered her his protection. That's when I headed for the back door."

He shot a hard glance at Crystal. "You got him to the hotel. The deal was, baby sister, you were supposed to stay there with him. Give him reason to hang around town longer than he'd planned. Remember?"

She glanced down at her ill-fitting dress. "What was I supposed to use for bait?"

The two men shared a look. "You've got bait, all right," said Royce.

"Why do you think I keep you out at Shingle Camp, away from town?" asked Edgar.

She shook her head in disgust. He'd hinted at her appeal a few times before, but she had paid him no mind. A few of the ranch hands looked her way, but she figured that was because they were lonely. They never did more than look. Royce saw to that.

The truth was, she was a plain spinster who rode and shot like a man, and she stayed at Shingle Camp because she was needed there. She couldn't foresee a time when she wouldn't be.

Edgar wouldn't let up. "I'd be willing to place a sizable bet that you can distract him for a couple of days. If you haven't already messed up." He threw his cup down in disgust, and it rolled around in the dirt. "You're your mother's daughter. It's time you acted it. Women know all about these things."

"I don't."

But he wasn't listening. "Two days. That's all I asked, hold him up two days, and if by damn—"

He broke off and cursed some more.

The cursing came unexpectedly. Her father never cursed. He always dressed for dinner, always behaved politely to everyone at the table, talking about the weather and the food, complimenting the housekeeper, Helga, while he suggested different dishes she might try. Not that Helga paid him much mind, but he never seemed to notice, no more than he did the way his unceasing innuendo sowed the seeds of hate.

"You didn't ask, Father. You said he was a villain through and through, that he'd abandoned his father and brother and sought safety in the north. That he'd refused to come home even when he heard his brother had been killed. That he'd changed his mind after Daniel O'Brien wrote he was near death."

Edgar came close, a trace of whiskey on his breath.

"Are you calling me a liar?"

She stood her ground, but it wasn't easy, not with the strange cast to Edgar's eye, like a hint of madness much more deep-seated than his usual greed.

The sight made her blood run cold. Never had

she defied him in such a way, except for that time when he'd been especially hard on Judge, taking a whip to him for some minor infraction, but then she'd been fighting for someone else.

In a way she was doing the same thing now, only this time she was fighting for a man she barely knew.

"I'm saying you're wrong about Conn O'Brien," she said, putting her feelings as strongly as she could, hoping she knew what she was talking about and fearing that maybe she'd let a pair of kisses and a little kindness turn her stupid.

Edgar raised his fist. In all her life he'd never struck her, but he was angry enough to do so now. "If he makes it back in time for that funeral, you'll pay as much as anyone."

"Well, well, well." Both turned to Royce, who had a wicked glint in his eyes. "Could it be our innocent Crystal is smitten? I was right. Something did happen between you two."

"Don't be ridiculous," she said, but her voice was not nearly so strong as she wished.

"Something sure made you forget about Mama and Judge."

Unfair, she thought, but still her conscience struck her. She felt pulled on a rack of torture, torn between two powerful forces of honor, knowing that whichever force won, the other would suffer a great loss.

When she'd fled the hotel that morning, shaken in a way she'd neither anticipated nor understood, she'd hoped Edgar would listen to what she had to say, ignoring the fact he'd never done so before. Now she saw the futility of that hope.

Royce glanced at his father. "Looks like another O'Brien has charmed one of our women. And this time a wealthy one."

Edgar's eyes turned mean, and Crystal felt anew the heat of his fury. "You *are* just like your mama, eh? I told you I'd go easy on her if you did what I told you, that I'd continue to support her, but not now."

Crystal tasted fear on her tongue, not for herself but for her mother. She hugged herself, then let go to touch her father's sleeve.

"Mama's never been unfaithful," she said, letting her anguish show. "She doesn't deserve this."

He shoved her away. Her boot caught in the hem of the unfamiliar skirt and she tumbled to the ground.

"Hit her again and I'll shoot you."

All eyes turned to the speaker. The youngest of the Braden clan stood at the edge of the clearing, a Navy Colt in his hand, the barrel pointed at his father's heart.

The only movement around the fire was Royce's hand edging toward his own holstered gun. Crystal sprang to her feet. "He didn't hit me, Judge. He just didn't want me to touch him, and I tripped." She tried to smile. "I'm a little awkward in this dress."

"What are you doing out here?" snapped Edgar. "We're having ourselves a regular family reunion.

You're supposed to be back at Shingle Camp with your mother."

"She's doing all right."

"You can't be sure about that. She's a frail one, remember." He spoke the words with bitterness.

"Yeah, I remember," said Judge. "Ever since I was born. You've told me a million times."

Crystal sensed a burning at the back of her eyes. Dear, dear Judge. He'd come along fourteen years ago, after Mama had lost two babies. She always said he was worth the trouble and the wait, though his birth had ruined her health. Slight of frame, gangly, with a length of arms and legs he didn't know what to do with, he was the best horseman of all the Bradens, or he would be once he learned more discipline. Crystal always told him he was too quick with a crop. And here he was with a gun.

She blamed herself. Like Mama, he was also her charge, the promises that made them so given long, long ago. And her father had sworn to go easier on them if she did what he asked.

The screws on the rack turned. She couldn't keep her word; she couldn't face Conn with more lies. She turned to tell her father how things were, but he was staring at Judge with the strange, hateful madness harsher in his eyes, terrifying her far more than when he'd looked at her. He moved toward his son slowly, his limp pronounced. The air turned chill. She hugged herself and felt the claws of panic once again.

The gun wavered in the boy's hand. Edgar back-handed him to the ground. Blood spurted from a cut to his mouth.

With a cry, Crystal ran to his side. Kneeling, she used the hem of her petticoat to wipe away the blood. Judge blinked away tears, stubborn in his show of pride, and stared past her to his father, a matching hatred in his eyes.

When his hand squeezed around the handle of the Colt, Crystal turned hollow inside. What a fool she had been to think she could decide her own fate. She saw what she must do. The promises, both old and new, would be kept. Duty would be observed. It was ironic that in the doing she would have to continue a lie.

"Put the gun away, Judge. Please."

His wide eyes turned to her in protest. She could read the determination in their depths, and the budding manhood that Edgar relentlessly suppressed.

"Please," she repeated. "You'll only make things worse."

He slumped in defeat and eased his hold on the Colt. She tried to help him stand, but he jerked away and scrambled to his feet, disappearing into the brush at his back.

She longed to follow in his path, but of course she could not. A quick glance at the sky showed streaks of yellow light lacing across an early morning blue. Like so many other facets of her life, time was her enemy. She must be moving on.

Before she lost her resolve, she turned to face the other Braden men.

"I can find Conn O'Brien again," she said with more courage than confidence, and something inside her died, a sense of herself that had guided her through the years. She took a deep breath. "I'll do whatever is necessary to hold him up a few days."

The image of his mouth descending toward her flashed in her mind. With a shiver, she replaced it with the memory of Judge's last glance.

"Good thing you came to your senses," said Edgar.

Her shame made her bold. "But I want some concessions from you."

"See here, girl, I already swore to more than enough. What you saw with Judge just now is only a part of what he'll get if O'Brien gets back too soon."

"I don't doubt it, Father. But I'm like you. I want more."

He came for her. "Don't you talk like that—"

Royce restrained him with a hand on his arm. "Let's hear what she has to say."

Her brother was an unlikely source of support, but Crystal took what she could get.

Edgar snarled in disgust as he nodded for her to continue.

"You said you'd toss Mama and Judge out, and I argued against it. I've decided your idea is best."

"Go on," he said. "I'm listening."

She explained her proposition bluntly, talking fast, working out the details as she went along. With only a few interruptions, she was able to get through to the end. To her relief, they agreed, though Royce had to do most of the talking and Edgar put in a growl or two.

She even got the details in writing, using the back of a wrinkled bill of sale Edgar found in his saddlebags. He scrawled his signature at the bottom, then thrust the paper into her hands.

"Swear you won't let me down, girl. I won't be responsible for what happens if you do."

She thought of the blood on Judge's young face. Her hand trembled as she tucked the agreement between her breasts. "I swear."

The words portended terrible times ahead; she felt it in her bones, though whether for her or for Conn, she couldn't begin to guess.

An unseen bird sang in the trees, and the sun, peeking over the tops of the April-green limbs, robbed the day of its chill. The scene was cruelly beautiful considering the events unfolding around her.

One whistle brought Trouble trotting to her side. Hoisting her skirt between her legs, she pulled herself into the saddle, checked her rifle and rope, then took the reins in her hands.

"I'll keep him away two days, or the deal's off."

"Make certain you do," said Edgar. "Surely the funeral won't be put off any longer. The way things are, old Daniel's going to be ripe by the time he gets into the ground, but you never can tell what that lawyer will decide."

"I'll do what I can," she said.

"Three days'd be better," put in Royce. "If you

get a bath, you might hold him up for a week."

But she'd had a bath last night, at the hotel, courtesy of Conn. And, for all his fancy talk, he'd been composed enough to end their embrace. What else would she have to do to keep her word?

She reined away from the camp, ignoring the two-fingered salute with which Royce sent her on her way.

Three days. If Conn O'Brien was already on the road, which she suspected he must be, then by the time she caught him they would be no more than a day, a day and a half at the most, from the ranch. Just how was she to detain him? It might be she'd have to let him kiss her again.

Would that be so bad? If he wanted her, if he touched her, if he teased her in his gentle way, would she let him take more liberties?

She feared the answer as much as she welcomed it, her anticipation of the coming days equal parts eagerness and shame.

Conn cursed himself for getting under way so late. He'd awakened early enough, gone down for breakfast, then returned to summon his Sleeping Beauty. But she was gone. Only the new clothes, spread upon the bed, gave evidence that she'd ever existed.

She must have got away well before dawn. It had taken him half an hour to find the stable where she'd kept her horse. The bill had been paid the night before by a man claiming to be her brother, which jibed with her story about Mister Mule.

What didn't jibe was her story about being broke. If she'd wanted so much to pay her way, she could have sold the horse.

Why had she gone? He must have come on too strong, at least from her point of view—holding her, opening his heart, kissing her the way a man should not kiss an innocent.

To his mind, he'd been a master of restraint. She had no idea how close she'd come to being tossed onto the bed and thoroughly loved.

Which he would have regretted. Enjoyed and regretted. A gentleman didn't treat his intended so crudely. He waited until after the wedding to do the tossing.

Except that the innocent Miss Braden, reacting to the lone kiss with an encouraging flare of passion, had shown herself capable of throwing a toss or two herself.

She would be the perfect wife. If only she hadn't run away. It was a complication that just might postpone his wedding plans, and he readjusted the odds.

Conn laughed at himself, though the laughter was not without pain. He liked to think of himself as a romantic, but it could be he was simply a fool. Instead of falling in love with the first pretty Texas woman he met, he ought to be thinking about the reunion with his father. In a way it never left his mind.

Anguish was inescapable, as well as awkwardness. He'd left after bitter arguments over the impending war, which he'd seen coming more clearly than anyone else. When he heard that James had been killed at Shiloh, he'd come close to tearing off his blue uniform and heading for Texas.

Instead, he'd written home to let his father know he hadn't been anywhere near the battle, indeed that he wasn't engaged in any fighting except with the cavalry horses that were in his charge. The reply had been curt and to the point: Daniel no longer considered him his son. Knowing the declaration was written in the midst of grief, Conn had continued to write through the years, but no other answer had been received.

Until the brief summons to leave Saratoga and come home. As profitable as the last few years had been, he'd never wanted anything but to do just that and take up the life that the war had interrupted. Nothing would replace the loss of James, but grieving for him on the land where they'd grown up might make the grief more bearable.

Being with his father again was the most important part of the return. If they could truly find their peace. They had to. Conn would never feel complete until they did.

Maybe he shouldn't have been thinking last night about taking a wife. But it was a part of what he wanted. A Texas girl to help him with his dreams for the ranch. The father he remembered would be pleased with her, if she were ever found.

One minute he was loping along, slowing for a

sharp curve in the road, thinking about Daniel and Crystal, about the land as he remembered it, smelling the clean Texas air, even liking the dust kicked up from the ride, and the next thing he knew a rope dropped over his shoulders and he pitched to the ground. Free of his weight, the mount surged on ahead, empty stirrups flapping, while Conn shook his head to figure out what in the hell was going on.

Cursing, ignoring the sharp pain in his shoulder where he'd landed, he got to his feet fast. The rope bound his arms tight to his body, keeping him from drawing his gun.

The rope fell slack. He followed its line backward along the dirt and rocks to a live oak growing close to the road, to a long-legged roan restlessly shifting half-hidden beside the tree, to the woman sitting astride and looking as skittish as the horse.

Crystal had been found. Or more accurately, she had found him.

"Are you hurt?" she asked. She sounded scared and nervous. She ought to be.

He couldn't hold on to his fury long, not with a pair of wide doe eyes staring down at him and a pair of full lips parted as she waited for him to respond.

The rest of her looked just as good as the lips, so much so that he forgot to assess her horse. Saints preserve him, as his mother had often exclaimed, he was a foolish Irish lad, green enough to have just come off the boat.

Slipping free of the rope, he stretched, then

caught his shoulder. He didn't have to feign the stab of pain.

"Oh," she cried softly, beginning to dismount.

"It's nothing," he said with a wave that cost him another shot of pain. He grinned. "Nothing a good rubdown wouldn't fix."

She blinked once, then settled back in the saddle. Smart woman, she'd figured out that she would be doing the rubbing, and his shoulder might not be the only part of him involved.

"I shouldn't have done it," she said with a nervous little laugh. "But you came around that bend so fast and I was afraid you might get away."

"And would that have been so bad?"

Her blush told him what she did not put into words.

Conn scooped up his hat, slapped it against his thigh, and settled it low on his forehead. A sharp whistle brought his horse back at a run. Always a man who liked things neat and questions answered, he bent to pick up the rope.

"It seems to my simple mind that staying at the hotel would have been a mite easier on us both if you wanted my company."

Slowly he wound the hemp into a thick coil, walking closer, handing it up to her. A glimpse of leg bared above the top of her boot stopped him for a moment. He glanced at the Winchester in her saddle scabbard, then back into her wide brown eyes.

"Or did you prefer bringing me down out here on the road? Are you a thief, Crystal Braden? And if so, are you after my cash or my heart?"

"I'm not—"

"No matter. They both are yours."

He glanced again at the leg. A man could be strong for only so long. His hands grasped her narrow waist and before she could protest, he swung her out of the saddle and eased her to the ground. Light as the air, she fairly floated to a stand in front of him.

The roan shifted nervously. Not Conn and, to his great pleasure, not Crystal.

Her hands rested on his shirt. She lifted thick black lashes and looked at him with eyes as deep as the world. He pulled her close and kissed her. Soft and sweet he made it, tempting them both, and then he smiled.

"You've caught me, lass. It's a scandalous thing you've done, lassoing a man like that. There's no way out for either of us. We'll have to be wed."

Chapter Four

With a soft cry, Crystal turned from Conn.

His breath was warm on her neck. He lifted the thick braid that fell down her back and kissed her heated skin.

She shivered and clung to Trouble's saddle for support.

"Tell me, Crystal, that you feel nothing between us."

"Don't."

"Don't what?" He kissed her neck again. "Is that what you're talking about?"

She managed to shake her head. "It's the teasing and the talk of getting married."

"Good," he said and kissed her one more time. "I'm not teasing you, Crystal. I meant what I said."

Her mind and heart begged for her to lean back into his strength. She wasn't tough enough for this. Her father should have known.

"Please go," she whispered. "Ride on. Please."

His hands rested on her shoulders. "Not until I hear you say I mean nothing to you."

Here was where she should lie, for his sake as well as hers. Here was where she should deny the bells, deny her pounding heart and the way he robbed her of breath, the way he made her think of no one and nothing but him.

Lie. It's the honorable way.

But it was not a way open to her.

Trouble bobbed his head and shifted out of her reach, as if he wanted nothing to do with her. Conn stayed close, rubbing her shoulders in light, insistent circles.

"You mean something to me," she whispered, leaning back on Conn for support. Crossing her arms across her breasts, she rested her hands on his.

"Then I should tell my heart to beat again," he said in the dear, provocative way that had become so familiar so fast.

"Tell mine to slow down," she said.

He turned her to face him, and for a while he just looked at her, catching her in his spell. Had a rattler coiled around her ankle, she would have held still and kept looking right back.

"Come with me to my home," he said. "Or what used to be my home. I've been away these ten long years and I'd like to have you by my side when I see my father again."

"You ask too much."

"Don't be distressed. The O'Briens are not such a bad lot."

All that her father had ever said about Conn and his family came back in a rush, and with it all his threats and the mean way he'd struck down his young son.

Even Mama had asked that she obey Edgar, though she'd not understood the vileness of his demands.

Crystal must do what she had vowed. Every sense told her it was so.

"It's not your family that bothers me," she said. "It's mine."

Pulling away, she paced at the side of the road, her legs weak beneath her. The words came in a flood, lie after lie, about how she had been on the road looking for Royce when Conn came along unexpectedly, and how she knew her brother would return for her once he sobered up, the importance of her being in town when he did, the obligation she felt no matter how badly he had treated her.

"Didn't he say he was leaving Texas?"

"He's said such things before. And he's never gone very far. He was supposed to arrange for the sale of our cattle yesterday, and when he couldn't find a buyer, he got drunk. He's still around somewhere. I feel it. That's why I asked you to go on. I have no right to hold you up."

She stood still, eyes closed, and waited for his response.

It came fast and was what she had expected.

"A day's wait is little to pay for finding you again."

"It may take more than a day."

"It doesn't matter. As long as you come with me when I leave. If, after a while in my company, you still want to."

"And you still want me."

"It would take more than my feeble brain can imagine to change my plans."

"Oh," she said in a small voice.

"And that's the last you'll hear on that subject for a while. You have my word."

The sound of approaching horses drew them back into the protection of the woods, along with their mounts. They watched as the Fredericksburg stagecoach creaked and swayed past. With the dust settling, they were soon on the road riding in the opposite direction, toward San Antonio, away from Kerr County and the Bushwhack Ranch, away from the father Conn thought awaited his return, away from his longed-for family home.

For all her sense of determination, Crystal felt lower than the ruts in the road.

She stole a look at him. The strong, tanned face, the sure hands on the reins, the natural grace with which he sat his mount brought a flood of pleasure to her heart.

Conn caught her eye. Skilled rider though she was, she almost fell off the horse. Bells rang, more sweetly than in the saloon. How different he was from the other men in her life. He would never threaten her, taunt her, bring her to harm.

He will when he learns the truth.

The happiness died. She looked away. Not he; she felt his glance as surely as she'd felt his hands last night.

She had every reason to feel lower than the ruts, to feel dirtier than the dirt Trouble kicked up with each trot.

"I've a question to put to you," he said. "If it won't disturb your thoughts."

She licked her lips. "All right."

"Are you as good with a rifle as you are with a lariat?"

She laughed. She couldn't help it.

"Better," she said. "When I'm roping, I sometimes miss a stray calf the first try. I never miss what's in my gun sight."

"Then I'm glad you chose the rope."

"So am I."

"I've another question. When you look at me like that, what's on your mind?"

Her heart rose to her throat. "How do I look at you?"

"In a way that makes the riding uncomfortable." He didn't explain what he meant, and she decided not to ask.

"I was thinking you remind me of Papa Stewart."

"Your father?" he said, clearly disappointed.

"My grandfather."

"You've a sweet-talking way about you, Crystal Braden. No wonder I've fallen in love."

"There you go teasing again. I meant it in a good

way. He's the only man in my family who is remotely like you. *Was,* that is. He and Mama Stewart have been dead a long time."

She closed her eyes to remember the Virginia plantation where she'd spent much of her first fourteen years. She knew the land was gone from the family, the house, too, and, most of all, the good times, but still she missed them and wished every day she could return.

It was there that she'd dreamed of being adored by a dashing young man and having a family of her own. The dreams had gradually died as the Bradens moved west.

"Papa Stewart had a confidence about him that made others know he could be trusted, but he was never arrogant, never demanding. He knew what he wanted and he was honest enough to say so." She warmed to both the memory and the man who rode beside her. "He was gracious and loving and kind—"

She broke off. She revealed far too much. Such forthrightness of speech was for people like Conn, honest people, and not for the likes of her.

"You make me sound like a Saint. Saint Conn. I'd rather you think of me as a man."

She remembered his kisses. "I do."

The horses fell to a slower walk.

"Why did you run this morning?" he asked.

She took a deep breath. "That's three questions. You said one."

"I could say, 'So shoot me,' but you might take me at my word."

"My brother, remember? He—"

"Not good enough. You could have told me good-bye."

"I know I owed you for the room and the food. I left the clothes. It was all I could do."

"That's not why I brought it up. And it's not why you left without seeing me again."

"All right, then. I was afraid."

"That's not the way I remember it."

His voice was thick and deep and gently mocking. It held a tone she wasn't used to hearing in her real life and it disturbed her as much as anything about him because she liked it so much.

Her feeling for him, whatever it was, showed no sign of weakening. Nor did her dilemma. The agreement paper burned between her breasts. The torture rack tightened another notch.

"All right," she admitted, taking a firm grip on the reins, "I left the way I did because I scared myself. A woman past her prime has no business getting so involved with a simple kiss. And don't look at me like that. I'm halfway through my twenties, and I understand the truth of my situation."

"I'm halfway through my thirties. Guess that puts me in my dotage."

His crooked grin set her heart to turning somersaults. "Are you never serious?" she asked.

He studied her for a long while, his high-noon eyes steady beneath the wide brim of his hat, putting out more warmth than the rising sun. "I was serious last night. Aren't you telling me that's why you ran?"

"I'll put it another way. Are you serious only when it comes to all that loving stuff?"

She blushed, knowing she sounded ignorant.

"Not necessarily. Sometimes during the loving stuff is when I'm most playful. I'd be glad to pull over into the stand of trees ahead and demonstrate."

Crystal started. Would she never learn?

"I'm sorry," he said. "I've embarrassed you, but you are such an incredible, delightful innocent. I had not thought to find your like anywhere."

His apology did little to soothe her.

"I suppose you're used to more sophisticated women."

"Ones more experienced with men, if that's what you mean. Women with more money, too, though I suspect your family once enjoyed a better life than they now face."

"What makes you say that?"

"Your gown, for one thing. It shows quality and care in the making."

"You seem to know a great deal about women's clothes."

He shrugged. "And there's your horse."

"Trouble is as fine an animal as you'll find."

"Exactly. Given the incident with Mister Mule last night, I would have thought whatever mount you came up with would be a nag." He hesitated. "I don't mean to embarrass you, but if we're to get on, we ought to be honest with one another, don't you think?"

"Of course."

Another silence fell between them. It remained unbroken for the remainder of the ride, all the way to the adobe shacks that marked the beginning of the town, through the narrow, winding streets, and on to a ramshackle establishment at the center of San Antonio, where they finally halted.

"The Alamo Arms," she said in surprise. "Why?"

"This is where you last saw your brother. I thought we should begin our search in here."

We won't find him. She couldn't say the words. *Let's ride on and never stop.*

"What's wrong?" he asked. "This is what you wanted, isn't it?"

"I want—" She could not look at him. "Royce is not a very nice man."

"This is not news."

Oh, but she had other revelations to make. She wondered how and when they would be said.

"You've got more problems than you've told me, love. I'll find out what they are."

She closed her eyes. He always seemed to read her mind.

"I'm sure you will," she said. But not just yet. As tormented as she was, she wanted these hours with him to stretch as long as possible, and keeping him from his father's funeral had nothing to do with it.

They both dismounted. He extended his hand. She took it and walked beside him through the swinging doors.

Her grasp was strong. Conn liked that in her. Reluctantly he turned his attention to the saloon.

The room had been cleared of the debris from the previous evening's fight, though the number of tables and chairs had decreased. Even at this midday hour, the saloon was half filled. Mister Mule was not among the customers. Crystal assured him that neither was Royce Braden.

He took her by the arm to escort her outside.

"Good day, sir."

He turned to face the woman who'd come up behind them.

Mrs. Truehart was the name she had given when she'd introduced herself yesterday. A redheaded, buxom woman of forty, she'd looked more world-weary than lusty when she'd asked if he wanted one of her girls.

But she'd also seemed honest and straightforward and respectful of his decline. He'd liked her right away.

Her dark eyes turned to Crystal.

"I understand why we couldn't do business yesterday."

Common sense told Conn to end the conversation fast, but before he could maneuver Crystal toward the door, she introduced herself and stuck out her hand.

The madam took it. "Mrs. Truehart here. You came in yesterday, didn't you? With that handsome rascal of a brother. The one who sold you for a mule."

"You heard about that?" Crystal said.

"There's little that gets past me, Miss Braden."

"I'd hoped no one knew."

"The few who did were either too drunk to remember it the next day or decided the story was a joke."

"Have you seen the brother today?" Conn asked.

Anger flashed momentarily in the woman's eyes. "No, and he'd better not—" She stopped herself.

"What's he done?" Crystal asked.

"He used one of my girls."

"Didn't he pay?" Crystal asked, with such innocence and awareness that Conn wanted to give her a great big kiss.

No shy violet was his intended bride.

Mrs. Truehart shot him a questioning look. He gestured for her to continue.

"That wasn't the problem. He . . . used her."

"He hurt her?" Crystal's voice turned small.

"I gave her the rest of the week off to rest."

Conn pulled a gold coin from his pocket. "If you see him, could you send word to the Menger?"

She waved the money away. "I saw you rescue her last night. You helping her look for him?"

Conn nodded.

"You staying until he shows up?" she asked Crystal.

"I have to."

"At the Menger Hotel, I'll bet. Your man looks like the kind who'd want the best."

"I have my own room," Crystal said.

"Didn't think nothing else. You got the money? Don't bother to answer. Of course you don't."

She looked Conn over, then it was back to Crystal. "He's a good one, I can tell, but no man's that good. Room's next to yours, right?"

Conn felt the need to protest, but for once in his life he couldn't come up with anything to say. Besides, Crystal didn't look offended. And he was curious as to where the madam was headed.

He soon found out. She suggested a nearby rooming house where Crystal could stay.

"Won't cost you anything. Not for a night or two. The owner owes me a few favors. It's time I collected."

Crystal protested, but Mrs. Truehart wore her down. Conn figured any arguments he put up would sound as if he were losing out on a good thing.

"You'll need some clothes."

"I'm all right."

"I'm taking care of her," Conn said.

"Don't want to be taking favors from any man, honey. Trust me on that. I'll get a couple of dresses over to you. Nothing fancy like the girls wear, never you fear. Owner of the dry goods store—"

"I know," said Crystal with a smile. "He owes you a few favors. It's time you were collecting."

Mrs. Truehart glanced at Conn. "She's a fine woman. You plan on keeping her?"

"I am."

Crystal stared at the floor.

It took all of his will not to toss her over his shoulder and carry her to the nearest bed.

First things first.

He left her at the Alamo Bed and Board, a respectable-looking place two blocks south of the

Menger, and went asking around for Royce Braden. Only the stablehand and the battered saloon girl remembered him, and they hadn't seen him since the previous night.

He gave up in the late afternoon and went back to Crystal. She met him in the parlor. They were alone. She was wearing a sky-blue cotton gown, high-necked, long-sleeved, simple in its lines, but there was nothing simple about the body it covered.

Her hair was loose and soft against her shoulders. Her eyes were deep and round and worried. Her lips parted when she saw him.

He kissed her because they both wanted him to.

She pushed herself away from him, but not right away.

"Someone will see us."

"Would you really mind?"

She thought a minute. "No."

He kissed her again, this time with more enthusiasm, getting his tongue and then hers into the process.

He was the one to push away.

"In case you're wondering, love, I didn't find him."

"Who?"

"Your brother."

"Oh."

"In case you were wondering."

"I wasn't."

Conn's heart filled to the point of bursting.

"Let's walk," he said, and she agreed, leaving

him briefly to fetch a matching bonnet and gloves and a parasol that she twirled becomingly over her head.

"I've never had one of these," she said. "Mrs. Truehart is very thorough."

"In her profession, she must find it necessary. Ah, I've embarrassed you. Forgive me."

"You haven't embarrassed me," she said as they strolled outside. "I was just wondering how thoroughness figured in."

He threw back his head and laughed, and he fell in love a little more.

They walked and talked. He told her of the years in Saratoga, the lean times of working for others, and then the good times when his knowledge of horses began to pay off. A few lucky bets, a few purchases, and he soon had a small stable of his own. And then a stable that was not quite so small.

"Did you never think of coming home? To Texas, I mean?"

"Every day."

"And why didn't you?"

"I had instructions to remain in New York."

"Who gave them?"

They were walking along the banks of the river. He stopped and listened to the moving water and the laughter of children across the way.

"My father."

"Oh," she cried out, covering her mouth with a gloved hand.

"Perhaps it was all for the best. Who's to say? I kept up with him through a Kerrville lawyer. Now he's sent for me, and I'm in a position to help him in ways I couldn't have managed earlier."

She stared past him, but he doubted she was seeing anything.

"Don't fret yourself. I'm a believer in fate and in happy endings, don't you know?"

She pulled away from him and began to run down the path. He caught up with her. "What's wrong?"

She looked as if she wanted very much to tell him. Instead, she took his hand and kissed his palm. No woman had ever done anything to him so tender and so loving. He began making specific plans.

Looking past her to the laughing children, he said, "Do you want babies?"

She followed his gaze. "I helped to raise my brother. The younger one, Judge. He's fourteen now and quite a handful."

"He's got a funny name."

"It's short for Judgement."

Something in her voice warned him not to probe further in that particular direction.

"So what about the babies?"

She lowered the parasol so that he couldn't see her face. "What difference does it make?"

"None, if you've a strong feeling against them. It's just that I've always wanted a large family. It comes from spending all those years alone."

"I've no feeling against them," she answered in a small voice.

"Remember I said a large family."

The laughter of the children washed over them. "It's what you ought to have," she said and hurried up the bank to the walkway that led back to town.

They ate at a small inn near the river and when she pleaded exhaustion, he returned her to the rooming house. Having things to do, he gave no argument.

The next morning she appeared in the parlor wearing a riding skirt and leather jacket, and her hair was pulled back in a braid.

"Mrs. Truehart," she explained.

They spent that day and the next riding around the town and out onto the surrounding roads, usually forgetting to look for her brother, just talking, she about Virginia and a little about Texas, and he about his plans for raising horses, both work and racing stock.

"That's a fine roan you've got," he mentioned early on. "What's with his name?"

"I raised him from a colt. Father said he'd be nothing but trouble, keeping me from my work, but I made sure he never did."

Conn's stroked his horse's neck. "This one I bought when I got to San Antonio. I've a fine stallion back in New York. I plan to bring him down once things are settled at the Bushwhack. To use for breeding and for racing should the opportunity arise."

She grinned at him. "Horse racing? In Texas? It might be arranged."

"Did you know you have only one dimple?"

She looked away, the grin faded. "I—"

"Two would be gaudy, don't you think? I like the one."

She fell to silence, and he did not interrupt her thoughts.

Conn hadn't completely forgotten his father. At one point he considered sending word to Daniel, or perhaps the Kerrville lawyer, that he had been delayed in San Antonio, that when he returned he would not be alone, but he decided against it. He would be at the Bushwhack soon enough. Crystal would be his splendid surprise.

On the third evening of their acquaintance, after she'd changed into the blue gown, they ended up back at the Menger, this time in his room, with dinner spread before them. They left the food alone. But not each other. For two days they had been little more than friendly, intimate in their talk but little else, touching hands on occasion, kissing good night at Crystal's door. Conn was about to explode. He'd had enough of gentlemanly courting. He suspected she felt the same.

He proved right. When they sat side by side on the small sofa, she came into his arms as naturally as if she did so every night.

"I can't keep my hands off you," he said.

Looking down, she made no response. But she kept her arms around his neck and he could feel the heat coursing through her just as it pulsed through him.

He lifted her chin.

"You love me," he said.

"We've known each other such a short while, Conn."

"Yeah. Great, isn't it? Now admit the truth."

She stared at his lips. "I love . . . your smile."

It was a start. "And why is that?"

"It rests comfortably on your face. And I'm not used to men who smile."

What kind of life must she have led? He kissed one corner of her mouth, and then the other. He kissed her eyes. He kissed her ear and pressed his lips to the side of her neck, letting his breath warm her skin, listening to her sharp intake of breath.

And then he backed away to stare into her eyes.

"Understand one thing, Crystal. I'm not letting you go until you tell me exactly how you feel."

Chapter Five

How did she feel? How many ways were there to tell him?

You look at me and my bones turn to butter.

My heart has taken to turning somersaults.

I'm hot when you're near.

I'm cold when you're gone.

If these were her only symptoms, she would credit the flu. But there was more. Much more.

I want to give you children.

I want you. In every way there is for a woman to want a man.

The past two days with him had been the happiest she could remember, and the most incredible. She felt like a runaway wagon, out of control, racing downhill on wheels with broken spokes.

And she felt more glorious than she could ever remember. If that was love, then she loved him, more than life itself. She'd rather die than bring him harm.

Impossible. Too fast. Insane.

And she harmed him every second she stayed with him.

She should speak out now, but the words wouldn't come, not while he was looking at her, not moving any closer, just sitting beside her in his hotel room and staring with eyes an incredible blue. A woman could look into eyes like that until the end of time.

There was only one way she could respond.

"I love you," she said.

He grinned. Her heart stopped.

"Good," he said. "That's settled."

"Nothing's settled. I don't want to hurt you."

"And how would you do that? Except to say you'll not be my wife."

"I won't marry you. I can't."

Before he could kiss her again, she jumped to her feet and put distance between them. When she turned to face him, she had to fight the urge to bolt back into his arms. He offered her safety and sweet release from her torment. He offered her all that she wanted in the world.

And what did she offer him? Betrayal. She had to tell him the truth. A man as good as he would understand the pressures on her, the threats, the promises she'd had to make.

Again the words wouldn't come. Not just yet. In her heart she knew that once they were spoken, all would be lost.

"I'll be your woman." For one night. "Isn't that what a man really wants?"

"Oh, is it now?" He stood and took a step toward her. "What do you think being my woman involves? Do you fetch and carry when I ask? Cook my meals? Wash my clothes?"

She cleared her throat. "You know what I mean. We sleep together."

He nodded. "There's little point in having a woman if she won't do that." He drew nearer. "We sleep naked, of course."

An image of Conn without clothes rose in her mind. She had trouble with a few of the details. She hungered to undress him and check for accuracy.

"If naked is what you want," she said. What an erotic word *naked* was. She'd never noticed that before.

"Naked is one of many things I want."

He was almost upon her.

"We'll do little sleeping," he said.

"Oh."

He took her hand. "And we might have to stay in bed for days. Just to make sure we're doing it right."

His words made her dizzy. "Days," she said, knowing how stupid she must sound.

"Aye. Your brother could come and go in that time, and we'd not know it."

"My brother?"

She couldn't recall so much as his name, not with sparks flowing from Conn's hands to hers, rippling across her skin, charging through her veins, igniting a thousand fires, burning their way to her heart.

He let go of her hand and worked at the buttons of her gown, laying back the folds of cloth, brushing his thumbs against her skin. His eyes found the lace of her camisole and found, too, the dark, tight nipples thrusting forward beneath the thin cloth, begging to be touched.

He did not disappoint. When he stroked her breasts, her knees buckled. He held her upright in his arms and she welcomed his strength, wishing it could overcome the weakness of her will.

Wrapping her arms around him, she rubbed her breasts against his rough leather vest. "Please, Conn, touch me again. Undress me all the way. Undress yourself."

His arms, his body were hard, sculpted by muscle. His hands found her waist, then moved lower to hold her hips tight against him. Through the layers of their clothing she felt a new kind of hardness pressing between her thighs. She felt a new kind of thrill.

Instinct took over. She parted her legs the better to know the shape of his body, and she began to shift back and forth, ever so slightly, just enough for the torturous tingles to grow more intense.

"Marry me," he whispered into her ear.

"No," she managed.

The tingles demanded she keep doing what she was doing. His hand somehow journeyed under her skirt and with unerring navigational skill located a very vital spot. She'd never before felt anything so demanding.

"Say yes." His voice was soft, insistent. He was a devil to do this to her, but she would die if he dared to stop.

The world grew still, the tingles melding into one long tremor and then an explosion. Her whole body throbbed, and she fell against him, stunned by what was happening to her.

"Say yes."

"Yes."

"Again."

"Yes."

"Again."

"Yes." Each word came out a broken sigh, except the last, which sounded close to a cry. She barely knew what she said except that he wanted her to say it and that made it all right.

He laughed and held her for a long and precious moment. Slowly her body relaxed, sated, but only briefly as the yearnings began anew. Doubt and desire caught like unshed tears in her throat. She was hopeless. She was helpless, too.

Her skirt fell into place. He cupped her face. She wanted to crawl inside his skin.

His hands worked once again at her gown, only this time he was fastening it closed. Her befuddled mind took a second to figure out what he was doing.

"What—"

"We can't have the minister seeing you like this."

"What minister?"

"The one who'll be marrying us. Did you really think I'd take you to bed before the proper words were spoken? What if our children learned of it someday?"

The question took her by surprise. "How would they know?"

"Ah, love, you admit there will be children."

Trapped again.

"No, I—no, there can't—" She gave up just as a knock sounded at the door.

"That'll be him now," Conn said. "You're a tough one, love. For a while I feared my timing would be off."

"Your timing?" Crystal's head reeled. She must be losing her mind.

"Aye." He kissed her quickly, smoothed her hair, and took a moment to adjust his own clothes. Most noticeably his trousers. He grinned at her, shrugged as if to say *what's a man to do with a woman like you?*, then opened the door to the summoned minister. Mrs. Truehart stood by his side.

Crystal stepped back, terrified, as if the small, birdlike man facing her had traipsed in with a pair of pistols blazing. Instead of guns, he bore only a leather-bound Bible in his hands and a militant look in his eye.

He introduced himself as the Reverend Theodore Powell.

Mrs. Truehart nodded in greeting, a smile of satisfaction on her face as she looked at Crystal. "I'll be the witness," she explained.

"But—"

"I've got the license," the reverend said, patting his coat pocket.

"Reverend Ted is a thorough sort," said Mrs. Truehart. "Like me."

In an instant Crystal found herself standing before the good, determined reverend, Conn at her right, the madam at her left. Iron bars could not have imprisoned her more effectively. All chance of retreat had gone.

"I'll not be party to any hanky-panky," Reverend Ted declared. "This wedding may be hurried and unorthodox, but it will be legal in the sight of both God and the law."

"Couldn't have put it better myself," Mrs. Truehart said.

The minister ignored her. He looked at Conn. "Do you love your young woman here?"

Conn's steady gaze was only for her. "Yes."

A dozen times over the last few days Crystal had seen an edge of darkness beneath his bright good humor. She saw no darkness now. He overpowered her by simply looking at her, leaving her weak and strong at the same time, proud and petrified.

The reverend turned to her. "And you, Miss Crystal Braden, do you swear you love this man?"

Outmanned and outmaneuvered, Crystal gave up the fight. "Yes," she said.

The ceremony was over in a minute. Conn had even come up with a ring. When he kissed her to seal their vows, she told herself that all would work out right. He loved her, and she loved him. Hadn't Mama Stewart taught her that love was the most powerful force on the earth? Just because she'd seen no sign of it outside of her grandparents' marriage, that didn't mean it didn't exist.

The papers were soon signed, and the reverend paid. Mrs. Truehart laid a package on the bed. "Something for the trousseau. You won't have it on for long."

And then they were gone, leaving the husband and wife alone. Nervous, desperate to hold reality at bay, she turned to the gift. Tearing the paper, she lifted a froth of ecru silk and lace she supposed was a nightgown. It wouldn't cover much.

"Mrs. O'Brien."

The sound of Conn's voice enfolded her. She didn't turn right away.

"Don't you know your name, lass?"

With a small prayer for strength, she dropped the nightwear and turned to face her husband.

"What's this? A cast of fear in your eye?" He shook his head. "When I first saw you, I gave myself better than even odds we'd come to this moment." He glanced at the nightgown. "Looks like I win."

Her small cry stopped him for only an instant. "We both do," he added. "The world sometimes plays tricks on us. 'Tis something every Irishman knows, no matter where he's born. This time the world is on our side."

He stepped toward the door. "I'll leave you to put that on. Don't be long. As you're no doubt learning, I'm not a patient man."

The door closed behind him. Panic struck. She looked around the room and her eyes settled on the bed, on the gown, on the wide gold band he'd slipped upon her finger.

The marriage really was legal. It was a fact. And so was the way she'd delayed his return home.

Images of her father and of Royce flashed across her mind, and in the background the ghostlike shapes of Mama and Judge. Tomorrow Daniel O'Brien would be laid in the ground. Tomorrow Bushwhack Ranch would fall into Edgar Braden's hands.

She had liked Daniel the few times they'd met, when she'd taken her mother across the creek for sympathy calls.

She loved his son.

What in the name of all that was right and honorable had she done? She ought to run out after Conn and confess the truth, throw herself on his mercy, tell him good-bye.

If she couldn't do that, then she could slip out without a word, the way she had before, saddle Trouble, and ride away, never seeing him again, never knowing what it was to be loved in every way.

She didn't move toward the door. Instead, she began to unbutton her gown.

Conn paced the hall for what seemed an hour but could have been no more than a quarter of that time. Crystal was as skittish as a filly. It must be normal for an innocent lass on her wedding night. He'd show her soon enough that she had nothing to fear.

So many things to show her. It would take the rest of their lives.

When he reentered the hotel room, he found his bride in bed, the bedcovers to her chin, her golden hair spread upon the pillow.

Coyness wasn't her problem. She looked at him straight on. Such a look it was, filled with a bride's unfathomable thoughts, that he could have dropped his pants and taken her right away. But she deserved better on their wedding night.

"Have you no wish to undress me?" he asked.

She stared and shook her head. Her eyes were the deepest brown he'd ever seen.

"Tell me what you want, darling. I'm here to please."

Something close to a growl, something most unCrystal-like, sounded in her throat. "Take off your clothes."

"Is it a show you're wanting? I can go fast or I can go slow," he said. "With or without the light."

Interest flared in her eyes. It was a glint he understood.

"Slow," she said. Her voice was shaky but she seemed to know her mind. "Leave the light as it is."

"Crystal, you torment a man."

The vest went first. He tugged the shirt from his trousers and made fast work of the buttons. She gasped when he dropped it to the floor.

"I can't go much slower or I'll expire," he said.

"Don't. Not either one. It's just that I tried to picture you without your clothes." She stared at his arms and chest. "I didn't get a few parts quite right."

"And I've only just begun. In what ways am I different? Do I disappoint?"

"No." She said it fast and sounded sure. "It's just that you're darker and broader and you have shape." The last came out ragged.

"Was it a whitewashed board you were expecting?"

"Of course not," she said and her smile, brief though it was, brought a flood of relief to him. "I like you the way you are. Hair and all."

"The hair on my chest surprises you."

"And pleases, too."

"Then I've got another surprise you're going to love."

He pulled off his boots and socks; next came the trousers. They were off in an instant, leaving him with ankle-length drawers that fit him like a second skin. Nothing to hide the contours of his body, nothing to disguise his shape.

He didn't want to frighten her, but he wanted her to understand what she did to him. She was looking at his sex. She licked her lips. She understood.

He stripped quickly, pulled back the covers, and joined her in the bed.

"Did you get other parts wrong, wife?"

"I didn't go nearly far enough." She stroked his

upper arm, his throat, his chest. "You're very strong. And hard." Her fingers circled an erect nipple. It was almost his undoing. He caught her hand and kissed it.

"My turn," he said. "Undress."

"I've only the gown."

"And a lovely thing it is. Take it off." He kissed her throat. "I'll get you started. After all, I've done some imagining of my own. Let's see how right I was."

He lowered the lace and stared at her bared breasts. "You're a lovely creature," he said. He licked the nipples. "And you taste good, too."

With a small cry, she threw her arms around his neck and held on tight. He embraced her for a while, enjoying the feel of her breasts against his chest.

"I'm not yet done," he whispered into her hair. She loosened her hold on him. He threw the covers back to the footboard and lowered the gown to her waist, easing her arms from the wide shoulder straps, then exposed her hips and navel, kissing his way as he went. He was close to his prize when she cried out, "No! This is wrong."

He moved back to kiss her lips. "Nothing between a husband and wife is wrong." He kissed her again. "I've moved too fast."

"I meant—" She shook her head. "Just get it done. Make me yours, Conn. Make me yours."

She seemed more desperate than eager, her tremors from some source other than passion, her eyes glistening with tears. But he was too far gone in his own passion to question why. If they didn't move fast, he would spill his seed on the sheet like some inexperienced schoolboy. And that would be wrong for them both.

She removed her gown for him. He parted her legs and nestled between them, using his sex to play with her, to bring her to the same point of mindless hunger that had overtaken him, but when he eased to the damp entrance to her chamber, she thrust her hips upward, taking him inside her all at once.

He wanted to ask how she'd managed the feat, but other matters took precedence. He climaxed an instant later, crying out as if it were his first time. The power and the quickness left him stunned, but only until he realized that she, too, had cried out, not in pleasure but in pain.

She clung tightly to him. He knew she hadn't climaxed with him, but there was little he could do at the moment except let the shudders of completion play out their course. He held her close, even when her own embrace eased. She felt soft and small and delicate and very much dependent on him to take care of her.

In this first coming together, he hadn't done a very good job.

He lifted his head. "I'm sorry."

Panic fluttered in her eyes. "About what? About making me your wife?"

"That's the best thing I've ever done, love. But I hurt you."

She sighed. "Oh, that. From the little I've been

told, I thought it was supposed to hurt."

"Only once. It gets better."

She nodded once and closed her eyes. Shifting to lie beside her, he could think of nothing to say except, "I love you," nothing to do but to stroke her hair and her arm.

"I'll make it better next time," he said after a while.

She smiled up at him. Something was amiss with the smile, a hint of sadness that should not have been there. A fist squeezed at his heart.

"It was perfect," she said. "I really am yours. In every way."

"Next time you'll see the difference."

She sighed. "I don't know that I'll want it different."

For the first time Conn felt at a loss with a woman, the one woman in all the world he'd wanted most to please.

Next time, he promised himself as she turned to nestle against him. She lay still and after a while her breathing grew even. He would let her rest. And then he would show her the way lovemaking should be between them, the way it could be every time. He would show her until dawn lightened the sky.

The trouble was, lying next to her was torture. He couldn't keep his hands to himself. Slowly he rose from the bed, dressed, and with a kiss pressed to her brow, turned out the light and went downstairs for a drink.

The Menger served its liquor in a dark and paneled room that opened onto the street. A half dozen men sat at separate tables, none of them speaking, each lost in private thoughts. Good. Conn had thoughts of his own.

The service was fast. The brandy went down smoothly. He would take just one. Liquor had never impaired his performance, but he was not just performing tonight. He was preparing his beloved for the rest of her life.

He grew restless. How long had he been down here? Not long. Maybe he needed a breath of fresh air to cool him down. Slow him down, too, so he could love his bride right. Five minutes of walking ought to do it. He rose from his chair to go outside.

"Conn O'Brien! I don't believe my eyes."

He looked toward the door, squinting to make out the figure coming into the dim light. He thought a moment. "Hamilton Gates. I'll be damned."

The two men shook hands.

"Ham," said Conn with a shake of his head. "You're the first old friend I've seen since I got back."

He stared at the man with genuine pleasure. He and his brother and Ham had grown up together, getting into trouble, getting out again, racing horses, chasing cows. Chasing women, too, when they got a little older. James and Ham had caught the cows best, but Conn had caught the girls.

The rumbles of war had changed everything. Ham had sided with Conn's father and brother, declaring that no matter what a man thought about the troubles dividing the country, Texas deserved their allegiance. Though he tried, Conn couldn't see issues the same way. When he headed North, they'd parted without rancor. The rift in the O'Brien clan had been deeper, too deep to consider on this particular night.

Conn looked his friend over. The cowhand was as tall and lean as he remembered, maybe a little more hard-bitten, more trail-weary, lanky as ever, loose-jointed as if his bones jangled disconnected inside his skin.

Ham dropped his hat on the table and ran a hand through his dark hair. "Damn, it's good to see you. Didn't expect you'd ever be back in these parts."

"I was beginning to doubt I'd ever make it."

"It's God's country, that's for sure, or at least it used to be. Had us some good times, didn't we?"

The grin on his face died and he mumbled regrets about James not being with them.

"Thanks, Ham. I appreciate the kind words."

"I'm not much for sentiment, but you O'Brien boys meant a lot to me, growing up the way I did without family. It's a shame I'm not hanging around. We could call us up a few memories worth holding on to. See if we still have some of the old vinegar in us. Truth to tell, Conn, I'm not sure I do."

Forgetting his walk, Conn gestured for Ham to join him. "So where are you headed?"

Eager as he was to get back upstairs, another few minutes wouldn't hurt. And it really was good to see an old friend again. It made him realize he truly was back home.

"I'm going west," Ham answered, taking the offered chair, stretching his long legs beside the table and crossing his spurred boots at the ankle. "I haven't decided exactly where, but life is hard here and it don't show no signs of getting better. Not for a poor old cowpoke like me. There's lots of cattle to run but no one's buying. I thought I'd leave Texas for a spell, try my luck in one of the territories."

He glanced around the Menger bar. "I decided to have me a drink at a fancy place my last night in town. You just ride in?"

"No. I've been here three days."

"Three days." Ham's grin was firmly back in place. "Same old Conn. Bet you found yourself a woman."

Conn couldn't keep the good news to himself a moment longer. "Not just any woman. You're looking at a married man, my friend."

It didn't bring the reaction he'd expected.

"You brought a Yankee woman back? It's gonna be hard enough on you, what with resentment about the war still hanging on. You always did ask for trouble."

"The war's been over for years."

"But not Reconstruction. That's what I've been trying to tell you. Those bastards in Washington won't let up until we're all flat busted broke. No one on either side's ready to forget or forgive. You had the right of it. We never should'a fought. Don't let that get around, though. I won't make it to New Mexico alive."

"Then it's a good thing my wife's not trouble. I met her here in San Antonio. It was what you might call a whirlwind courtship. Love hit me like a herd of stampeding beeves. There was just no way to step aside."

"So she's a Texas girl."

"My Texas Crystal. She's upstairs waiting for me right now."

Conn would have gone on, but something about the way Ham sat up gave him pause.

"That her name? Crystal? Kind of unusual."

"And as pretty as she is. Crystal Braden. O'Brien now."

"I'll be a humpbacked mule. You married the Braden girl."

"You know her family? I thought they lived somewhere in north Texas."

"Not the Bradens I'm familiar with."

Ham scratched at his bristled chin. He seemed to be thinking matters over, an exercise he'd never managed with much ease. Conn let him think. Something was wrong, something he didn't want to hear, but he couldn't see walking away without finding out what was eating at Ham.

"You've been here three days, you say."

"That's right. Crystal and I will be starting out tomorrow for the ranch."

"It'll take you two days of steady riding."

"I haven't forgotten."

"No, don't suppose you have. Pardon me for

seeming a little cotton-headed. It's taking a while to put things together. Mind telling me what brought you back?"

A chill whispered through the room. "I got a letter from my father asking me to come home. I'd been waiting years to hear from him. I didn't stay away because I wanted to. Until a month ago, he didn't want me here, and I decided the best thing I could do for him was honor his wishes."

"I can see why you'd feel that way."

"The letter changed everything. I've got plans for taking care of him and for the ranch. Hell, this marriage has me so befuddled, I'm not thinking clearly. There's no need for you to ride west looking for work. I can give it to you at the Bushwhack."

"Then you haven't heard. Didn't want to bring it up unless you did. You seemed to be taking the matter mighty calm. Now I can see it was because you didn't know."

"What matter?"

But Ham seemed in no rush to pass on his information.

"Let me get this straight. You got here three days ago and met the Braden girl. One thing led to another, and you're just now planning to leave."

"What's going on, Ham? Spit it out."

"It don't spit easy. I know you're eager to get back to your bride, but you'd best hold up a spell. Order us a couple of them drinks, too. Make 'em doubles. I got a few things to tell you and it might take a while."

Chapter Six

Crystal heard the door open and close. Conn was back. It seemed to her he'd been gone for hours. She'd been half fearing, half hoping he had ridden away without her, giving up on her as a love partner, deciding he didn't want a wife after all.

Especially one he barely knew.

Such thoughts had been tearing at her ever since he'd left. She'd been lying in the dark, cold and awake, pretending to be asleep in case he returned, pretending to be the loyal wife he thought she was.

Pretending was second nature by now. She hated herself as much as she loved him.

The one thing she'd wanted to give him was a good time. In that she had failed. Even in the dark his presence filled the room. A familiar warmth curled low in her stomach. Another try might be in order before confessing.

No. That would be as bad as everything else she had done. And she'd probably do things wrong all over again.

He turned up the light. The smell of liquor surrounded her. She sat up to face him, brushing the hair from her eyes, holding the covers close to her chin.

How to begin? Straight out. No more lies.

"I've got something to tell you," she said. And then she got a good look at him.

His hands were clenched at his sides. The look in his eyes was something she never wanted to see again.

She thought about the dark-edged light she usually saw in those blue depths, and about the love that had overpowered the ugliness of his past only a few hours before when the minister guided them in their vows.

The light was gone now, and so was the love. Darkness reigned. No need to confess. He already knew. Her heart died, and along with it all hope.

He pulled back the covers and stared at her naked body, pale against the white sheets except for the dark triangle of hair above her thighs and the dark tips of her breasts. He made no move to join her in the bed. No longer was nakedness erotic. She felt cold and ashamed, and terribly exposed.

Which must have been his purpose. She'd known from the beginning that he was a clever man. She saw now that he could be cruel if sufficiently provoked.

Good. She deserved whatever he decided to do. All she hoped was that he would do it quickly and put them both out of their misery.

Hurriedly she grabbed her gown from the foot of the bed and pulled it on. He made no move to stop her.

"How did you find out?" she asked as she leaned back against the pillow. Nothing inside her was still. Her voice sounded as if it came from a bottomless cave.

"I ran into an old friend downstairs. Ham Gates."

"I've heard the name."

"He's heard yours. He told me how your family bought the spread across the creek right after I left. Ever since then you've been the talk of Kerr County, riding the range, tending the herd like one of the hands, keeping to yourself, never going into town. A real beauty, he said. Many a man wanted to court you but was discouraged by the Braden men."

She barely listened. "I was going to tell you."

"I'm sure you were."

"I love—"

She didn't finish. He didn't care.

"Why did you do it?" he asked.

Do what? Meet you? Marry you? Fall in love?

He meant it all, except the last.

"There's not a simple answer. I gave my word."

"You gave it several times."

He wanted to hit her. She could see it in the way he clenched his hands. She hoped that he would.

Instead, he kept on staring with eyes as cold as death.

"What did your friend say? Besides the part about me, I mean."

"Why? Do you want to get your story right?"

She winced at the harshness in his voice. Until now, she'd heard only softness and teasing provocation in it. Like the light in his eye, the softness was gone. She wanted to die.

But such an escape was not open to her. She looked at him straight on.

"My father threatened Mama and Judge if I didn't keep you in town for a while."

"He was going to shoot his wife and son? That's some family you come from."

"I tried to tell you about my family. But you've got it wrong. He wasn't going to shoot them. He considers himself too much a gentleman for anything so violent. What he threatened was to throw them out. Mama isn't well. She couldn't have survived, and Judge would have grown wilder than he already is. I was protecting them."

She saw no need to bring up the old promises to Papa and Mama Stewart. He was not in a mood to care.

"Did you not think I would do the same?" he asked.

"Is that what you would have done if I'd told you everything?"

"I'd like to think I would have tried."

"I couldn't take the chance." Her voice dropped to almost a whisper. "I'm not used to kind men."

"You thought I was like your father and brother. Ham told me a little about them. I'm not flattered."

She tried to swallow the lump in her throat, but it would not go away.

"I know you're not like them."

"No. I'm more stupid."

He knelt beside her on the bed, all grim hardness in his leather and rough clothes and smelling of alcohol. And she, weak and vulnerable in her flesh-colored gown, the scent of their lovemaking still on her. Hysteria bubbled in her throat. She fought it down.

"My father's dead," he said. "I should have been told."

She wanted to touch his cheek, to take him to her bosom and offer words of consolation.

Instead, she stared past him into the empty air and gave him the facts as she knew them.

"It happened a week ago. His heart was bad. He'd been bedridden the past few months. The doctor said the excitement of your return was too much."

Her voice broke. She closed her eyes and fought back the tears. This was far worse than anything she had ever imagined, and she had imagined horrible things.

"I'm sorry, Conn. About your father, I mean."

He made a wordless sound that tore at her soul. "Enough about him."

She barely heard him. "I liked Daniel. He was a good man and kind to Mama."

"I said enough."

But she couldn't stop. "Father thought there was something going on between them, but he was wrong. He died before you and I ever met. I didn't keep you from his side."

"But you kept me from his burial. It's in a few hours, right? We could never make it in time."

He wrapped his hands around her throat. His thumbs pressed against her pulse. "But of course you know that. It was part of the plan."

She lifted her chin high. "Go ahead. I deserve it."

"Did you work out the details the night you ran from the hotel? God, how foolish I must have appeared, letting you rope me and then babbling on with sweet talk about marriage." His fingers tightened. They were hot against her skin. "I could kill you."

"Then do it," she said and meant every word.

The pressure increased, then lessened. She stared at him. The tears came. She made no attempt to brush them aside. They trickled down her cheeks and onto his hands. He jerked away as if she'd burned him.

"Damn you to hell," he said, pulling away from the bed. "Wife." He snarled the word, and her heart shattered a little more.

From somewhere deep inside her she summoned a fragment of tattered pride. "I didn't want to marry you. I tried to tell you it was wrong. But you wouldn't listen. That's why I ran."

"I figure that was more of your cleverness. You made me want you more."

"I don't know anything about making a man want me. You're the only man I've ever loved."

"Then pity me. And congratulate the rest of the men for their good fortune."

She stared down at her hands. "They told me you were greedy. That you came back only for your inheritance."

"But I'm wealthy. Hadn't you heard?"

"Sometimes men who have things want more."

"Your father."

She nodded.

"So you thought I was a villain. A man who had to be taught a lesson. You did your job well, lass. You taught me to be the bastard you thought I was."

He turned from her. She couldn't let him go this way. She sprang from the bed after him. She touched his sleeve, but when he turned to face her, the look on his face drove her back.

"Where are you going?"

"To the bar, if it's any of your business. To get riproaring drunk."

"I love you."

"You don't know what that means."

"I'm still your wife."

"More's the pity."

"When you return—"

"It won't be back to your bed."

They stared at one another for a long and agonizing moment. Conn broke the silence.

"When I return, be ready to ride. We'll leave at dawn. We'll be riding hard."

"But we can't—"

"Make it in time for the funeral? Of course not. Never fear. Bushwhack Ranch will soon be in Braden hands, if it's not already. Ham knew all about the will. So does everyone in the county. The Bradens have beaten the Yankee traitor. It's what they will all be saying in a few hours. You'll get most of the credit, of course, as you so richly deserve."

Each word cut like a knife. "I can talk to Father."

"And what would you say? That you snared yourself a rich husband who has vowed to love and honor you? Don't plan on my keeping those vows, wife, any more than you plan on keeping yours."

He left her. She fell to the floor and the tears gave way to sobs that could wake the dead, though they would have little effect on Conn's heart.

He'd left her, and she was alone. Much as she'd always been. In years past she'd had her duty to keep her going, and she'd had her occasional dreams. She had nothing now.

Who was to know of her sacrifice? Not Mama, so lost in her own problems she could see aught else. Not Judge, who was too young to understand.

And not Father, who cared for only his own dreams.

Royce would see her heartbreak. Royce would laugh. Let him. He was the least of her worries, the least of her pain.

What was Conn planning? She had killed the gentleness in him, the ready laughter, the joy. A moment ago he'd been ready to choke the life from her. She wondered if he planned to shoot them all.

Sometime before dawn, she fell asleep, still curled on the floor. A knock on the door awakened her.

She shook the cobwebs from her brain. The world and all its harshness rushed in.

"Conn?"

He made no response, but she knew he was out there standing in the hall. She stood and held onto the bedpost for support.

"Give me a minute to get dressed. Then I'll be ready to ride."

As Conn had promised, they rode hard all day, stopping only to rest and water the horses. He'd brought along hardtack and jerky and a canteen for them both. He turned his back to her while she forced down a couple of bites, but he didn't wait for her to relieve herself. She had to scramble into the bushes and back again, throwing herself into the saddle as she struggled to catch him on the trail.

By dark they'd reached an inn near the small town of Comfort, close to the Kerr County line. He got them separate rooms. Crystal expected nothing else.

Her belongings were in a bedroll tied behind her saddle. In the privacy of her room she stared at the nightgown. She chose to sleep naked, wrapping herself in blankets instead of her husband's arms. But she didn't cry. She had used up all her tears.

The next morning they were on the road again, drawing closer and closer to the creek and to the pair of ranches that were now in Braden hands.

Once she tried to ask about his plans. He didn't answer. She decided she didn't want to know.

The truth soon became apparent. He was taking her to the Bushwhack. Even after an absence of ten years, he chose the trails unerringly.

They arrived late, just after sunset. On the balmy April evening, the windows of the two-story ranch house were open. Light and sound spilled into the night. She heard her father's laughter, but his words were indistinguishable. She heard no one else.

Despair grew, just when she thought it had reached its limits. Already her father had taken over his new possession. She should not have been surprised.

Conn strode inside, not bothering to knock. It was up to her to follow. She'd never taken more reluctant steps in her life. The front door opened onto the parlor. Conn made it halfway across the room before stopping. Each piece of furniture caught his eye, each lamp, each hanging on the wall. For a long while he stared at a painting over the hearth.

It was a portrait of his mother, Bridget, the Irish immigrant who had borne twin sons on a Texas beach the first day in her new land thirty-five years ago. She'd died years before the Bradens had come to the hill country. On her few visits to the Bushwhack, Crystal had listened while Daniel talked lovingly about her. Dark-haired and blue-eyed, she looked like Conn.

The air grew so heavy that Crystal thought it might break. She reached out for her husband, but he was already moving on. A side door led to a long hallway. An opposite door opened to the dining room. It was from there that Edgar Braden's laughter came.

Conn strode inside, Crystal close behind.

Edgar Braden sat at the head of the table. One glance at the intruders and his laughter died. He looked at Conn, at his daughter, and last at Conn's holstered gun. His sideways glance picked out a rifle propped in the corner.

Conn shook his head. Edgar settled back in his chair. "You're too late," he said.

"Was there ever any doubt I would be?" asked Conn.

Silence descended. Crystal took her place by Conn's side, though she knew he wouldn't like it. But it was where she belonged.

Her mother sat at the far end of the table, looking more frail and colorless than ever. Her gray-streaked dark hair was twisted in a tight knot at her nape. Dark brown eyes lay sunken in her pale face. Her black gown washed out her complexion. Annabelle never wore black. Edgar didn't like it. The gown must be in recognition of yesterday's funeral. Her gentlemanly husband would have insisted that the rules of society be observed.

Judge sat at the side, a look of disgust on his young face as he stared at his sister. He was well named. Knowing what was going on, he had judged her and he had found her at fault.

Royce was not to be seen. It was the one good thing that had happened to her in days.

The door from the kitchen burst open and Helga Werner came into the room. Dear Helga, tall, sturdy, outspoken, an immigrant like the O'Briens, except that she came from a village in the Black Forest of Germany. Housekeeper to the Bradens these past five years, she was the one person Edgar could not intimidate.

"Mein Gott," Helga muttered as she surveyed the scene. She set a steaming soup tureen on the table. Edgar glared at her, but she made no move to leave.

Behind her in the kitchen, Crystal spied Graciela, the Bushwhack's house servant. Dark, sullen, and voluptuous, she was as different from Helga as night from day.

So her father now had two servants, did he? He must really think he was in high cotton. But only for a while, if he lived up to his part of the agreement with her. And only if Conn let him live.

Edgar cleared his throat. "You know about the terms of the will." He glanced at Crystal.

"I know, all right, but she didn't tell me." He put a world of hatred in the *she.*

Annabelle half rose from her chair. "Crystal, dear, what's going on? What have you done?"

A knife turned in Crystal's heart. Even her mother thought her at fault.

Edgar glared at his wife. She fell silent.

"I'm a reasonable man, O'Brien," he said. "I've got a few things that belong to you. Personal belongings of your father's. Letters, clothing, that kind of thing."

"Do you now? You're including the portrait of my mother."

Edgar cleared his throat. Crystal could see his confidence grow stronger each minute that Conn failed to reach for his gun. She'd never considered her father a stupid man. She was fast changing her mind.

"Technically, the painting belongs to the ranch. But as I said, I'm a reasonable man."

"And so am I. I'm returning your property, too."

"What have you got that's mine?"

"Your daughter. My wife."

Annabelle cried out. This time Edgar made it all the way from his chair.

"Your wife!" he said. He glared at his daughter. "You weren't supposed to marry him."

"Ah, well," said Conn, his voice as steely as it was low, "no plan is perfect, is it?" For the first time in hours, he looked at Crystal. "She's a temptation for a man. But then, you know that already. I'm returning her in less than perfect condition, of course, a husband taking his marital privilege as it offers itself." He looked her over. "And she did offer herself, that she did. Even before the preacher appeared."

"See here," said Edgar, "you can't just storm into a man's house and insult him that way."

"I thought I was insulting her."

He stared at her for one long and bitter moment. He opened his mouth to speak. She awaited the assault of his words.

For an instant, she saw the pain deep in his eyes. But then it was gone and the anger, the disgust, the hate returned.

He left the room. She listened to his footsteps as he walked across the hall and through the parlor. The front door slammed. She listened to the sounds of hoofbeats as he rode away.

"Are you really married?" her mother asked.

She found her voice. "Not now, Mama."

She looked at Judge. The swollen lip where their father had struck him still bore a slight cut. He looked so young, yet so worldy-wise. And the disgust was still in his eyes.

She scarcely cared. The sound of Conn's parting words and of his leaving thundered in her head. He was gone.

Reaching inside the collar of her gown, she pulled out a wrinkled piece of paper and threw it onto the table in front of her father.

"I kept my word," she said. "Now I expect you to keep yours."

She glanced at her mother. "I hope you haven't moved everything across the creek."

Annabelle's hand fluttered to her throat. "There's scarcely been time."

"Good. You won't be staying here. Your husband agreed to let you live at the Shingle Camp. You and Judge and Helga. He and Royce will stay here."

"But that's breaking up the family."

"We're not a family. We're people related to one another, that's all." Her attention moved on to Judge. "And get that mulish expression off your face. I can and will tell you what to do, Judge. Until you've proven yourself capable of handling matters for yourself."

"My, my," said Edgar. "Hasn't our little Crystal changed?"

He was gone.

Her heart lay leaden in her breast. "In more ways than you can ever know."

It was a grand moment for an exit. And she didn't think she could stand another moment. Falling into a heap would not be smart. Her father would think her weak. She was weak, devastated in ways he could never understand, and so she hurried into the hall.

Helga met her and gathered her into her arms. Crystal let herself fall lax. Indeed, she had no choice.

The housekeeper muttered something in German. "I've a room prepared for you, *mein liebes Kind,*" she added.

But Crystal wasn't her dear child. She'd failed on every count.

"Could you call me Mrs. O'Brien? Just between the two of us, of course."

"*Ja,* Frau O'Brien," Helga said, and the two of them moved slowly toward the stairs at the back of the hall.

They didn't get far before the front door opened

and closed. Footsteps moved through the parlor. Crystal's heart began to beat. He'd returned. He was taking her with him after all.

Royce walked into the hall. A grin curled its way onto his handsome face. "Sorry to disappoint you, baby sister. Your man rode out of here lickety-split. I made sure he was gone."

She gripped Helga's hand. "You're a coward."

"I'm cautious. He was like a wounded wild boar. There was no telling what he might do. Besides, I would imagine there have been enough dramatics around here for one evening. At least that's what it sounded like from outside."

"You beat up women."

"How did you—"

He broke off, and a mean light glinted in his eyes. "I give them what they want." Slowly the grin made its way back again. "Congratulations. You've caught yourself a rich man. And you've done all right by the rest of us, too. But please, get some rest. You look terrible. Never can tell when we might need you again."

He tipped his hat and headed for the dining room, saying something about checking on the kitchen help since Helga wasn't doing her job.

Crystal could only sigh in relief that their first meeting was past. If he'd thought to insult her, he had failed. She was beyond caring for the opinions of anyone but Conn. And he was gone.

She looked at her left hand. He hadn't taken the ring. He was the one who looked for signs, and she decided maybe he had a point. The ring gave her hope. A few minutes ago in the dining room, when all her life was crashing around her, he could have had it if only he'd asked. He'd have to cut off her finger to get it now.

The hope gave her a kind of vitality and purpose she hadn't had before. She couldn't let matters end this way. She couldn't and she wouldn't. Tomorrow she would come up with something. The thought added to her strength. Separating herself from Helga's supporting arm, she led the way up the stairs.

Chapter Seven

Conn came to consciousness and wished mightily that he hadn't. Everything about him hurt. He lay on his stomach in what felt like a bed of nails, face trapped in a pillow, unable to breath. Worst of all was the thousand-pound stallion prancing on his head.

He groaned. The sound of his voice was not encouraging. It meant he was alive and the odds were better than even he was growing more awake.

He shifted his head, but the stallion remained in place, its hooves finding purchase in his skull. He dared to crack one eye. Light pierced his head.

And so did reality. The image of a honey-haired woman flashed across his tormented mind. He cursed. He seemed to recall spending the past hours, days, weeks—hell, he didn't know how long—drinking himself into oblivion, and now, after a little sleep, he woke to the one memory he wanted to forget.

He hadn't forgotten a thing. Except where he was. And how he'd gotten there.

He forced himself to turn to his back and, with effort beyond reckoning, to sit. Cradling his head in his hands, he looked around. His clothes lay in a heap on the floor. The usual bedroom furniture surrounded him, all of it serviceable and without decoration. A mockingbird sang outside an open window. He wanted to shoot the bird, but his gun and holster were draped across the corner of a dresser mirror, too far away to reach.

He scratched at his bearded chin. He must not have shaved in days. He sniffed. Neither had he bathed.

He needed another drink if he were to tolerate himself.

The bedroom door creaked open. He moaned in pain.

"Glad to see you're alive. If that's what you are."

He squinted at the speaker. "Don't shout."

"You're a pitiful sight, Conn O'Brien. I like a drop of whiskey on occasion same as most men, but two days and nights of the poison is beyond my limit. Beyond yours, too."

Conn identified the man. "Stoke Price," he muttered and a measure of relief washed over him. Like Ham Gates, Stoke was one of his old friends. One of the best. His mentor as well as his friend. He'd taught Conn all he knew about horses, and that was more than any man in the entire country.

"We said our hellos when you first rode up late Monday. Glad to see you remember."

"What day is it now?"

"Thursday noon."

Conn didn't need to ask how he'd passed the time.

"I got you some hot water here and some soap for a shave. Then I'd be most obliged if you'd take a dip in the creek while I air out the room."

"You're turning old-maidish on me, Stoke."

"I got to breathe, Conn. Ain't nothing old-maidish about that."

He left his guest to his misery. Conn managed to make it to the dresser, where the basin of water awaited. He wet his face with great care, then lathered on the soap. The extra weight hurt, and so did the razor. Dragged across his whiskers, it screamed like a banshee at his head.

Somehow he lugged his naked body out the door, out of the house, and down the twenty yards to the creek, a pair of hound dogs nipping at his heels. A plunge into the cold water almost finished him off. He scrubbed hard with the soap, trying to get his blood moving again.

Stoke met him on the bank with a towel and a cup of coffee. He offered a pile of clean clothes, too. Conn took it all. Stoke had always treated him like the son he'd never had, showing a friendliness and concern he kept from the rest of the world.

A long time ago, in better times, Daniel had given him a small parcel of land up the creek a couple of miles, in gratitude for his kindness to Conn. It had taken a while for him to accept the gift. He'd built the house himself, with a young lad hanging around, asking questions, getting in the way more than he helped.

No wonder Conn had headed straight for Stoke's Place, as it was commonly called. It was home now, or as close to a home as he was likely to find.

Dried and dressed and only semi-comatose, he followed Stoke into the kitchen at the back of the house. Having lost interest now that he was clean, the dogs dropped away to find shade under a tree.

A short, bandy-legged horseman, his old teacher still walked with a limp from where a mustang had thrown him years before. Though he was in his sixties, his hair remained dark, his eyes sharp, his craggy face as brown as bark.

And he could cook better than the finest Saratoga chef.

He set a plate of bacon, eggs, and biscuits in front of Conn, who swore he would never eat again, then gobbled down the whole mess and asked for more biscuits.

Conn hunkered over the table for a few silent minutes, letting the food do its work.

"Monday night," he said at last, "when I got here, did I happen to mention what's going on?"

"Some, before the whiskey took charge." Stoke shifted a plug of tobacco from cheek to cheek. "I filled in the omissions."

"I must have turned stupid up in New York."

Stoke sent a stream of tobacco into a cuspidor beside the woodstove. Bullseye.

"I've seen your wife. Nothing stupid about wanting her."

Conn almost came out of the chair. "You've seen her? Was she here?"

"Nope. But she rides the range on the Shingle Camp and sometimes she brings her roan down to the creek for a drink. She usually just stares into the water, like she's a thousand miles away, and then she'll talk to the horse, soft and low the way you used to do. I don't bother her, even if she's strayed onto my land. But I can't help noticing what a fine filly she is. Roan ain't bad, neither."

Conn couldn't bring himself to disagree with either judgment. He pictured Crystal the way he'd first seen her in the saloon, looking gentle and fair and struggling to be brave. Or that's the way it had seemed. The truth was she'd been waiting for him to come to her rescue, her worry being that he would pass her by. The bells he'd taken as a sign of an upcoming wedding had really been tolling his doom.

"I was stupid all right. The worst thing was, I didn't have to marry her."

"That's one way of looking at it. Don't forget you've been through hard times. I'm not such a foolish old bachelor I don't know what it's like to want family. For that you need a wife."

"You're making excuses for me. That's not like you."

Stoke shifted the chaw again and pondered the matter.

"You're right. You were a fool."

Conn did not find the affirmation comforting.

"Do you mind putting me up a while until I decide what to do?"

"I'm insulted at the question."

"Sorry. A woman told me recently she wasn't used to kindness. Guess you could say the same for me."

"Nothing kind about it. This place is half yours. I figured you always knew it."

"After all these years? You know I fought for the North, don't you?"

"Whole county knows. The way I see it, a man does what he feels is right. And that's what I've done. The land and all that's on it is half yours now and yours outright when I'm gone. Don't take to arguing. I've already got the papers drawn."

Conn choked up for a minute, but kept his feelings private, Stoke not being a man for expressing sentiment. He let the matter go with a nod of thanks, then pushed away his plate.

"Speaking of papers, I'll need to ride into town and take care of a few matters. I'm not looking forward to it. Bankers and lawyers are not my favorite people, but I guess at times they're necessary."

"Like a scrub-down and a shave."

In the old days Conn would have grinned. Now all his grins were gone.

He took time to walk with Stoke around the

place. Over the past years, his old friend had obviously worked hard, buying and clearing land for pasture, adding corrals, building a new barn. He had a few dozen longhorns grazing in one of the pastures and an equal number of horses in another. He even talked about adding hogs and sheep.

"Doubt if I'll do it. Too old to take on new problems, though there's some who say hog and sheep is the way to go."

Stoke talked mostly about the horses and about the mustangs still running wild and available to whoever could catch them—"if the Injuns don't get 'em first."

"Whatever happened to that bay mare you used to ride?"

"Alice? I got her a small corral back behind the barn. She's too old and ornery to be set loose anywhere else. Kinda like me."

Conn gave a moment's thought to the mare and to the horses he had ridden as a youth. One or two of them might still be at the Bushwhack. He didn't think about them long.

The house itself was much as it used to be—cedar shingle roof, a rock base and split-cedar walls, a porch across the back looking out on the creek, shaded by pecan and oak, and inside a large kitchen taking up the back half of the cabin, a small parlor and the one bedroom dividing the front.

Conn walked through the kitchen and into the parlor. A yellow horsehair sofa backed up close to the door. The hearth and a couple of chairs were to the left, the bedroom to the right. Across from the sofa a window looked out onto a small clearing, and beside it was the seldom-used front door.

Nothing about the room looked any more worn than Conn remembered from before the war.

"I put this room in for you," Stoke said as if he read his mind. "Thought maybe the time might come when you'd want to hang around a while."

"You always were smart."

The furniture was all hand-hewn, all Texas-made of hill-country oak. Conn said he felt guilty over taking the only bed, but Stoke replied he'd slept in the barn many a night when Alice had been ailing and there was no need for him to do anything else now.

Stoke's Place covered a hundred acres, small by Texas standards, but adequate to support a single man, if times were not so hard.

"Lately I couldn't have even paid the taxes except that I had some money put by from before the war. It was taxes did your pa in. I tried to give him what I could, but he wouldn't take it, and besides it wasn't enough."

"If I had known what was going on—"

"Son, you don't have to flail me with that parcel of news. I shoulda' got in touch with you somehow. Never writ a letter in my life, but I coulda' learned how."

"I'm blaming no one but myself. It was my place to get down here and check things out."

"He'd 'a taken Edgar Braden's money before

yours. The rascal just showed up at the Bushwhack one day offering to help him out. Took me by surprise. I thought Braden didn't care for your pa. Don't know why, just a feeling I got."

"If times were hard, where did Braden get so much money?"

"That's another peculiar thing. He brought it with him, the story goes, pulled out of Virginia before the times got really bad, but how he held on to it after the war is a puzzle."

Conn was not in a mood to express gratitude for the sudden Braden generosity.

When he finally saddled his horse, Stoke sent him off with a warning:

"You won't find people so friendly as they were. More'n likely, they'll not be sorry you lost your land. I understood how you felt about the troubles all those years ago and finally so did your pa, but we were the only ones. Us and a few German hardheads, but you know how ornery they are."

"There weren't more than fifty slaves in all of Kerr County," said Conn. "I said let them go and keep the peace."

"After Lincoln set 'em free, most stayed on to settle here peaceably, but that weren't the point. It was Yankees telling us what to do that riled folks. Braden ain't the most liked man around, but at least he stayed in the South. Couldn't fight because of his bum leg, same as me, but that oldest boy of his did. Leastways he claims so."

"You doubt him?"

"He was too young to join up during the early

years, and then he went out to West Texas. Said he joined up with one of the Confederate outfits fighting Injuns. I can't see him risking his hide to protect a few settlers, but I keep the opinion to myself."

He spat in the dirt. "I won't keep it from you. Royce Braden is the slickest, meanest son-of-a-bitch ever to ride these hills. And that includes some fiercesome Comanches still roaming about. But he ain't the only sorry son in these parts. No matter what folks think, and they don't talk much, leastways about him, his pa's not viewed the same."

Stoke had given him things to think about as he made the hour-long ride into Kerrville. Most of them only added to his troubles. He half expected a vigilante committee to meet him at the edge of town. But all he got were stares as he rode down the main street of town.

A more sensitive man might have worried at the hard looks. Conn was fast developing a thick skin.

He went first to the bank. There were hard stares here, too, but they softened considerably when he mentioned the funds he would be transferring down from New York. His papers were in order. The banker was practically his best friend by the time he escorted him out the door.

The lawyer was next on his short list. Hugo Ridley kept a small office near the courthouse, which was housed in a former general store and was about as crude and unofficial looking as Conn remembered.

Ridley had been the family attorney for years. Through him, Conn had kept up with the family news. He must have been the one who'd drawn up the will giving Edgar Braden title to the Bushwhack. Among other matters, Conn wanted to hear the details.

Ridley met him on the street and hustled him inside, as if he'd been waiting for his arrival and didn't want anyone to see him walking in. A short, portly man sporting a gray moustache and sideburns, he gestured for Conn to sit and settled behind his desk.

"Can I get you something to drink? I've got some fine brandy that'll go down right smooth."

Conn's head pounded at the thought. "I'll pass, thanks all the same."

"A cigar, then." He reached for a humidor at the corner of his desk.

"No. But help yourself."

"Trying to give up the smokes. The little woman, you understand. They can be hard on a man, that's for sure. I meant the cigars, of course."

"Women can be, too."

Ridley cleared his throat. "For a lawyer, I've got a bad habit of misspeaking. There's no need to pussyfoot around. I'm a man believes in getting right to the point. What I'm trying to say is, I heard about what happened in San Antonio."

"What did you hear?" Conn asked, thinking he was better off hearing the gossip right away.

"Now, Conn—you don't mind if I call you that, do you? We've been corresponding for so long I feel like I know you. Anyway, I heard you married the former Miss Crystal Braden. There's been many a man who wished he could have been in your shoes."

"They're welcome to them."

"What—Oh, I see you're joking. You always were one to tease. Welcome to your shoes. That's a good one."

Ridley pulled a pocketwatch from his vest, but instead of opening it to check the time, he stroked its etched surface with his thumb. It seemed to give him some kind of comfort. Conn wondered if he shouldn't get one for himself.

"I guess congratulations are not in order," Ridley said. Conn chose not to respond.

"I suppose you're wondering if the transfer of title to the Bushwhack was legal. No need to pussyfoot around. It was, and it is. There's not a court in the land, not even a Reconstruction court, that'll void your father's will. Braden loaned him money to keep going, when the bank turned its back. The only thing he asked was the title if and when Daniel should die."

"He wasn't taking much of a risk. My father was a sick man."

"That he was. But sometimes men linger long after the rest of the world has given them up. I swear to you, when I delivered your letter to Daniel, the one saying you were on the way back to Texas, I thought he was going to rise out of that bed and kiss me. All in a manly way, you understand. But the excitement proved too much. And don't blame yourself. Doc Rivers had given him up a year ago."

"He died alone. You should have let me know he was ill."

"He made me promise not to. I was to keep quiet about the will and his financial woes, too. He didn't want you coming back feeling sorry for him. Now don't get your dander up. We had an argument over it, but because of his heart I didn't argue long."

"Still, he died alone."

"Graciela was there. She took care of him the past few years. I don't suppose you've seen her. A fine-looking woman from south of the border. Graciela Gomez is her full name. When the men haven't been thinking about courting Crystal Braden, they've been considering taking Graciela to bed. Damned if I haven't—"

He was practically wearing the etching off the watch. "That's another story. As far as I know, she's led a virginal life, though she surely doesn't look it. It's none of my business, you understand, her sleeping habits, that is, but I was concerned that she take good care of Daniel. And she did. Doc Rivers says she was the reason he held on for so long. Not that there was anything between them. Your father might have looked a time or two, but—"

Conn's patience ran out. "I didn't ride into town to hear about my father's personal habits."

"Well, now, of course not. I understand that."

"And I didn't expect to hear we could break the

will. My father owed the money. I didn't get here in time to pay his debts."

"You're taking this well, I have to hand it to you. Why, any other man—"

"Wouldn't you like to hear what it is that brought me here?"

Ridley did one of his quick about-faces and gestured for Conn to continue.

"I'm a married man now and I've got obligations."

"You're—"

"I know. I'm taking this very well. You don't know the half. What I want is to settle a sum of money on her at the bank in her name. I want a monthly transfer of funds into her account from mine."

He named an amount.

Ridley whistled, but he was wise enough not to say a word.

"I've seen the banker. You draw up the papers and he'll do the rest. Except for letting her know. That will be up to you. Write the letter. Make it legal and binding. This is what she gets from me and nothing more. Unless there's a child, of course. I'd want to care for a child."

Conn kept the words even, as if they were not tearing at his gut.

"If you're sure. It seems to me the woman has played you false. Grounds for divorce, though from what you say an annulment is out of the question."

"Whatever happened between us is our business

and no one else's. Just draw up the papers, write the letter, and deliver it to her yourself."

"I doubt if she'll come into town. She never has before."

"You'll be amply compensated for your journey to the Bushwhack. You went there many times to see my father."

Ridley agreed that he had, then went on to explain just how the papers would read, what he would say in the letter, when the matter might be taken care of. They were points of no concern to Conn, and he left before the lawyer found another topic he could beat to death.

Outside he was met with more cold stares, although how the upright, moral citizens of Kerrville knew his identity remained a mystery, most of them being strangers to him. Probably one person had recognized him and word had spread. He'd forgotten how gossip worked in a small town.

Stubbornness made him linger. A block away he found a general store. He stepped inside to the sights and smells of his boyhood, when he and James would ride into town for supplies. This particular store, proprietor by the name of John E. Ochse according to the sign above the door, had the usual assortment of goods for sale: brooms and horse collars and trace chains hanging on the wall, shelves behind the counter with rows of snuff figuring prominently, barrels of apples scenting the air, men's hats and work clothes, bolts of cloth, boots and brogan shoes.

A row of rifles figured prominently, too. On the

counter was a jar of stick candy, a sign listing such medicines as paregoric and camphor, and beside the sign a tobacco cutter for measuring off plugs.

There were people there, too, a dozen men and women and children scattered throughout, but they stopped what they were doing when he walked in. None seemed eager to step up with a friendly *hello*.

One particular woman caught his eye. She was dressed in black, including an imposing black bonnet that fit tight around her face. Middle-aged and formidable of figure, her lined features drawn, her eyes narrow and cold, she stared at him hardest of all.

Beside her was a younger woman, close to thirty, dressed also in black, her dark hair and bonnet making her look paler than she already was. She had delicate features, too, and a timid, beaten look about her, as if she bore the weight of the world on her shoulders.

He nodded at her in sympathy. She ventured him a small smile and he saw how pretty she was. Her companion jerked at her arm and she looked down at her hands.

Conn recognized the older woman as Dora Weathers. She and her husband had a ranch on Green Creek, the Double D; their son had been one of his friends. His name was Dalworth, like his dad, but he was known as Stormy and he could raise hell with the best of them. Mrs. Weathers had welcomed Conn into her house and at her table many a time.

Removing his hat, he strolled over to say hello and to ask about her son. She saw his intent. Gathering herself together like a thundercloud, she took the hapless younger woman by the arm and with a loud *humph* strode past him and out the door.

Well, thought Conn, that pretty much summed up how things would be. He turned to the clerk at the counter.

"Mrs. Weathers lost a boy in the war," the clerk said. "Dal Junior. That's his widow Jennie with him. Don't expect them to hug you hello."

"Damn," Conn muttered, not because of the slight but because of Stormy. Damn the loss and damn the war. It seemed as if the hurt would go on forever.

He made his purchases fast: a couple of plugs of tobacco and a gallon of whiskey to pay back what he must have drunk. He bought a half dozen sticks of candy, too, figuring Stoke would take pleasure in the treat. He would come back later for more basic supplies, although for a couple of single men out in the country, tobacco and whiskey and candy seemed basic enough.

He made the return trip faster than the riding in, not bothering to look around the countryside. The effects of the past few days were beginning to tell, and the whiskey sounded tempting as it sloshed around in the jug.

He'd better hold off. He still had some thinking to do.

He tied his horse to the rail at the back of the

house and took down the saddlebags holding the purchases. Stoke strolled out the back door. The hounds were nowhere in sight.

"See you made it back all right. Have any trouble?"

"No. But you were right. The fair citizens did not greet me with gifts and a parade."

"Ought to be glad they didn't greet you with a necktie party."

"I think a few of them are considering it."

Stoke fell silent. Something about the way he was standing there blocking the door and staring made the hair at the back of Conn's neck prickle.

"What's going on?" he asked.

"You got a visitor."

"Is he armed?"

"Not that I noticed. Not the usual kind of weapons, that's for sure."

"Where is he?"

"In the parlor. Except that—" Stoke shook his head. "In the parlor. You best go right in."

He took the saddlebags from Conn. "Feels like you bought yourself a load of granite. Nope. That's a jug of whiskey in there. I'll keep it handy. You may be needing it before long."

Conn hung his hat on a nail by the back door, but he kept wearing his gun as he strode inside. He passed through the kitchen but he didn't make it into the parlor before he figured out who the visitor was. Crystal's scent was in the air. He felt like someone had kicked him in the groin.

She was standing by the front window staring

out. He stopped in the doorway between the two rooms, and she turned to face him. She was wearing a split buckskin skirt and vest and yellow blouse, and her hair was twisted into a thick braid down her back. Her gloved hands were holding tight onto her hat.

One look and everything inside him tightened. Damn her black soul.

"What are you doing here?" he asked.

She swayed, so slightly he would have missed it if he hadn't been staring hard.

But then she straightened. He'd married a strong woman. She just looked weak.

She walked toward him. Damned if he would run, but that was the second thought that sprang to mind. Fool that he was, his initial inclination was to bound over the sofa and kiss her until they were both spring-silly and groping each other on the floor.

She came closer. He could see the dark shadows under her eyes and the bleakness in their depths. But there was determination, too. It angered him. She had no right to be here.

"You don't look so good," he said.

"Neither do you."

"Now that we've got the amenities out of the way, what are you up to?"

She tossed her hat onto the sofa; then she took off her gloves, pulling at the fingers one by one, revealing the ring on her left hand, tormenting him, driving a knife into his gut with each pull. She dropped the gloves beside the hat.

He leaned against the door frame. "You planning on stripping all the way?"

"Do you want me to?"

"No." He lied.

He'd lied, too, about her looking terrible. Except for seeming tired, she looked better than he remembered. And he remembered a great deal.

She came around the sofa and like a bullet came straight for him, only she was moving slowly.

"If you knew anything about me, I mean really knew me, you'd not be surprised I'm here. Whether you want me or not, I'm your wife, Conn O'Brien. My rightful place is with you."

Chapter Eight

Crystal had lied about Conn looking bad. Except for seeming tired, and maybe a little hung over, he looked wonderful, dark and solemn and strong and mocking, too. She wanted to kiss a smile back onto his face, kiss his lips, his eyes, his throat, and though he didn't want her to strip naked, she would just as soon he undressed. That way she could kiss him south of his neck.

But her lot was to stand firm, declare herself, and await her sentencing.

"You're not my wife, Crystal, not in the true sense of the word, and we both know it."

He said no more than she expected, but still the words hurt. She had to stand tough. Conn was worth a thousand such pains.

"The law sees it otherwise."

"What kind of game are you playing?"

She glanced at the gun resting against his thigh. At least he hadn't shot her. Not yet.

"It's not a game. I'm here to stay." *Until you toss me out, which might be any minute considering the look in your eye.*

"This isn't my house. It's not my place to say move right in."

"Stoke said it's yours as much as his."

"So you two already talked. I should have known."

"You weren't here and he was. And I didn't say anything to him I wouldn't say to you."

"You're already lining up my property, right? Seeing what else you can take?"

She winced. He knew how to wound without using the pistol. She had no defense, except that she loved him in a way he couldn't begin to understand.

"You're confusing me with someone else," she said. "I don't own anything of yours."

"What happened? Edgar won't give you a share?"

"I deserve everything you say. But I'm not leaving. Not so soon." She turned and sat on the sofa, her back to him. "What I'm telling you is the truth."

His scornful laugh almost stopped her. Almost. But she still had things to tell him, hurtful private matters that she could scarcely put into words.

"Father doesn't want me any more than you do," she said, beginning soft and slow, hoping to make him listen all the harder. She didn't want him thinking of anything but her.

"He calls me tainted property," she went on. "I was supposed to go to bed with you if necessary, but that was all. Marriage wasn't in the deal."

She could almost feel his breath ruffle her hair, though he stood several feet behind her, and she could picture the set of his mouth and the scorn in his eyes as she spoke. But she didn't hear him walk away. She could almost breathe a sigh of relief except that the worst of her revelations was yet to come.

"I messed things up by making an honest woman of you, did I? Nice man."

"Of course he's not. I never claimed that he was. I'm an O'Brien now, and he hates all O'Briens. I told you he thought my mother and your father were having an affair. They weren't. When she heard about your brother's death, Mama had me drive her across the bridge to offer sympathy and take some food, the way she'd been taught in Virginia. They talked about James and your mother, that was all. They never even mentioned you."

"If it's all the same, I'd rather you not be quite so truthful. Your lies went down easier."

"Not from my end."

An uneasy silence fell. Crystal didn't mind it terribly, not if the silence was brief.

But it went on too long. She took a deep breath. "Would you mind sitting where I can see you? I've got some more things to say."

"Ordering me about, are you?"

His voice was hard, but he came around to take

a chair by the hearth, turning it to look at her while she talked. His legs stretched out in front of him, long and lean, and she pictured the muscles working beneath his fitted trousers. She pictured other parts, too. She knew no shame. Conn had educated her beyond all maidenly thoughts.

He crossed his boots at the ankle. He was still wearing his spurs; they jangled whenever he moved. It seemed to her that her nerves jangled just as loudly.

He appeared relaxed enough, sitting back the way he was, but Crystal knew he was wound as tight as she. Funny how she'd learned that much about him, about the way he held his shoulders when he was tense, about the way his eyes crinkled in the corners when he was concentrating on what he heard.

Funny, too, how all she wanted to do was stare at him, to feast on every detail until the memories of the past few days away from him faded to insignificance.

But feasting was a luxury not meant for her, and she forced herself to go on.

"I was born in Virginia, but of course you already know that. My father had been a worker on my grandparents' plantation. The only thing he ever said about his own family was that they were poor white trash from farther south and he never wanted to see them again."

She waited for Conn to say something sarcastic, but he kept quiet and she hurried on.

"He and Mama fell in love. She says he was quite

the dashing young man in those days, a hard worker determined to succeed. He moved up to foreman, and when she told her parents he was the man she wanted, they didn't put up too much of an argument. She was an only child and they tended to spoil her, I suppose. Royce came along first, and then two years later I was born."

She closed her eyes for a minute, remembering details of her childhood she'd wanted to forget.

"As I was growing up, Father changed. He had his own farm by then and he was working hard at it, but he started accusing Mama of . . . ugly things. She lost a couple of babies, and when my younger brother was born, her health broke down. Father claimed the boy wasn't his, no more than the stillborn babies had been. He named him Judgement, saying the effect of his birth on Mama was punishment for her sin."

She felt Conn's eyes on her, pinning her to where she sat, but there was no warmth in the stare, no sign of sympathy. Perhaps she should have told him just how ugly those years had been, but she doubted his stare would have changed. Her nerves jangled louder than ever. She wanted to stand and pace, but at the moment simply staying in the same room with her unwilling husband took all her strength.

She wanted, too, to tell him how difficult all this was to reveal, but smart man that he was, he must already know.

Fixing her gaze on the stone fireplace, she hurried on.

"Things were getting ugly in Virginia and he sold out, saying he was getting Mama away from her family and her lovers. He'd fallen, you see, turned over a carriage when he was chasing a man he thought had been sniffing Mama out, as he put it. It left him damaged, though he got over the worst of his injuries. All he's got now is a limp. And his bitterness, of course. He brought that to Texas with him."

She stopped and held her breath.

"So what's the point in telling me all this?"

"Before we left, my grandparents took me aside and asked me to take care of Mama and Judge. 'You're the strong one in the family,' they said. 'You'll have to be there in our stead.' I could see why they didn't ask Royce. He was irresponsible at times, even then. But I was only fourteen, a girl child in a world ruled by men. Still, I promised to do what I could. It was for Mama Stewart and Papa Stewart that I agreed to . . . do what I did with you."

"Very touching."

"You're not touched at all. I don't blame you. I should have confided in you the minute I saw the way things were between us. And that was right away."

His lips twitched. "Don't give me any of your blarney, Crystal."

"Call it what you will, it's the truth. The bargain with Father was that if things went his way, Mama and Judge would continue to live at Shingle Camp and he and Royce at Bushwhack. I hadn't thought of asking about myself. I guess I just assumed I could live where I wanted. Father saw the flaw in our agreement right away. He said as soon as I shed myself of the O'Brien name, I'll be welcome to live at either ranch. Until then, I'm not welcome on Braden land."

She tried to laugh, but it came out weak. "He doesn't want me here, either. He doesn't want me anywhere. The truth is, he's never known quite what to do with me." And in a softer voice: "None of the men in my life do."

Conn straightened, his eyes never moving from her. They were as cold and hard as the stone hearth.

"I'm trying to put this all together. You're wanting a divorce, I assume."

"That's not what I said," she said with a cry.

But he wasn't listening, just staring and judging and viewing things in the worst possible way.

"We can arrange it. You'll need cause. I've already abandoned you. I could find myself another woman, and you could add the charge of adultery. Surely we can find something in all of this that even a Reconstruction judge will listen to."

"I don't want a divorce. Not ever, even if you find another woman. You would have to file the papers." Her voice rose in defiance. "But I don't think you will. You're Catholic."

"Lapsed. I haven't been to mass in years."

"But the old teachings are with you. That's why you were so upset when you learned the truth. Marriage is forever. You wanted a wife. I was it.

But then you found out you didn't want me."

"I wanted a wife with pride."

"As I said, I'm it. No pride, no honor. I'm your wife and I have no place to go." Circling the ring on her finger, she summoned the dregs of her strength. "You have to take me in."

"Are you pregnant?"

The bluntness of the question stunned her. "I . . . don't think so. I had proof the last few days that I'm not."

"Your time of the month came?"

She felt herself blushing. "I didn't know men knew about such things. I barely say anything about it to Mama."

"The Southern lady. You lie, you betray, you steal, but you don't talk about normal bodily functions."

His words slipped out slow and easy, but each one was edged with steel.

"I'll talk about making love all you want."

He shot from the chair, muttering a few familiar profanities and some inventive obscenities she'd never heard.

It took a minute for him to get control. And when he did, he looked at her with eyes that showed no mercy.

"You tell a good story, lass. There's Irish in you for sure. The only problem is, your timing's bad."

"I—"

He cut her off. "You should have confessed while I still loved you. Such a tale would have torn the heart from my chest. I would have slain dragons had you but asked."

He moved close to her and drew himself to his full height, making her feel small and weak and afraid. "But there are no dragons except the ones you've created yourself. I have no heart left, Mrs. O'Brien, and I have no love."

Each syllable was a hammer blow, but he didn't linger to study their effect, instead stepping wide around the sofa as he left the room.

She collapsed against the sofa cushion. He'd given her the ultimate rejection, or so he thought. She had tried to prepare herself for it, but she hadn't come close to succeeding. Hollow inside except for a leaden heart, she listened as he stormed through the kitchen. The back door slammed, and in a moment she heard him ride away.

For the second time in their brief marriage, he was gone. She wondered if he would do the same everywhere she turned up. If that was the case, considering her determination to follow him, he would soon run out of houses to flee.

Crystal blinked back tears. She had failed, but only for the time being. She wasn't done with him, nor he with her.

Somehow she found the strength to stand. She was pulling on her gloves when Stoke Price appeared in the doorway.

"He'll be back," Stoke said.

"I don't think so. Not while I'm still here."

"I know him better than you. He'll be back,

maybe not for a spell, but I'll bet a week of cooking that even with you in the vicinity he'll be back tonight. He just needs to think things through." He looked back into the kitchen and spat a stream of tobacco juice. It hit the spittoon with a *ping*. "I heard you talking in here. Ain't apologizing for it, neither."

"I'm glad you listened. I have no secrets anymore. You must hate me, too."

"Ain't my place to judge. A week of cooking. Is it a bet?"

She almost smiled. "Conn likes to gamble."

"He picked it up from me. You're a big gamble right now, the biggest he's ever had to take, but he's not one to run from bad odds. I'm thinking that's the way he'll be looking at it."

"That's not very romantic."

"If it was romance you was after, you messed things up for sure. Not that I'm judging, understand. Just saying the obvious."

"I'm after a life, Mr. Price. And the only life for me is with my husband."

"Glad I never got tangled up with a woman. You're all stubborn as a tick on a hog's butt."

"I'll take that as a compliment. It means we're strong."

She thought she saw a hint of admiration in his eyes, but she couldn't be sure. Admiration was one thing she hadn't expected ever again.

"So what about the bet?" Stoke asked. "You gonna ride out of here or hang around for a while?"

She walked to the front window and stared out into the trees. "I wonder what staying would be like. It's what I want, of course, more than breathing. And it's why I came, hoping against all common sense that my stubbornness would win out over his."

She turned to face Stoke. "I'm not the woman Conn thought I was, not as good and not as bad. The question is, am I still the woman he wants?"

"You're asking the wrong man. Is it stay or go?"

"It's stay. You knew it would be. The problem is, I don't know how to cook."

"Let's get into the kitchen, then. This is one bet I'm going to win, and I don't take much pleasure in eating swill."

Conn returned shortly after sunset, hungry, grumpy, tired, and sore. He'd had a long day dealing with a hangover, a banker, a lawyer, a town that didn't want him, and a wife he didn't want.

He could deal with everything but the wife.

Thank God she was gone.

And then he saw Trouble in a back stall of the barn, right behind Stoke's old bay mare.

There was trouble in the house, too. For the woman. She had a hell of a nerve staying after all the things he'd told her. He'd spoken the truth, too, except maybe for the part about not wanting her to take off her clothes. But that was just the man in him lusting after a naked woman. Neutral, so to speak. He didn't specifically want *her*.

He took care of his horse, washed up at the edge

of the creek, and headed for the kitchen. Spoke was sitting in a rocker on the back porch. The hounds were sprawled beside him, their eyes glistening from out of the shadows, their tails thumping against the floor in greeting.

"I didn't see you at first," said Conn. "What are you doing here in the dark?"

"I sit out here every evening, which you would'a known if you hadn't been skunk drunk every night since you got here."

"Don't start in on me. I've had a bad day."

"It's gonna get worse."

"I know she's here. I saw her horse in the barn."

"That's part of it. But there's more that's worser still."

"Let me see. What could possibly be worse? I know. Edgar Braden's in there, too."

"Nope. She's alone." He hesitated. Conn girded himself for the bad news.

"She did the cooking tonight," Stoke said.

"Is that what I smell?"

"Like hair off a singed dog? Yep, that's it. Welcome home."

Conn ran a hand through his damp hair. He would be a coward to run from a hundred-pound female, even though the idea had its appeal. Hanging his hat on the back nail, he went inside. The kitchen was deserted. A mountain of dirty pots and dishes sat by the sink. At the back of the stove awaited a cloth-covered plate, the source, he assumed, of the singed-dog aroma.

She walked in through the parlor door. She'd

brushed out her hair and put on the blue dress Mrs. Truehart had sent her in San Antonio. She was tying on an apron, staring at the floor as she walked, but when she came to a halt and slowly lifted her eyes, he knew she'd known he was there.

A lantern hanging on a peg by the sink cast a golden glow across her face and gave him a good view. The light caught in her yellow hair and in her dark eyes. She took his breath away, as well as a beat or two of his heart. Maybe he should have run after all.

He cursed her to perdition, but only in his mind. He couldn't let her know she affected him this way.

And he absolutely refused to stare at her breasts, no matter how closely the gown followed her form.

"Your supper's waiting." She moved past him, giving him a wide berth, and set the plate on the table; then she went over to the sink. "I'll wash up if you don't mind my being in here."

"Of course I mind your being here. Why did you stay?"

Turning her back on him, she set the plates into the bucket of soapy water in the sink. "Stoke and I had a bet about whether you'd return tonight if I was still here."

"And I was expecting you to declare your feelings again."

She scrubbed at a plate. "There's that, too."

"Here I am. Did you win or lose?"

"Technically I lost. I said you wouldn't show up. He said you would."

"Technically you won. I didn't know you were here until I saw Trouble in the barn."

"And you're seeing trouble in the house, right?"

"The thought crossed my mind."

"I've got more bad news. Not only do you have me underfoot, I'm doing the cooking. For a whole week. Those were the terms of the bet."

Conn lifted the cloth from his plate. Whatever the offering had been in a former life, it was indistinguishable now. "What is it?"

"Beef and beans. I made biscuits, too, but I threw them out to the dogs."

"Did they eat 'em?"

"They tried." She washed another plate.

"No wonder they're resting out on the porch."

He lifted a rock-hard bean and twirled it between his thumb and forefinger. "I've figured out your plan. I'm supposed to break my teeth and then I won't be able to bite you."

She turned and dried her hands on the apron. Her eyes locked with his. "You can bite me anytime you want, Conn. And anywhere."

He tried not to react, but he was only human. If he stood, she would know just how she affected him. He didn't love her, but he wanted her. Curse his weak hide, he wanted her as much as he ever had.

It took all his strength not to bound across the table and take her on the kitchen floor.

"I'll pass," he said, but his voice sounded unnatural to his ears. "On you and the beans."

She went back to the dishes fast, but not before he saw the glistening in her eyes. Let her cry. He could take it. He'd suffered through a lot worse than a betraying woman's tears.

She stood with her back to him. He could see her shoulders shaking. He felt mean inside. He didn't like himself, even knowing he was the one who was wronged.

He shoved away from the table and slammed out the back door, shedding clothes as he went, knowing Stoke was watching, and probably so was she through the back window. Let her see his bare backside if she had a hankering for such a sight. There would be a summer frost in Kerr County before he would look at hers.

He dived into the creek. The water was colder than he'd expected. Good. He needed cold. The kitchen had been too hot.

He swam until his skin puckered, until Stoke made his way toward the barn for the night, until the light went off in the house.

Where was he supposed to sleep? His bed was already occupied, he knew for sure. He was not about to recommence matters that had begun in the Menger Hotel.

He let the air dry him, to make sure he was good and cold. There was safety in cold. Grabbing his clothes, he went inside. Moonlight streamed through the parlor window. He would sleep on the sofa, and tomorrow they could talk about other arrangements. But she was already there, wrapped up in covers so tightly that she looked like a cocoon. Her hair spread out everywhere. She should have had the decency to sleep with it braided.

The covers were turned back on the bed, and she'd laid out clean underwear for him to sleep in. He threw them on the floor and crawled into the bed. He'd be damned if a woman would tell him how to sleep.

He tossed and turned for what seemed hours. Every time he came close to sleep, he heard her stir and it was open-eyes time again. Against his will, against all common sense, he began to wonder if she was sleeping naked, too. Sometimes he decided yes, sometimes no. The question became a burning issue in his mind. Did she have the nerve to take over the parlor and flaunt her body like that?

Of course she did.

Her staying here wasn't going to work. She needed to hear it now.

Wrapping himself in a blanket, he made for the parlor. Throwing a log on the banked coals in the fireplace, he turned to find her sitting up. The log caught right away. Moonlight and firelight played across her face and tangled hair. The covers fell aside. She was wearing the prissiest gown he'd ever seen, high-necked and long-sleeved.

"Aren't you hot in that thing?" It wasn't what he'd planned to say.

"I'll take it off."

He wanted to say no, but the word got lost in

the growl in his throat. Tucking the blanket around his waist, he found himself standing beside the sofa. "This isn't going to work," he said.

"You've got the bed. I'm fine sleeping out here."

"It wasn't your comfort that got me worried. Look, Crystal, I don't know why you're here—"

"I'm your wife. And I love you."

"I'd say it was a guilty conscience, or maybe the fact you have no place else to go."

A tear caught on one of her lashes.

"Don't you cry. Whatever it is you're feeling, love or guilt or lost, it's no more than a burden to me."

He meant every word. But then the tear fell on her cheek. Her very soft, pale cheek. Something exploded inside him. She started to speak, but he gave her no chance. He gripped her by the shoulders and pulled her to her feet. He stared at her lips, moist and parted.

Touching her had been a mistake. He'd planned to shake and curse her. Instead he crushed her to him and claimed her mouth with his.

Chapter Nine

Crystal fell into Conn's arms, stunned, thrilled, jubilant with a hope she had no right to feel. Reasoning with him hadn't worked as proof of her love. If she worked at it thoroughly enough, maybe kissing would.

His lips felt good upon hers, sweet and right. Until he ground their mouths together and his fingers dug into her shoulders, her arms, her back. He wasn't kissing her, he was punishing her. She welcomed everything he did, no matter its purpose, praying in her heart that the rage burning within him would transform itself into another kind of heat.

His tongue forced its way inside her mouth. She splayed her hands against his bare chest. His skin felt hot and tight. She wanted to rub her hands all over his body, to visit the places she'd scarcely begun to know, to explore and please him until he accepted her as his wife.

And then she forgot all else but the way his tongue was dancing with hers and his hands were playing down her back. Each stroke was rougher than any she remembered from before. This wasn't the Conn she knew. But he was the Conn she had created, and he was above all else the man she loved.

His assault was like a summer storm, filled with heat and lightning shocks, desire a rumbling thunder inside her that blocked out everything except where he touched her and where she touched him. She stroked his chest and along the sinews of his taut neck, lacing her fingers in his thick, dark hair.

The blanket dropped from his waist. He pulled her to the floor and they lay on top of the warm fibers, their arms and legs in a tangle as he continued the kiss. He covered her face and throat with kisses, sucking the breath from her at the same time that he gave her life.

Hard hands found her breasts, and even through the nightgown she knew he felt their pebble tips. He stroked and squeezed and hurt her more than he'd ever done before, but she wouldn't have stopped him even if she could. Abandonment and loneliness hurt far worse than any physical pain.

Tears burned in her throat. She held them back. A moment of gentleness would be worth her life, but there was no returning to their marriage night.

He had come to her then with tenderness, his

body scented with a splash of bay rum and on his lips whispered words of love. Tonight he smelled of sex and sweat, and the only sound she heard was heavy breathing and the shift of their bodies on the floor.

Fool that she was, the scent and the sounds drove her as wild as he. He hardly let her touch him, so intent was he on his own gropings, but she still managed to find the tight muscles of his arms, the contours of his chest, his narrow waist.

Shyness and shame had kept her from boldness on their wedding night, but she was without either now and somehow she worked her hand past his waist, to the flat abdomen, the thickening hair, and at last his sex. When her fingers wrapped around the hot, hard length, he moaned and jerked at the hem of her gown, his hand working its way up her thigh.

Her first thought was regret that she was wearing underdrawers, the second that they would be no barrier to Conn. She parted her legs. He kissed her lawn-covered breast and thrust his hand between her thighs, a magic thumb working its miracle against her own throbbing sex. The wet readiness came through the cloth. She thrust her hips upward. Impatience was a growl in his throat.

"Tear them off, Conn. Quick."

She felt his fingers grip the cloth, and then he stopped. She urged him on with more frantic thrusts, but his only response was another growl, this one filled with disgust instead of desire, and he rolled away, abandoning her to a fear that was more potent than any she had ever known.

Each breath came forced and her head reeled. She felt foolish and lost and more alone than she'd ever been. Worst of all were the aching that lingered in her private parts and the chill that shivered through her soul. It took her a minute to comprehend what was going on. Too much had happened too fast—his sudden appearance in the night, the harsh words, the kiss and all that went with it. He'd hungered for her as she had hungered for him, but he'd thrust her away as if she were a piece of too-ripe meat.

He sat with his back to her and stared into the fire. Moonlight from the curtainless window cast a ghostly light upon his head and shoulders. For the first time in their brief relationship, she could see each section of his spine. The sight was as intimate as anything about him, but it was rejection, too. He was the one who was naked, but she was the one who shivered and who took the blanket as a shield against the cold.

His silence screamed its terrible message: His wanting her was a curse he must overcome. The tears burned more insistently, but she would not give way to them. He had said he wanted a wife with pride. It was all she had to offer now, though whatever pride she summoned would be a sham and a lie.

Miraculously she found her voice. "You knew something like this would happen."

He took a moment to answer. "It's always a possibility when we're together. I knew it as well as you. What I didn't know was whether I would come to my senses in time."

"Well, you did. Congratulations. You're much stronger than I."

He looked over his shoulder at her, his eyes as dark and deep as a starless midnight sky. She felt foolish sitting on the floor like this, so close to him and yet a world away. They were like a pair of children playing games before the hearth, but the innocence of childhood was lost to them both and whatever name she could put to what they were doing had nothing to do with play.

He turned more in her direction, putting his face in shadow. Had she wished, she could have seen much of his nakedness. Of course she wanted to feast on every inch of him, but that would have been more punishment, and she kept her eyes trained on the column of his neck.

"I get it," he said. "You wanted to take my seed and bear my child. That would bind us together for sure, though why you're so insistent about it is a mystery."

He made it sound like an evil wish instead of something so sweetly wonderful she hadn't dared put it into words, even to herself. He wounded her beyond imagining. He angered her, too. He went too far.

The pride came easier than she thought. She raked the hair back from her face and gathered what dignity she could, letting the blanket fall from her shoulders.

"Good for you, Conn. You've finally figured me out. A baby would trap you more than any vows. That's why I dressed so provocatively and lay waiting for you in your bed."

"You're too subtle for anything so obvious."

"When have I ever been subtle? When I roped you on the road? Or maybe it was just showing up here today and declaring I'm your wife and there's nothing you can do about it."

She saw the flash of hurt in his eyes. The words had found their mark. For a moment she wished she could call them back, just as she would call back much of what had passed between them during their brief and stormy union.

"You've made your point. There's little about any Braden that's close to subtlety."

"I'm an O'Brien now."

He glanced down at her hand. She realized she was twisting the wedding ring round and round. She refused to stop. The ring was hers as much as his name.

When his eyes met hers, she could read his thoughts as if he'd spoken them aloud. Divorce might be the answer for them both, whether or not it was right. She fought a rising panic as ferociously as she'd fought the tears.

"I was rough with you tonight. For that I apologize."

"You didn't hurt me, not in the way you're talking about."

He showed no sign of relief. "I'll not touch you

again," he said, "and it doesn't matter that legally I have the right."

"Do you think staying away from me will be easy?"

"There's little that passes between us that's easy."

He spoke almost sadly. She felt the breach between them widening, though he was but a few feet away.

"I've settled money into an account for you at the bank," he continued. "You can use it to find a place to live."

He seemed calm enough, a businesslike and reasonable man, unlike the Conn who'd courted her from the moment they first met. Unlike, too, the Conn who'd come to her this night not because he wanted to but because he could do nothing else.

Somehow he'd found control. She must do the same.

"Where might this place be?"

"I've no idea."

"Please. Give it a try."

"Crystal—"

"Are you going to say I'm no concern of yours? That it's my problem and not yours?"

He growled something unintelligible. "Take the coach to San Antonio. The Alamo Bed and Board ought to do for a while. Or the Menger, if you want to go back there."

"I can always confer with Mrs. Truehart on ways to occupy my time. Is that what you mean?"

His answer was another growl. If she'd done

nothing else, she'd shaken him from his calm.

"I don't want your money," she said.

"It's not a small amount."

"No matter. It's not what I want."

"And what is that?"

"My husband."

"It's sex you're after, Crystal."

"Maybe . . . all right, of course I am. That's part of it. But I'm not the only one."

The answer seemed to infuriate him.

"I like stick candy, too. But it's nothing I can't do without."

Liar, she wanted to cry. She'd never seen a man attack any sweet the way he had attacked her.

He raked a hand through his hair. "If you really want to make amends, take the money. I don't want it said I've abandoned my responsibilities."

"Since when do you worry about what people say? You're the O'Brien who argued against the war when all the county felt otherwise."

"I've still got myself to answer to."

"And of course you're a person filled with honor. As opposed to your wife."

She stood and dropped the blanket beside him. What she wanted to do was launch herself into his arms with orders to finish what he'd started. He was right. She wanted sex. But she wanted it from only him.

She forced a small smile onto her lips.

"I'm staying the week. I've still got the bet to pay off. But I'm leaving your money alone. Whether you believe it or not, I've still got myself to answer to."

She headed toward the kitchen, almost tripping over the hem of her gown.

"Don't tell me you're going to get started on breakfast," he said.

She paused in the doorway. "You almost sound afraid."

"I'm terrified. And I was thinking, too, of the dogs."

"Don't worry. Stoke is going to help me with the biscuits, and that's hours away. I'm going to sit out on the porch for a while and try to calm down. You may not plan on touching me, but I'm not so strong as you. Wrap yourself in that blanket if you don't want to be attacked."

Just as she'd threatened, she stayed the week, continuing to clatter and bang around the kitchen when she wasn't feeding the chickens and sometimes playing with the dogs, who'd forgiven her for the first biscuits she made.

She also tidied up the parlor and kitchen and back porch, and even did the wash. Conn insisted she stay out of the bedroom, except to store her clothes. She said that was fine with her. Her chores kept her busy enough without waiting on him. It was one of the few exchanges of opinion that they'd had.

The food she served was edible enough, after a few of Stoke's suggestions, but Conn had lost his appetite, maybe because she didn't have the decency to leave the kitchen when he came to eat.

Actually, the food went down more easily than the sight of her in her aproned dresses with her hair in a braid, looking far more awkward at the stove than she'd ever looked on a horse, but with a determined light in her eye.

Once he might have said she looked endearing, but that was a lifetime ago.

In the afternoons she changed to her riding clothes and disappeared for a couple of hours astride Trouble. She never said where she went and he didn't ask, but she was always back early enough to start her evening assault on the kitchen.

The worst part of the day came after the last meal was done and the clatter and bang had died away in the kitchen. Then, she went down to the creek to bathe and prepare for the night. Conn busied himself inside the cabin or in the barn, while Stoke usually chose to take a stroll.

Conn never could keep occupied enough so that he didn't picture what was going on at the creek.

His sleep was off, too. He tried moving to the barn at night, but Stoke kicked him out, claiming he snored too loudly and upset the stock. Conn knew it was a lie. Curse her devious hide, she had won over the old bachelor, probably because she doted on everything he said.

So Conn slept inside, or what passed for sleeping. But he kept the bedroom door firmly closed. He felt like some tremulous virgin fearing assault. Sometimes he wondered how he could be in the right and yet feel so wrong.

During the day he kept himself busy away from the house, helping Stoke repair a few fences, moving the stock, hunting for game. He also took a lot of cold swims in the creek, sometimes early in the morning, and again late, after she had settled down for the night. Most important of all, he didn't touch her again.

Stick candy could ruin a man's teeth, just as surely as a bad woman could turn around his life.

"Sure are a man for cleanliness since you got back from New York," Stoke commented one evening when they were sitting on the back porch. It was just the two of them and the hounds; Crystal had already gone inside. On this particular night she'd washed her hair, and he knew she'd be drying it in front of the fire.

Every long, golden strand.

Stoke cleared his throat. "You listening to me?"

"I'm listening. I take too many swims. You complained so much about the way I smelled I was afraid to do otherwise."

"Given up drinking, too."

"I never was much for whiskey. Besides, I like to keep a clear head."

"Is that so?" Stoke sent an arc of tobacco juice into the night. "Hard to do sometimes. What you got to work on, Conn, is moderation."

"The advice comes a little late."

For a change, Stoke didn't come back with an answer. Conn was grateful. He'd taken to appreciating silence around his old friend lately.

Two days later, Crystal's week came to an end.

Conn tried not to think about it too much, and he'd said not a word except to exclaim once or twice in her presence that he thought the bet would never be paid off.

At breakfast on the last cooking day, she was wearing the buckskin riding clothes, the first time she'd done so in the morning. Her custom had been to wear one of the Truehart dresses until her afternoon ride. The sight stirred an uneasiness inside him he didn't attempt to explain. She watched him walk in and take his place at the table.

A plate of fried beef, biscuits, and gravy was waiting for him. He poked at the beef with a fork, but his eyes were on her. She stood across the table by the sink, facing him, watching the hand holding the fork.

She'd said once as they were riding along, when things were better between them back in San Antonio, that she liked his hands, blunt and broad and callused though they were. She liked the way he used them, she'd said, claiming to mean the grip he had on the reins.

But she'd looked at him with eyes that told a different story. The eyes were saying the same thing now.

He tried a slice of the beef. It stuck in his throat. A swallow of hot coffee washed it down.

"I see you're dressed for leaving," he said.

"Are you going to eat more than one bite?"

"I haven't decided. And you haven't answered the question."

"I didn't know you asked one."

"Well, I did."

"So did I. You're looking puny, Conn. You need to eat. My cooking's not so bad."

There were other things about her that weren't so bad, either, but he'd put them off limits. He started to tell her just that, but moderation dictated he keep the thought to himself.

"No, your cooking's not so bad. The dogs aren't turning it down."

Her lips flattened. "Thanks for the compliment."

She turned back toward the sink and the dirty dishes that waited. She might be improving in the cooking department, but she still hadn't mastered how to fix a simple meal without messing up every kitchen utensil she could find.

If things were right between them, he ought to be teasing her, and sometimes helping out. But things weren't right, and they never could be. The realization was as painful for him as he knew it was for her.

He wasn't such a clod that he didn't know she was suffering. But the fact was that as much as he wanted her, he didn't love her anymore. He probably never had. He'd been hungry for a wife, and he'd thought—

Hell, there was no point in going over all that again. He'd done it a thousand times. Keeping her around was too bitter a reminder of what they could have had and what they'd lost.

She made a lot of noise in the cleaning. Conn tried to concentrate on his food and forget how soft buckskin could follow the lines of a body. The way she shifted and moved and stretched, it was almost like staring at her flesh.

Not that he was staring, of course. He wasn't doing much eating, either.

He took advantage of a lull in the slams and bangs.

"Leave, Crystal. It's not going to work."

She held herself as still as death. All he could do was stare at her back and fight the urge to take her in his arms and tell her how sorry he was the marriage hadn't worked out; but then, once he held her, he doubted he'd be able to talk.

Sitting like this was torture. He stood, plate in hand, and headed for the back door.

"Where are you going with that?"

She was facing him now, and her eyes were a bright, shiny brown. He didn't look at her straight on like this very often, and he saw once again how lovely she was. And he saw she was close to tears.

Everything inside him twisted. He cursed himself for being weak.

"I'm feeding the dogs and then there's something I've got to do." He turned to leave.

Her low cry startled him, and he whirled back around.

"You're not the only one."

She came at him fast and knocked the plate from his hand. Beef and biscuits went flying, along with splats of the gravy.

"Forget the damned dogs."

It was the first time he'd ever heard her curse.

Hands on hips, she glared at him. "I can't stand

all this politeness and quiet talk and walking a mile around each other and wanting you so much I'm all empty inside."

"Crystal—"

"And I'm tired of wondering where you are during the day and hearing you in the creek and wanting to strip naked and join you until we join each other, and making a baby has nothing to do with it, you bastard, and don't say that it does."

The last was punctuated with a shove at his chest.

"I can't," he said hurriedly, "you won't let me get a word in."

She was magnificent in her anger and more dangerous than she'd ever been, a wild filly who was begging to be tamed. Or maybe not tamed, but wanting a stallion with a wildness to match her own.

He felt that wildness rise in him. He fought it down.

"Lord, I've been *trying* to change, cooking and cleaning and being the dutiful wife, though the duties I'm called upon to perform are not especially satisfying. You want to know what I do in the afternoons? Do you?"

He opened his mouth to answer, but to no avail.

"I ride off to keep my sanity. And lately I've started meeting Judge, to make sure Mama's all right and to send word that I'm doing just fine. I feel like I'm trying to juggle two different lives, the one here and the one I used to have, and I'm making pretty much of a mess of both. Mainly because

I'm not getting a whole lot of help."

"Crystal, I'm sorry. Really sorry. If this is so hard on you, you know what to do about it."

"And what is that? Go jump in the creek and wait for you to join me? We both know you want me to just go away and not bother you again."

He expected the tears to come, but she seemed too lost in her fury to cry. Her color was high and so was her chin, her lips so close, it would take only the slightest bend of his head to taste them.

"Maybe I just decided I don't want you after all, not like that." She squeezed her fists and pressed them against her cheeks. "What I really want is to hit you. I want it so bad right now it hurts."

"Then do it."

"I've never raised my hand to another living being."

"I have. It's not so bad."

He knew she was remembering his fight with the man who'd traded her for a mule. He shook her, not so hard it would do her harm, but enough to get her attention. "Hit me back. Defend yourself."

She did. He'd expected a slap, a woman's kind of attack, but she socked him in the jaw, then yelped and shook her hand.

He rubbed at his face. She was stronger than she looked. But then, he should have known she would be.

They looked at one another. She was breathing hard and her face was flushed, and a few strands of her hair had worked loose to curl against her cheeks. Hunger for her burned in him like a branding iron. He grabbed her, not thinking of moderation or of how dangerous touching her was, and he kissed her hard, just once, but he made it long, no tongue involved, just mouth crushed to mouth, and then he thrust her away. She had to know he was saying good-bye.

Her lips were wet and already beginning to swell. She just stood there staring up at him, her arms at her sides, hands no longer curled into fists. Anguish tore at him, and a longing for what could never be. He left before he did the thousand other things he wanted to do. The dogs yipped and ran for cover when he stormed out the door.

Grabbing his hat off the back porch nail, he jammed it on his head and marched a dozen yards from the cabin before coming to a halt. What had he ever done to deserve this torment? Ah, yes, he had fallen in love at first sight.

He could go off into the trees somewhere and give himself the release he needed, but his aching hardness was a punishment he wasn't ready to get rid of. He needed punishment for wanting her. He had to get over her. And he would.

Out of sight meant she would eventually be out of his mind. But that didn't mean he wanted to hang around and watch her leave. Instead, seeking another kind of pain, he did something he'd been putting off, something he needed to do.

Sometime during the restless night he'd considered how to spend the day. Now he knew. He would visit his father's grave.

Chapter Ten

Instead of flowers, Conn carried two guns to his father's grave, a holstered pistol riding against his thigh and a rifle in the saddle scabbard. In dealing with the Bradens, he'd messed up too many times already. He didn't want to be caught unawares again.

He made his way slowly from Stoke's land onto the neighboring Bushwhack, trying to forget his wife, concentrating hard on picking out the overgrown path that had once been well worn; at the same time he listened for signs that someone was close by.

He half expected a gunshot to come at him, but all was silent. Dark clouds hung low in the April sky; he could smell approaching rain.

The ride was not without torment. In happier days, he'd gone this way a thousand times. But then the land had been O'Brien land. He hadn't realized how much it meant to him until he'd left Texas. He realized it even more keenly today.

The small cemetery was away from the main house, high on a hill overlooking much of the ranch, a white fence marking the boundaries. Bridget O'Brien was buried there, and he assumed so was Daniel, but there would be no others. Hugo Ridley had written that the remains of his brother lay in an unmarked grave in Tennessee, much like thousands of other fallen Rebs.

No one stopped him as he rode, and he could see no activity on the land, but then it was a rugged part of the country that Daniel had selected for his wife's resting place. The ranch's pastures, gentler and more benign, were closer to the creek and on the far side of the house.

"She always liked the wildness," he explained when her sons questioned the site. "And her spirit can look out on the Bushwhack and see that all is well."

Conn remembered those words with bitterness. He prayed his mother's spirit had gone to a happier place.

When he finally found the overgrown hillside path, he saw right away that the fence needing painting. Just as he'd expected, two graves occupied the space, one overgrown with weeds, the other freshly turned.

A rock headstone rose from the weeds:

BRIDGET MURPHY O'BRIEN
BORN 5 AUG 1805 IN COUNTY KERRY, IRELAND

DIED 3 NOV 1850 IN KERR COUNTY, TEXAS
BELOVED WIFE AND MOTHER
SHE SINGS WITH THE ANGELS NOW

The words were as familiar to him as the Irish ballads she used to hum for her "lads," as she called the three men in her life. He knelt to pull a few weeds before he forced his eyes to the freshly turned dirt close by. No headstone had been erected to present the pertinent facts about Daniel. He would talk to Ridley about the oversight.

He tried to picture how Daniel had looked the last time he'd seen him, but they'd been arguing and the image wouldn't come. Instead, he remembered other, happier times when Bridget was alive, and then later, when she was gone and Daniel had tried to make up her loss to their sons.

The pair of them had been brave pioneers; life in Ireland had prepared them to be. They'd married young. As Catholics, they'd had to rent the land they worked and pass the profits on to the British landlords. Three babies lay buried in Irish soil. Daniel had taken work in town to earn money for passage to the New World.

Texas had been a dream. Bridget had barely made it to shore before giving birth to two healthy boys. She'd always said it was a sign that life would be good in their new home.

She claimed the sign had proven true, that their life had been better than her wildest expectations, even though she never again conceived.

Conn remembered nothing of their early years in the coastal settlement of San Patricio, although Bridget assured them they'd been happy there with their fellow Irish immigrants. He and James had been barely past their second birthday when the war against Mexico came. Along with many of the other settlers, Daniel had taken his family to safety in Nacogdoches in far East Texas, then joined the Texas Volunteers.

"He was a fighting man, your father," Bridget once said, "so brave and handsome it like to broke my heart just to gaze upon him. Not that he's lost either the bravery or the looks, praise the saints."

"I fought at San Jacinto beside General Houston himself," Daniel put in, "though by Irish standards it wasn't much of a fight. When I went back to San Patricio, I found our home looted and the livestock gone. They took just about all we owned in the world—your mother's lace tablecloth she'd brought from the old country, the Bible she'd forgotten in her rush to leave. And what they couldn't take, they destroyed."

"Who, Papa?" Conn remembered asking. "Who would do such a thing?" In his innocent, protected world he couldn't imagine anyone being so bad.

"Thieves, drifters, bandits who crossed from south of the Rio Grande. 'Tis a shame, lad, but there's bad 'uns everywhere."

All those years after the war, his voice had still held the bitterness of the family's losses. Daniel had never been a man to forgive and forget.

He'd used his soldier's land grant to claim what

became the Bushwhack, or at least the beginnings of it. He and his sons had worked hard to help it grow.

"It's your legacy," he'd told them. "No one can take it from you because of your religion or even if you have none. You take care of the Bushwhack and it will take care of you."

He'd been right on that point. For over thirty years, the ranch had stayed in O'Brien hands. But wars and taxes could exact a terrible toll, and banks and scheming men were even more harsh. Worst of all were women who could turn a man's head.

Conn stopped himself. High on this hill, with the clouds hanging so low he could almost touch them, he felt his mind clear. He'd blamed Crystal long enough. She was what she was, and so was he. Like his father, he couldn't forgive and forget.

He'd wanted a marriage like the one his parents had known. He'd wanted a woman like Bridget Murphy O'Brien. He thought he'd found her, but he'd been wrong.

He walked to the fence and stared at the land stretching out on all sides—at the rocky, rolling hills, at the thick brush, at the creek snaking through the trees. He could see a wisp of smoke curling from behind one of the hills. It would be from the chimney of the ranch house in the valley beyond.

He loved it all, as much as he had ever loved anything, but he'd traded his legacy away, and for what? For a gamble on a woman. A gamble he'd lost.

A sense of loss overwhelmed him. He could have wept if he were a man for such a release, but he kept his worry inside him like a cancer, letting it spread and eat away all the dreams he'd held for so long. Gone, too, was every chance he'd had to know peace.

"I ought to leave Texas," he said.

He'd carried the idea in the back of his head for the past week. It needed to be said aloud, to hover in the air where he could see it as a real possibility. There were friends back in Saratoga, and a horse racing business he knew well. And there were women who would welcome him back, women who wouldn't care that he'd left a wife behind.

Saratoga was surely an option, with its fine hotels and high-stakes gambling and prime thoroughbred stock. He'd led a good life there, even if he'd felt at times that he was playing the part of Yankee wheeler-dealer and losing the truest part of himself.

"Leave," he said again.

Even repeated, the word had a hollow ring to it. He couldn't go. The hill country was where he belonged. His carefully honed plan to turn the Bushwhack into a thriving horse ranch needed a few adjustments, that was all. If the decision didn't bring him peace and joy, at least it kept him from the damnable curse of self-pity.

Adjustments. They didn't come as a new idea. He'd been thinking of them, too, along with the option of leaving, throwing a few of them out to Spoke when they were caring for the stock or mending the fence.

He turned back to his father's grave. He ought to talk to him now, at least to his memory, the words coming as easily as they had with Stoke. He ought to explain what he'd done, to ask Daniel's pardon, to tell him good-bye. Through the years, he'd said a thousand words over his mother's final resting place, but he could say nothing to his father. Nor could he grieve. The fact of Daniel's death and the manner of it, in excitement over his estranged son's return, were still too raw for Conn to deal with just yet.

Instead, he threw himself into cleaning up the area, pulling weeds, tossing rocks over the fence, eventually taking off his hat and shirt and even his holster, letting the occasional rays of sun heat and the breeze cool his bare skin, wondering about putting in some flowers, though he'd never been a man of the soil and knew little about planting things.

The toil was therapeutic, occupying his thoughts at the same time it cleared off the mind-fog that had settled on him since he'd left San Antonio. He was feeling good, or at least telling himself he was, brushing sweat and dirt from his eyes, when he heard the click of a gun behind him.

He froze. His own pistol was hanging from the fence a dozen feet away, and the rifle was propped against a distant tree beneath which his horse was cropping grass.

He stood slowly, hands at his sides to show he was unarmed, and turned.

The man stood just beyond the fence, a ready shotgun in his gloved hands. Almost feminine in his leanness, a hat pulled low over steady eyes, he stood with feet apart and stared at Conn. His features were even and, like his build, almost feminine; he was a handsome man except for the weakness of his mouth.

Something about the insolent way he held himself and the cut of his clothes said he was no ordinary ranch hand. Conn would swear he had never seen him before, yet he seemed familiar. It was the eyes—a shadowed, unreadable brown.

"Royce Braden," Conn guessed.

The man gave the barest of nods. "And you'd be Crystal's man."

"You know me from San Antonio. You were watching."

"Only at first, in the saloon. Then I saw you headed for Crystal. We knew she wouldn't fail."

Conn wanted to bound over the fence and knock the smug grin off his face. He must have telegraphed his intent, for Royce lifted the shotgun. Conn didn't doubt he'd use it if threatened. Or even if he weren't. A man like him would have no qualms about gunning someone down and claiming self-defense.

He'd certainly had no qualms about duping a man out of his land.

He could see why Stoke judged him so harshly.

And Royce was family. Conn wanted to puke.

A trickle of sweat ran down his neck and chest, but it was from the humid heat and not fear. He'd been through too much to be afraid even of death.

He turned his back to Royce and bent to pull the last weeds, then took a quick survey of his work. "This place needs better care."

"Why should we bother? I doubt any Bradens will be buried here."

Conn faced him again. "If you are, I'll open the grave and feed your bones to the buzzards."

Royce smirked. "Talk's cheap."

"It's more than talk. Die and find out."

"My, my. You seem a trifle upset."

"Put down the gun and you'll find out how much."

A darkness close to fear flickered in Royce's eyes. He wasn't stupid, just mean.

"Now wouldn't I be the fool to do that?" he asked.

"You'd better keep yourself armed, Royce. You never can tell when I'll be around."

"I always do. Except when I'm with a woman, of course. I never let a woman play with my gun. Well, not this one at any rate."

"Crystal says you're not much of a shot."

Royce drew himself up, and Conn was reminded of a coiled snake. He could almost see the narrow tongue darting from between his weak lips.

He suddenly felt very weary. He was sick of bandying words, sick of his situation, sick of himself. With a shake of his head, he went to put on his shirt, and he didn't care if Royce shot him in the back. He slapped on his hat, buckled his holster in place, and swung himself over the fence, heading for his horse and for his rifle, leaving Royce behind.

Settling in the saddle, he dropped the rifle back into its scabbard and then looked once again at his brother-in-law. He had planned to ride away without saying another word, but Royce wouldn't let him go. The insult about his shooting must still rile.

"Crystal did her work well." Royce's voice was oily, insinuating. "As I said, we knew she would. We'd been saving her for just such a situation."

"It's my understanding she went too far."

"The marriage, you mean? That's my father's opinion. I think she did everything right. Look at the money you're giving her. Lucky bitch. You must be as wealthy as we heard. Too bad you don't have any land to spend it on."

Conn considered running him down, but the bastard would probably get flustered and shoot his horse.

"Is she good in bed?" Royce asked. "I'll bet she is. The quiet ones often are."

Bile rose in Conn's throat. "My God, you're talking about your sister."

"Yes. It's the only reason she was still a virgin when you met her. She was, wasn't she? I'd hate to think I'd stayed out of her bed if you weren't the first."

Rage broke through Conn's control. He threw

himself off the horse straight at Royce. A blast from the shotgun creased a shoulder, but he barely felt it. The barrel was hot when he wrested the weapon from Royce's grasp and tossed it into the brush.

Royce tried to fight, but he was no scrapper and Conn was. He smashed the too-even nose and felt it break. Blood spurted onto his hand. He hit him again. Royce fell to the ground and covered his face.

Blood lust fed Conn's anger. He wanted to kick him while he was down, to pound him with his fists and kick him some more, to let loose all the demons of contempt and disgust that had built in him since he'd first learned the truth.

But Royce just sat there in the dirt, moaning, blood spilling onto his hands, and Conn turned the disgust onto himself. He'd come home thinking himself a gentleman, but the wildness of his youth was in him yet—only now it was tempered with hate.

He whistled for his horse, but fired off one last parting threat.

"Don't ever talk about her like that again. I'll kill you if you do."

"Ouch!"

Stoke clucked his tongue and poured another dose of carbolic acid onto Conn's shoulder. The liquid ran down his bare chest. "You turning into a sissy?"

Sitting on the stoop of the back porch, Conn

glared up at him. "Have you ever poured that stuff on yourself?"

"Every time someone shoots me."

"It's no more than a crease. Besides, I don't imagine you've ever been shot."

Stoke shifted his plug of tobacco from cheek to cheek. "If it happens, you can be the one to tend me."

"Good."

Stoke covered the wound with gauze and taped it down. "That'll smart right sharply for a while."

Conn waved him away and winced. "It's the poison you treated me with that's the problem."

"I'd say it was a bullet coming a mite too close. You want to tell me now what happened?"

Conn considered how much to say. In the end he told it all.

Stoke handed him a glass of whiskey when he was done.

"That's some family you got yourself hooked to. Told you Royce was a bastard."

"You were right. And I'm not hooked." He swallowed the whiskey straight. "Is Crystal gone?"

"Went into town not more than a half hour before you came limping in."

Conn kept his voice even. "Did she say exactly where she was going or what she was going to do?"

"I figured you knew."

Conn shrugged. The pain in his shoulder almost brought him off the porch.

"The week's up," he said. "She's making arrangements to leave."

"You two must have had a humdinger of an argument about it this morning. After you rode off, she slammed and banged around in the kitchen until the dogs ran for cover. Broke two plates."

"Crystal's not what you'd call a genteel lady."

Stoke nodded admiringly.

"She socked me in the jaw and her brother shot me. I don't think I can take another run-in with a Braden today."

He was speaking calmly, trying to sound as if he didn't feel as if the bottom had dropped out of his stomach. He ought to be throwing back the whiskey in celebration. At last she'd shown some sense. She was gone.

But the day was without joy. His mood was as dark as the clouds hanging over the trees.

He stood and pulled on the clean shirt Stoke had brought him, to go with the clean everything else. Though he taunted Conn with the same charge, the man was a demon for cleanliness. He'd made Conn bathe in the creek before he would treat the wound.

Worse than a New Yorker, that's what he was.

"I made a few decisions today," he said as he was strapping on his gun. He was going slowly, taking each movement with caution.

Stoke raised his brows but he kept quiet.

"Do you mind if I work on some changes around here, the ones we were talking about? I won't do anything specific until we confer."

"I told you, boy, the place is half yours. I got no plans to object."

"I need to ride into town to get matters started."

Stoke's brows stayed raised.

"I'm not checking on her," Conn said.

"Didn't say you were. But you're forgetting that shoulder."

"I wish I could. But I've put things off too long. I need to go by the bank and then talk with Hugo Ridley."

"No need to make excuses. You go into town and do what's needed to be done."

"I don't remember your nettling a man this way."

"Times change."

"So they do, old man. So they do."

Conn made the ride quickly, taking short cuts, slicing a good portion off the hour it usually took. Stoke had been right. The shoulder hurt like hell. Not a man to welcome pain ordinarily, he found it helped him focus on the journey, rather than what he might find at its end. He took few precautions. If Royce Braden wanted to waylay him, let him try.

But he'd bet the horse under him that his brother-in-law was home nursing his broken nose and moaning over his maimed good looks.

When he got to Kerrville, he saw no sign of Crystal or Trouble, but he didn't look hard as he made for the bank. On his first visit, he'd dealt with the second man in charge—a vice-president, he'd proudly called himself. This time the president himself led him into his office with offers of a drink and a cigar.

Bankers and lawyers were much alike, Conn observed.

His request was straightforward enough. He wanted a list of ranchers who might be in need of a loan.

"That's just about everybody," the banker said.

"Isn't there talk of driving cattle to the railheads north of Texas?"

"There's talk of course, being there's more cattle in Texas than the buyers can handle. Some are interested. Others think it's a foolish idea."

"And what do you think?"

"I'm not a cattleman."

"And you're not willing to help them out if they need some financing to make the drive."

"I've a responsibility to all my customers, Mr. O'Brien. I can't take risks with their money."

"Any of these ranches up for foreclosure?"

"That's private information, sir."

"Which means yes. They're customers, too. The ones that got this bank started, if I remember right."

The banker tried to bluster an answer, but Conn paid no attention. He'd thought things through, and he was prepared to refute any argument the man put up. Being rich was a major part of his preparation.

It took no more than a half hour to work out a deal. Conn would finance the drives and the ranchers would think the bank was putting up the money. He'd take the profit, too, when the debts were repaid, minus the bank's cut. The few who wanted to sell out would find a ready buyer, one who would give them a fair price. They didn't need to know right away that it was the Texas traitor they'd be dealing with.

"You're taking a big risk, Mr. O'Brien," the banker said.

"I know these men, even if they don't claim to know me. They won't let me down."

A visit to Hugo Ridley came next.

"I went out to the Bushwhack with the letter for your wife, but she wasn't there."

"You left it?"

"I had no choice."

"So her father knows about the money."

"The letter was sealed and addressed to Mrs. Conn O'Brien. Surely he wouldn't—Oh, but of course he would. I shouldn't have left it. I see your point."

Conn let it go. At least he knew now how Royce Braden had learned of Crystal's bank account. He cut the meeting short with specific orders for Daniel O'Brien's headstone; then he went out to the street and almost collided with Dora Weathers and her daughter-in-law, Jennie. Tipping his hat, he apologized. Mrs. Weathers was almost gracious in her acceptance until she got a good look at him and realized who he was.

"I should have known you'd be lurking around," she said with a sniff.

"I'm sorry about Stormy," he said before she

could *humph* her way past him and cross the street.

The feather in her black bonnet shook and her eyes shot out a venomous hate. "How dare you say his name?" she hissed.

"He was my friend." His gaze slid to her companion. "Ma'am."

Her acknowledging smile was fleeting, but long enough for Conn to realize once again that Stormy had married a lovely, delicate woman.

"Come, Jennifer," her mother-in-law ordered, "we've more important matters than lollygagging around with riffraff who by all rights ought to be hanged instead of allowed to stroll about harassing decent folk."

"But—"

"No arguments, girl. Maybe we can get our business done in peace this time."

Like a ship in full sail, Dora Weathers set off across the street in the direction of Ochse's General Store, her full black skirt flapping around her. Jennie started to follow, then paused.

"Mr. O'Brien, Stormy always spoke highly of you. He wrote me before the last—"

"Jennifer!"

Again came the smile, accompanied by a small shrug of apology, and she hurried to take up her customary position at her mother-in-law's heels.

Conn smiled after her. With his shoulder throbbing from the gunshot and his gut tight from wondering what his maybe-wife was up to, he was in a mood to accept small acts of humanity such as

Jennie Weathers offered. There was character in her. Stormy had indeed married well. Why was it a good man like him died and trash like Royce Braden thrived?

Because that was the way of the world.

The cynic in him tightened its claws. He shook his head in disgust. It was time to ride on back to Stoke's Place. He knew it. The trouble was, he couldn't get his feet to move across the street and head for the stable where he'd left his horse.

Something was keeping him here, unfinished business that had nothing to do with banks or lawyers. A fair-haired, brown-eyed someone who wouldn't leave him alone no matter how near or far she was.

He glanced to the right and to the left. A few wagons were making their slow way down the street, along with a half-dozen men on horseback. He barely gave them a glance, trying instead to figure out how that someone's mind might work.

He hadn't gotten very far in his thinking when one of the wagons halted directly in front of him. Crystal stared down at him from her perch on the wagon seat. She was dressed in the buckskin skirt and vest, and her hat rested at the back of her head. Wisps of yellow hair framed her face, and her dark eyes were flashing fire.

"So you haven't yet gone," he said, telling himself he was a fool to feel relief.

"Are you picking out the woman?" she asked. She sounded about as angry as she had in the kitchen hours ago.

"What woman?" he asked, genuinely perplexed.

"You know what woman. You're the one who came up with the idea. I've been watching you from across the way, wondering how far you'd go, and with her of all people and today of all days."

It must be the shoulder wound, Conn decided, that made him so dense. He had not a clue as to what or who she meant.

"I don't know what's got you so upset. I'd say get down and explain a few things, but you might hit me again."

"I'm done with hitting. I only hurt myself."

He was about to tell her that wasn't strictly true when a shot rang out. A commotion commenced on the street, and a woman's cry sounded out. Crystal, tight-lipped, fought to control the reins, and he looked past her to see Edgar Braden riding straight for the wagon, brandishing a pistol in the air.

"Hold up, you bastard," Edgar yelled.

Conn had an idea who he meant. He shook his head in disgust at the same time that he rested his hand close to his gun. Here was another Braden to deal with. And that could mean nothing but trouble ahead.

Chapter Eleven

Crystal watched as her father reined to a halt and holstered his gun. She hadn't thought he would shoot Conn. Directness wasn't his way.

She closed her eyes for a minute and wondered what she had done to deserve the run of rotten luck she was having today. First she'd made a fool of herself by hitting Conn and almost breaking her hand. Then she was openly sniffed at and generally ignored at Ochse's store when all she was doing was buying a few supplies. And here she was, a witness to her husband's carrying on with the two women who'd done the most sniffing.

Not that Conn had paid Dora Weathers much attention. It was Jennie he was considering as her successor, thinking his unwanted first wife was probably already out of town. He could deny it all he wanted, but she wasn't as stupid as he thought.

Her father's dramatic appearance was the final blow. He just sat there glaring down at Conn, and Conn just stood there looking up at him, calm and self-assured, as if half the town wasn't watching from along the street and through a dozen storefront windows.

She truly didn't think Conn was in too much danger, not physically. But she would have given her beloved Trouble to spare him more embarrassment, more pain. Even if, had they been by themselves, she was ready to wring his neck.

"Haven't you done enough damage to my family?" Braden's voice boomed loudly enough for the words to carry past the bank.

Crystal stared at him in amazement. He never spoke loudly like this. His face was flushed a bright red, and his normally impeccable suit was covered with trail dust from a clearly hasty ride.

She looked back at Conn. "Did you do something?"

His dark brows rose a fraction. "Other than the woman you were talking about?"

"Aha!" she snapped. "Then you admit it."

Conn shrugged and regretted it. "I'm not admitting anything, since I don't know the charges."

"Then why did you wince if it wasn't from a guilty conscience?" A new and terrible thought struck her. "You're hurt."

"It hasn't been a particularly good day."

"With that I agree."

"Gawddamn it," Edgar yelled. "I'm right here ready to draw my gun again and you two keep jawing at each other. Answer the question."

Conn smiled apologetically up at Crystal. "I forgot what it was," he said, keeping his voice low so that only she and her father could hear. The onlookers must be gnashing their teeth in frustration. A half-heard argument was difficult to report to the ignorant souls who hadn't made it into town.

Crystal helped him out. "He wanted to know if you'd done enough damage to the Bradens."

Conn glanced at Edgar. "You must have seen Royce."

"You broke my boy's face."

"What?" Crystal said.

"Not all of it," said Conn, as if that explained things. "Besides, he shot me. If fighting were like a horse race, I'd say he was the winner by a nose. No pun intended, you understand."

Crystal came an inch or two off the wagon seat. "Royce shot you?"

"He grazed me. You were right about his aim. He's not too keen with a gun."

"He should have shot you down. You were trespassing," said Edgar.

"I was visiting my father's grave. It seemed time to make up for having missed the funeral."

Suddenly the whole day took on a new meaning. Whatever anger Crystal had felt toward her husband evaporated, and her heart swelled with love and sympathy.

"I'm sorry, Conn. That must have been difficult for you."

She knew where the family plots were located; Daniel O'Brien had pointed them out once when he was showing her and her mother around the Bushwhack on one of their courtesy visits. She tried to picture what it must have been like for Conn, standing high on the hill, looking out over land that was supposed to be his, trying to tell his father good-bye.

She should have been there with him, close and comforting like the wife she wanted to be. She felt more useless than she had ever felt in her life.

Thunder rumbled in the distance. Her father growled. Conn stared at her for a moment, then looked past her to the rain-dark clouds.

"Stay away from my boy," Edgar said. He was speaking low now, as if he realized the performance he was putting on for the crowd.

"He's twenty-six years old," Crystal snapped. "He's hardly a boy."

"True enough. He's a better man than any O'Brien could ever be."

"So who's home nursing a broken nose?"

Crystal found that talking back to her father was getting easier all the time. Being out from under his roof was making her bold.

But she should have known he wouldn't let her have the last word.

"It gives him time to get in some target practice." He looked from her to Conn with such hatred that the heat came from him in waves.

"Stay away from my land, too. I've got title. That gives me the right to kick you and yours off, alive or dead. Alonso Rees is a good sheriff. He'll back me up. Matter of fact, I'd be talking to him right now about what happened today, but he's out of town, and that deputy of his is stupid as a mule."

Conn gave no sign of backing down. "I don't care what the sheriff says. I want access to the graves."

"Move 'em."

"No."

Edgar started. The dray horse stirred restlessly in his traces, and Crystal gripped the reins tightly, all the while watching her father's gun hand.

"Father, that's little enough for him to ask," she said.

"Defending him, are you? I thought he didn't want you."

Stung, she blinked back a sudden rush of tears. From the corner of her eye she could see Conn staring up at her. She could see, too, that he was about to speak. Things were bad enough without hearing what he had to say.

It could be the men would find themselves on the same side, opposing her.

"I've been with him the whole week," she said, too brightly. "You must have figured out where I was."

"I knew right from the start. One of the hands followed you. I wanted to see what you'd do after I threw you out. You did just what I expected, like a dog that's been kicked a few times and still runs to the man that did the kicking."

Crystal's face burned with shame, not because

her father was wrong but because, from the way he was looking at things, he was right.

She looked at Conn, wanting to let him know her father's words didn't hurt, thinking that surely he cared a little bit. But she couldn't bring herself to meet his eyes.

"Crystal, you don't have to take this. I can end it."

"Can you? I doubt it. Unless you take a cue from Royce and shoot every Braden you come across."

"Not every Braden deserves it."

His voice had a trace of gentleness to it, and she almost let loose with the tears.

But Edgar put a different meaning to the words.

"Face the truth, daughter. To him, you're not worth the bullet. Judgement said you were little more than a housekeeper. I didn't know you were liking it."

"I didn't tell him anything like that."

"He figured it out from the little you said."

"And told you? That doesn't sound like him."

"I convinced him to tell me where he's spent the past few afternoons."

She drew in a sharp breath. "You didn't hurt him, did you?"

"I didn't have a chance. Your mother came out blubbering and even Helga pushed her way into it. I'm going to get rid of that squarehead before long. I like women who know their place."

As he looked back at Conn, his eyes glinted with a malice that didn't seem quite sane. "I'm surprised you took my daughter in. You seemed eager enough to get rid of her before. She must be good in bed."

Crystal wanted to die. Conn's hand eased closer to his pistol. Trembling inside, she tried to laugh, but her attempt rang foolishly in the heavy air.

"Father, this ought to be between you and me. I won't be staying around much longer, anyway."

She threw the words out recklessly, trying anything to distract him from Conn.

"Is he tossing you aside again? Maybe you're not so good after all."

"Maybe I'm not. Maybe what we did to him—"

Before she could finish, Conn had jerked her father from his horse and relieved him of his gun, tucking it at the back of his own waist. He held Edgar close, hands tight on the lapels of his coat.

"You ever insult my wife like that again and I'll kill you. There's not a jury in the state that'll convict me. Half the town heard the filth you've been spewing out."

Edgar made signs that he would bluster a reply, but as he stared at Conn, the words died in his throat.

Conn let him go, brushed at his lapels, and smiled. But there was a coldness in his expression that made Crystal shiver. As furious as he'd been with her, she'd never seen the ruthlessness in his eyes that she saw now.

"Go on about your business, Braden, and I'll go about mine."

"We're not done," Edgar growled, but much of the bravado had gone out of him.

"We are for today." Conn's gaze slid to Crystal. "A storm's coming. We'd better start for home."

She stared at him in surprise.

"But—"

"You're a woman who likes arguing, that's for sure." He spoke up louder so that a few eavesdroppers could hear and pass the words on. "I'm looking forward to one of your fine meals this evening. Afterwards, we can build up the fire and listen to the rain."

Crystal managed to wipe the stunned look off her face. "That sounds nice," she said, wondering which part of his declaration was the bigger lie, the part about the fine meal or the one about sitting with her after it was done.

Conn pulled himself onto the wagon seat and took the reins. "Mind if I take over? We'll swing by the stable and pick up my horse, then be on our way."

And then, with a crowd of onlookers gaping and Edgar looking as if he'd eaten a piece of bad meat, Conn did exactly that. But he didn't touch her or smile with any real warmth or indicate in any way that things were truly changing between them.

"You don't have to do this," she said as they stopped in front of the stable.

He secured the reins and dropped to the ground. "Don't I?" he asked. Not waiting for an answer, he left to get his horse.

Crystal brushed a tear away, glad he hadn't seen it fall. He didn't like her to cry, and why should he? Seeing things the way he was seeing them, she felt sick inside with more regret than he could ever realize. Once again she had trapped him into keeping her by his side. What she was going to do about it, she did not know.

They were a mile down the road before Crystal spoke.

"I went into town to buy supplies. They're under the tarp in the back."

Conn let the remark go with a nod.

"I used your money," she added after a time, "but I intend to pay it back."

He growled in disgust. "I told you it was yours."

"You also told me to leave, and here you are taking me back."

"We'll talk about it later."

"You didn't have to defend me," she said in a small voice.

"Later." He didn't mean to sound so harsh, but since he didn't understand too much of what was going on, he needed to do some thinking. Of course she had to leave. It would be better for them both. But the details, being more complicated than he had first figured, needed working on.

He hadn't realized what a thorough scoundrel Edgar Braden was, even to his kin.

One of the wagon wheels dipped into a hole and she was thrown against him. She righted herself quickly.

"I'm sorry," she said.

He looked at her. She was dressed in the high-necked, sky-blue gown that fit her with such efficiency. The matching parasol lay at her feet beside her rifle. She was wearing a bonnet, but it sat high on the back of her head and didn't provide much protection from either the elements or his glance.

How she managed to look small and vulnerable and strong and proud and altogether maddening all at once was a mystery to him. She'd been through hell back there in town. He knew few men who could take such insults and not break.

When he'd pulled Braden from his horse, he'd wanted to beat the shit out of him, but he'd had enough common sense to know that humiliating him with the town watching had been punishment enough. At least for a while.

He'd been half hoping Crystal would take the rifle from its resting place and shoot him between the eyes. But all she'd done was try to play the peacemaker. She'd tried hard and she had failed.

She needed comforting now, and a few words of praise, but he had an idea where the comfort would lead.

Where she was concerned, he was a pure-bred fool. He reached for the canteen under the seat, thinking it should contain whiskey instead of water.

"Did you hear me?" she asked. "I said I'm sorry."

"No need to apologize," he said.

"I didn't mean just for falling against you. I'm sorry about a lot of things, but then, you've heard all that before. Right now I'm remembering what my father said. I'm sorry for not being better in bed."

Conn choked on the water. "What are you talking about?" he asked when he could speak.

"I'm talking about our wedding night." She was sitting up straight, looking down the road, not seeming in the least embarrassed for bringing up such a subject. "Don't you dare tell me it was the most glorious experience of your life."

He fought to keep from remembering, but the image of Crystal the way she'd been that night flashed in his mind, of her lying in the bed with the covers pulled to her chin, honey hair spread on the pillow, her sweet lips urging him to get undressed.

He remembered, too, joining her beneath the covers and taking her too fast.

"It almost was," he said, speaking more to himself than to her. "And it was going to be."

"It already was for me."

"Crystal—"

"I shouldn't have started carrying on like this," she said in a too-bright voice. "When I saw you in town talking to those women, I was about to check on when the next stagecoach would be leaving for San Antonio. In case I decided to give up."

He tried to imagine her traveling far, far away. It was what he wanted. It was the only way he could rebuild his life.

His insides were so tight, a knife wouldn't have cut them, and other parts were growing hard just from her being so close and looking so good.

"What would it take to get you on that stage?" He knew he was being mean, but he couldn't help himself. Meanness was the only defense he had.

"Not much more, Conn," she said softly, staring up at the dark clouds. "Not much more."

She fell silent and remained so for the remainder of the ride. He spent the time alternating between telling himself he was doing right bringing this marriage to an end and thinking about how he wasn't much better than the other men in her life.

And all the while he was arguing with himself, he was wanting her so badly and hurting so much that he would have welcomed another shoulder wound to give him a moment's peace.

Another wagon awaited them when they arrived at the cabin. She jumped to the ground and ran inside just as the rain was starting. Stoke came out and helped him unload the supplies.

They worked without speaking, neither mentioning the second wagon. Conn was grateful for the chance to do something besides think, and the effort kept his shoulder from getting stiff.

Still, he couldn't help wondering why Stoke set the parcels on the porch instead of carrying them inside.

"I'll take care of the horses," Stoke said when the last load had been deposited on the porch out of the damp. "The company's yours."

Conn tossed his hat onto the nail and raked a hand through his hair. "Who is it this time?"

But Stoke was not of a mind to communicate

any details. Grumbling something about a square-head and needing to go to the barn where he could enjoy a chaw in peace, he jumped off the porch, grabbed the reins of the dray horse, and, as fast as his uneven gait would allow him, headed for the barn.

There was nothing for Conn to do but take the supplies inside. A matronly, middle-aged woman in black dress and apron stood at the sink. Her fair hair was divided in two, braided and rolled in circles over her ears. The part down the back of her head was so even it could have been drawn with a straightrule.

He made several trips, having to keep each load light. Only when he was done did she turn to stare at him with eyes the color of blue ice. Her brows were as fair as her hair, her nose generous, her lips pinched, and her skin surprisingly pink and smooth for a woman her age. Here was the square-head he'd seen briefly at the Bushwhack. Edgar Braden didn't like her. It was a point in her favor, no matter the look in her eyes.

"You're Helga," he said.

"Helga Werner."

"I'm—"

"*Ja.* I know." She turned back to the sink.

He looked around the kitchen. Everything had a shine to it, from the wall behind the stove to the sink to the floor.

But something was missing.

"Where's the cuspidor?"

"*Kuputt*. Gone."

"Gone?"

"*Ja.* A kitchen is no place for such filth."

No wonder Stoke had headed for the barn. Conn wished he had witnessed the confrontation between the pair of them. It would be nice for a change to see someone else going through hell.

With that uncharitable thought, he edged past her and went to the parlor door. Crystal and her brother Judge were sitting on the sofa, their backs to him. She had taken off her bonnet and shaken out her long hair. As she looked at the boy, she was actually smiling. Genuinely smiling. He hadn't seen such tenderness on her face in a long, long time. Wrapped up as she was in her brother, she didn't know her husband was so close.

The rain was coming down hard outside the front window, and the fire had been built up against the storm's chill. It was just the homey scene he'd described to Edgar Braden, except that Braden's two offspring were the participants, and Conn was very much on the outside.

"I wish I'd had me one of them cameras," Judge was saying. He talked with animation, his dark hair shifting where it fell well past his slight shoulders. He rested a bone-thin arm along the back of the sofa. His shirtsleeve hit him three inches above the wrist.

He was laughing. It was a boyish sound. Conn stood back to listen. Judge didn't look a thing like James, who'd had a stockier build, even at fourteen, but he sounded like him. Listening to the laughter should have hurt, but it didn't. Instead, it took him back to happier days. The journey felt good in a poignant kind of way.

"The first time that tobacco hit the spittoon, I thought Helga was going to explode right there in the kitchen. You know how that German of hers sounds. She scared the bejeebers out of me and I was clear out on the porch."

"It's his house, remember," Crystal said, but she didn't put much force into Stoke's defense.

"He commenced to tell her just that, but she came at him with more German. 'Gol-dern it, woman, talk English,' he told her and she rolled her eyes—you know that way she has—and said she would if he would."

Crystal's smile broadened, and then she caught sight of Conn in the doorway and the smile died.

Conn felt an unreasonable irritation. Hell, all he'd done was come into the room.

Judge, too, looked around at him. If he'd been smiling, he wasn't now.

The boy jumped to his feet and faced him, his brown eyes narrow in a face whose features weren't quite yet formed. His skin was nut-brown from the sun and he was taller than Conn had first thought, almost as tall as Crystal, but he didn't look like he would weigh a hundred pounds soaking wet. He kept the sofa between them, not offering his hand. But shaking hands would be the way of a man. He was just a lad. And a Braden, at that.

Crystal stood beside him. "This is my brother Judge."

"He remembers me," the boy said. "I was there when he brought you back."

Judge made it sound as though Crystal was an unwanted purchase he'd needed to return. As Conn recalled, the youngest Braden hadn't made her feel any more welcome than the rest of the clan.

"Judge and Helga brought some of my belongings," Crystal said with a small shrug. "Clothes and things. Mama sent them. She thought I would be in need."

Her eyes pleaded in silence for him not to say anything about her leaving soon.

"That was good of your mother," Conn said to them both.

Crystal's sigh of relief was audible, but the boy didn't seem to notice as he spoke up.

"She was afraid Papa might burn everything, angry as he was over Royce. When he stormed out, she sent us over fast." Judge hesitated a moment. "He was going to see the sheriff about bringing charges against you. I don't suppose he did."

"He tried. And then when he saw me, he got so upset, he forgot everything else. By the time Crystal and I rode off, he wasn't in a mood to do much but get back home."

"You hit him, too?"

"I thought about it. But no."

"How is Royce?" Crystal said. "I forgot to ask."

"Not as pretty as he used to be." The boy's eyes sparkled. "Face is bruised and his nose won't never be the same."

"Ever," Crystal corrected. "Won't ever be the same."

"However you say it, it still won't."

They both giggled, and Conn experienced a stab of jealousy at the easiness between them. Had he and his wife ever been like this? Maybe. Before they'd taken their vows.

The two of them seemed suddenly aware he was watching. Judge wiped a hand on his britches. "I'll get out of here."

"Do you have to leave so soon?" Crystal asked. The begging was clear in her voice, but her brother didn't seem to notice.

"There's no need to rush," Conn put in.

Judge eyed him warily. Conn could read the distrust in his expression, as if he were waiting to be criticized.

"I prefer Shingle Camp. There's just women there."

"Not all men are bad."

"Maybe not." But everything about him said that experience had taught him otherwise.

He looked at his sister. "He treating you all right?" He spoke as if Conn wasn't in the room.

"Of course. He's my husband."

But Edgar Braden had a wife, too, and there couldn't be a person in the world who thought Annabelle Braden's life was one of peace, at least not anyone who knew much about the family.

The joy that had been in the room a moment ago was gone. Judge came around the sofa and stood a couple of feet from Conn, staring at him in defiance. Conn stepped aside. The boy's long stride took him across the kitchen fast. He slammed the back door as he went outside.

Helga paused in the unpacking of the supplies long enough to shake her head.

"What set him off?" Conn asked, wondering why he should be feeling guilty for the unhappiness of someone else's son.

Without answering, Crystal hurried past him and followed her brother outside.

"He thinks you're like his papa," Helga said.

"Or his brother?"

"*Nein.* No one is like that *Schweinehund.*"

Without knowing what a *Schweinehund* was, from the way Helga said it, Conn agreed.

"Helga," Crystal called from the porch, "come on. Judge is determined to leave, and he's right. The rain's let up for a while. You need to get back before it starts up again."

Cold Teutonic eyes assessed Conn once again. "Do not harm her, Herr O'Brien."

It wasn't exactly a threat, more like an order. She hurried past him. Conn went out on the porch to watch the wagon roll away, the boy at the reins, the strong, blunt woman sitting stiff-backed beside him.

"Tell Mama I love her," Crystal called out. Judge gave her a wave without looking back. Both hounds ran along snapping at the wheels, then gave up the game and came back to the porch.

Crystal stared at the tracks the wagon had made in the mud. "He's getting wilder, Helga was saying.

He doesn't always come home at night."

"He didn't seem so wild back in the parlor."

"He's not that way with me. But he will be, if something isn't done."

She looked at Conn. "Did you know he was furious at me for lying to you the way I did? He thought I was weak, buckling under to Father that way. But he's decided that maybe it was for the best."

And so should you. He could almost hear her say it.

She squared her shoulders and disappeared around the corner of the cabin. In a minute she was back with a mud-spattered cuspidor in hand.

"I really owe Stoke an apology," she said.

"Are you going to put it back where it was?"

"Of course."

"Then let me clean it up to go with the rest of the kitchen."

"It'll only get dirty again."

"So will the kitchen."

She came close to smiling, but when she looked straight at him, she turned solemn again.

"I better put the rest of the supplies away and get to supper. I'd planned to try making a pie for Stoke, but I'm not sure there's time. Maybe I could settle for stewing those apples, or—"

Something prompted him to touch her arm. "You don't have to go in right away. Sit out on the porch and relax."

She stared at his hand, which to him looked blunt and coarse against the blue cotton sleeve.

Maybe that was because she felt so small and soft.

She closed her eyes for a minute, and then looked away.

"I'd really better start cooking. It's been a long day for us both, and neither of us knows what tomorrow will bring."

She hurried inside, leaving him with the cuspidor, leaving him to reflect that he could handle whatever came tomorrow as long as he could get through the night.

Chapter Twelve

A midnight clap of thunder jerked Crystal awake. She sat up on the sofa, her hand clasped to her mouth. It took her a minute to realize the noise had been just the storm and not the gunshot she'd been dreaming about.

The gunshot that killed Conn.

She shuddered and, wrapping herself tightly in her blanket, tried to slow the pounding of her heart. Shadows played across the room. She'd been having a nightmare, she told herself, nothing more. Her husband wasn't lying crumpled against the hearth, his life's blood flowing onto the stones as it had in her dream. Her brother wasn't hovering over him, ready to shoot again.

No, nothing like that. The room was peaceful, empty except for her and the shadows, and the fireplace held nothing but a pile of glowing coals.

But outside the night was dark and wild, and the effects of the dream lingered. Sleep became impossible. She needed reassurance that Conn was all right. He really had been shot; she couldn't forget that. A light came from under the closed bedroom door. Was he hurting? Had the wound become infected and caused a fever?

He wouldn't let her clean it or even look at it before he'd gone to bed. He'd seemed unwilling to let her near him, as if, like the rest of her family, she would bring him harm.

Her imagination ran as wild as the storm. Covering herself with the blanket, she padded barefoot to the door and knocked, then went inside the room, knowing that if she waited for him to admit her, she could be waiting long past dawn.

He was kneeling in the corner where she had stacked her possessions. Except for taking off his boots and socks, he hadn't bothered to undress. When he caught sight of her, he stood hurriedly, his hands thrust behind his back. She didn't know which one of them looked more embarrassed.

His unkempt hair fell low on his forehead, and his cheeks were darkly bristled. His shirt was only half buttoned; his trousers fit with their usual efficiency. Everything about him looked tousled and wonderful. Involuntarily she swayed toward him.

"I couldn't sleep," he said.

"I couldn't sleep," she said.

They spoke at the same time, and then they laughed. Nervously, neither of them close to being at ease.

She brushed her hair back from her face. Could he see the way her fingers were trembling? Did he know she wanted to brush back his hair the same way?

She usually wanted him to look at her. Not now. Though she was covered from neck to bare toes, she felt terribly, foolishly exposed.

He smiled sheepishly and her heart squeezed into a knot. "I thought maybe there was something here that needed to be put away in the wardrobe."

She stared at his lips. "I said from the beginning the floor was good enough. I've inconvenienced everyone too much as it is."

He held out his hand. "You ought to take better care of this."

"Oh," she said, staring at the cameo he was offering. "I didn't see it. I guess I was so excited to see Judge and Helga, I just dropped everything in the corner."

He came close. She stared at his feet, bare like hers. They were long, though his toes were blunt, like his hands. She remembered on their wedding night how he had rubbed those toes up the side of her leg. She had thought to tease him later for being so nimble. The time for such silliness had never come.

She took the cameo from him, taking care that their hands didn't touch, and looked lovingly at the delicate silhouette resting in relief on a bed of thinly cut amethyst, and all of it surrounded by a circle of scrolled gold.

"My grandparents gave this to me for my thirteenth birthday. I don't know who the woman is supposed to be, but I always thought she looked like Mama Stewart."

"Beautiful."

Something in his voice caused her to look at him. The hunger in his eyes was stark enough to take her breath. She stepped away, stunned, knowing she wanted him as much as he wanted her.

The trouble was, he was strong and she was weak. He wouldn't give in to his hunger, and she was ready to throw herself at his very nimble feet.

If only he would stop staring at her like that, she would have an easier time controlling herself.

She concentrated on the cameo. "It's my dearest possession." Except, of course, for her wedding ring.

He nodded toward her belongings in the corner. "Judge must have left most of your things behind at the ranch."

"No. I don't have much."

"But he brought only some riding clothes and extra boots." He reached inside his trousers pocket. "And this."

He held up a wrinkled, lace-trimmed camisole. A few such pieces of feminine finery were her weakness. Only her mother and Helga knew she wore them beneath her plain shirt and buckskins.

She blushed. "What are you doing with that?"

"I came across it just as I heard your knock. I felt guilty, like I was doing something dirty."

"Were you?" She barely got the words out.

"I imagined what you would look like wearing it. And nothing else."

She recognized the tone of his voice. It was the one he'd used the night he took her to bed.

I could show you.

The words almost came out, but her bold suggestions had been rejected far too many times for her to risk another hurt. Not after all that had happened the past day.

He might take her up on the offer, even get started with the procedure, but he would come to his senses in time.

She turned from him. "I wasn't checking up on you, Conn. I had a bad dream. Even after I woke, it wouldn't go away. The light was shining under your door, and I wanted to make sure you were all right."

Stop babbling, she warned herself. *Say what you have to say and get out.*

She spared him one quick glance, then gave the doorknob more attention than it could ever deserve. "I guess you are. You're not favoring your shoulder. Tomorrow—"

"Why don't you own more?"

"What?" she asked, unsure she'd heard him right.

"You said Judge had brought everything. Where are the old photos? Miniatures. A diary. I thought girls always hoarded such things."

His voice was low, probing, insistent.

"Some do, I suppose." She ran a hand down the door frame. "I had a diary once, back in Virginia, but when I caught Royce reading parts of it to some of the help—"

Her voice broke, but she forced herself on, letting the almost-forgotten memory return in all its bittersweet detail.

"One in particular, a young man who had me completely smitten, was listening right along with the rest. I had mentioned him, more than once. He must have been surprised since we hadn't even spoken. Coward that I was, I ran away before anyone could see me, but that night I threw those silly scribblings in the fire, and I never looked that young man in the eyes again. He must not have been very important to me after all because I can't even remember his name."

She tried to laugh; it came out weak.

"After that, I never was much of a collector. I guess I thought I'd start the real part of my life later and then I could gather things I wanted to keep."

He started for her. "Crystal—"

She held up a hand to stop him. "I didn't mean to sound so pitiful. Such things mattered a long time ago. Once I got to Texas, I was too busy to worry about such foolishness. Too busy and too realistic."

Her gaze fell to the rumpled bed and moved hurriedly on. She looked at the bare walls of the room, at the high, stark wardrobe, at the top of the dresser, which held only a basin and pitcher, at the bedside table with nothing more than the low-burning lamp.

"What about you? Where are your keepsakes?"

"I left them behind at the ranch, the few I had. That was before the war. Rocks and a rusty knife and an amber glass bottle I found floating in the creek. Boy things. I'm sure they're long since thrown away."

"Didn't you accumulate anything in New York?"

"Money and horses."

She took a deep breath. "And women? I always wanted to ask."

"There was no one who mattered. I planned to start my life later, when I got back to Texas."

"Then we've something in common."

Her eyes met his. A cry caught in her throat. She couldn't go on being so calm, so self-controlled. Suddenly he was beside her. She had the door half open when he slammed it closed. His hands rested against the panel on either side of her, pinning her in.

She kept her back to him, but she could picture exactly what he looked like standing so close.

"Don't go," he whispered against her hair.

"I didn't come in here to trap you."

"I know. You don't have to be in sight for that. I lied a minute ago. I wasn't worrying about your clothes. I wanted to touch them, to smell them because they were as close to you as I would allow myself to get."

She shook her head, trying to ignore the soft, seductive words and the fire of banked passion they ignited inside her.

"You'll hate yourself tomorrow." Her voice was

almost a sob. "And worse, you'll hate me."

He turned her to face him. His eyes raked her face and his breath warmed her cheek.

"We're beyond hate and love, you and me. Whatever is between us goes past such considerations to something far more basic."

She wanted to tell him there was nothing beyond love, that it was the deepest, the most vital connection that existed between a man and a woman.

But if she did, she would drive him away, and then she would die.

A crack of thunder shook the cabin. He kissed the corners of her mouth. "I want you more than I've ever wanted anyone or anything in my life. I want you more than I did when we first met, and I didn't think that was possible."

"You've got me."

It was her heart that spoke, but it was her body that pulsed and burned.

"To do with what I want?"

"I don't know all the possibilities."

"I'll teach you." She couldn't breathe. She couldn't think. This moment was too precious for such trivialities. She didn't want it to shatter; she didn't want it to die.

Holding up the camisole, she gave a little laugh, trying to keep things light and hot at the same time, trying to flirt though she didn't know how.

"Would you like me to put this on?"

"I was thinking more along the lines of your taking something off."

All the lightness went out of her. "Don't start this and then stop, Conn. Not again."

"I couldn't, even if I wanted to. If you hadn't come in here, I'd have been out there."

She wrapped the cameo in the camisole and dropped them both to the floor. Every fiber of her body screamed for things to get going. She touched his chest where his half-buttoned shirt was parted, kissed his throat, licked the curls of dark chest hair, and finished the unbuttoning, tugging the shirttail free of his trousers as she worked. He didn't stop her, but his breath was growing more ragged, and through the folds of her gown she could feel his body heat.

"Let me," he said, easing the shirt from his shoulders and dropping it to the floor beside the camisole. She stared at the bandage. Tears came to her eyes.

"So I'm a little damaged," he said, as if he needed to apologize.

"Maybe I like you that way. You're a lot stronger than I am. It evens the odds."

He grinned. She almost collapsed.

"You sound like a gambler," he said.

"I am. Otherwise I wouldn't be here."

She worked at his belt buckle, all the while studying the contours of his chest and the way the hair swirled around his nipples, then thickened on the way to points below.

It was the points below that beckoned, but having waited this long for him, she didn't want to rush. The problem was, she was so nervous and eager and afraid this would turn out to be another dream, she fumbled at her task.

Again he helped her by taking off his belt, but when he went to the fastenings of his trousers, she covered his hand with hers.

"I'll do it," she said. And she did, letting her fingers brush innocently against his erection as she opened the placket. She knew what she was doing. And so did he.

His gaze took in everything. Surely he saw the concentration and eagerness in her eyes, the rise and fall of her breasts as she pulled in deep swallows of air. He must know what she was feeling, understand her tension, must draw pleasure from her fumbling anticipation.

He took her fingers and kissed them, then opened her hand and kissed her palm.

"You're driving me crazy," he said.

"Good. That's how I am all the time."

"Crystal." He whispered her name as a sigh. He lifted her hair and kissed the side of her neck. "Let's get in the bed."

"But you're not undressed."

He stepped back, got to work, and in little more than an instant was done. "I am now."

She looked down. "Yes, you are," she said softly, but she could add nothing more. His body seemed to flow in a single tapered connection of muscle and sinew and tight, smooth flesh from chest to waist to flat abdomen and powerful thighs. And then she came to the center of all that marvelous manhood.

She tried to be casual, subtle, sophisticated, worldly like the women he'd left behind, but she caught herself licking her lips.

She didn't remember him as being so formidable, specific memories of his anatomy having grown fuzzy over the past days. And she really hadn't gotten a good look at him. At least not all his parts.

She made up for the omission now.

Sleek and hard and slick and even sinewed, like his arms, and with folds at the tip—

She shook her head and looked up. "You must think I'm terrible."

"I think you've got on too many clothes."

"You're right."

Following his example, she got to work, lifting the gown over her head and tossing it aside as if she did such a thing every day.

"Not now," she said.

She had to force herself to stand naked before him, to drop her hands and let him look at her the way she had looked at him.

He didn't appear much more casual, more subtle, more worldly than she had. She especially liked the heat in his eyes.

"You weren't wearing anything but the gown," he said.

"The last time, the underdrawers stopped you. I've been sleeping in just the gown for a long time, should you ever—"

He stopped her with a kiss, a good one, a long and wet one, probing the inside flesh of her mouth with such intensity that she thought he might crawl inside. Frenzy coiled within her as she danced her tongue against his and rubbed her aching breasts against his chest.

Their bodies seemed to glide naturally against one another. She knew no shame.

At last she broke away. "Let's get to the bed."

They did. He threw back the covers. They lay on the cool sheets. Outside the cabin, the storm raged. Inside the bedroom they both went wild. He touched her everywhere, studied her, kissed her, ran his tongue around the tips of her breasts and around her navel, and even went lower to her thick triangle of hair.

She stopped him there. Parting her thighs, he stretched himself on top of her.

"This time I'll do it right," he said, stroking her hair as he looked down at her.

She gripped his shoulders.

"You already are."

"Not yet."

He plunged inside her. She bent her knees and lifted her hips to welcome him. A sense of rightness and such sweetness as she had never known washed over her. She didn't care that he no longer loved her. He wanted her, and that was enough.

Best of all, he accepted her as his wife.

Their bodies rubbed together in all the good places; she saw what he meant about doing it right.

Nothing in all the world could be better than this.

She was wrong. He made it better. On this wild night, with the problems between them fading to insignificance, he taught her what ecstasy was really like.

A long time afterward, when the storms had abated, both inside the cabin and out, she lay in his arms beneath the covers and listened to the evenness of his breathing. He hadn't once complained about his shoulder, but she knew it had pained him. Once, if she recalled correctly, though she hadn't been thinking clearly at the time, she'd tried to tell him to take it easy, but he had ignored her.

At least he'd ignored what she said. There wasn't a square inch of her body he hadn't given his full attention. She had tried to do the same for him.

Making love was exhausting. She was sore between her legs, and in general so languorous she could barely lift a hand. So why couldn't she sleep? She knew the answer. She didn't want to miss a second of lying in his arms. When he woke, there was little predicting what his attitude might be.

Propping herself on one elbow, she leaned across him to check the bandage, to see if the wound had started bleeding again.

His eyes opened. Her face was close to his. Lantern light flickered across his bristle-shadowed cheeks. He looked almost harsh, and she felt as if she were doing something wrong.

Then he smiled, and the world seemed good once again.

"It's all right," he said.

"It doesn't seem to be bleeding."

"I meant between you and me."

"Oh," she said.

Flustered, confused, telling herself not to hope for too much, she nestled beside him and rested a hand on his chest, letting her fingers pick up the beating of his heart.

So tell me that you love me once again.

He played with a lock of her hair. "I was as much to blame as you, carrying on that way about falling in love the first time I saw you. I expected too much, I guess."

You expected me to be what I seemed.

"We're married, Crystal, and we're fools to keeping fighting that fact."

The heart that had begun to heal shattered again.

Stop, please, she wanted to cry. He'd come so close to saying the words she needed to hear, so close but not nearly close enough.

"We both come with problems," he said. "We need to help each other work them out." He jostled her. "Hey, are you listening? You haven't fallen asleep, have you?"

"I'm listening."

She swallowed her hurt and again became the woman she had to be, the sensible one who did what she had to do.

"I'm wondering about what happens if I conceive. That seemed to bother you before."

He was a long time answering. "We'll leave that up to fate. If it happens, then we have children. You'll be a good mother. I saw the way you were with Judge."

He sounded so practical, so reasonable. He had no idea how commonsense could wound.

"Is that why you changed your mind tonight?"

"Because of Judge?" He laughed and kissed her forehead.

For a moment she was certain there was the sharp edge of hurt in his voice, of pain that equaled hers. But she must have been wrong. His laugh did not sound forced.

"I've always wanted you," he said. "And now I have you, as you have me. That's the only thing that matters. I'll take care of you. That's a promise. If you're sure this is what you want."

I want you to call me love.

She asked too much, but then, she was a fool. Wanting to be the most important part of his life, she would have to settle for second best.

Enough talk. He'd hurt her as much as he'd pleased her, but she must keep that sad bit of reality to herself. At least she didn't have to worry about her mother and Judge. They were safely moved back to the Shingle Camp, and her father rarely saw them, or so her little brother had said. If he hadn't gone over to the Bushwhack to get Annabelle's new sewing machine, which Edgar had ordered a long time ago, he wouldn't have known about the injury to Royce.

At first Mama had worried that with his only daughter gone, Edgar would come in a rage across the creek and take vengeance wherever he could. Judge didn't much think that would happen, busy as their father was lording it over everything and everybody at the Bushwhack, and Crystal agreed.

Besides, she'd never been very important to her father, and he had more than enough compensation for her loss.

Conn stroked her hair. She kissed him fast, fearful he might start to speak again.

"Make love to me," she said, bold as she pleased. "I always preferred daylight to dark, but right now I never want this night to end."

Chapter Thirteen

Annabelle Braden rose early from a restless sleep. Neither Helga nor the sun was up, but the storm had moved on, leaving the predawn hour still and, except for the drip of water from the eave outside her bedroom window, as quiet as she could remember it ever being.

The silence did not bother her. She was comfortable in this room, or as close to comfortable as she could be anywhere, in no small measure because she had never shared it with anyone else.

It was the one place she viewed as hers, private and inviolable. With her own hands she'd made the quilt, the curtains, the needlepoint pillows in the bedside rocking chair. With Helga's help she'd even hooked the rug. Such activities helped to pass the years.

Turning up the lantern, she sat before her

dresser and began to unbraid her hair. Her reflection in the wall mirror stared at her with solemn contemplation. She looked so old, so thin, her skin papery and translucent, almost as if she were not made of flesh and blood.

What was she, forty-four? The years had taken their toll. She'd started childbearing at such a young age, and had ended it in a great deal of pain.

Judge had been worth it. He was the joy of her life, together with Crystal, of course. But Crystal always seemed so self-sufficient, so private, so distant. She loved her daughter with all her heart, but she'd never thought the girl needed her the way her younger son did.

Even though in his youthful pride he would never admit it.

He'd reported that his sister seemed contented enough with her situation. Did Crystal love her husband? Or was her acceptance of him something forced upon her because of circumstance?

Annabelle couldn't put the questions to her young son, and, sad to say, she didn't know her daughter well enough to understand how she felt. She *did* understand the sacrifice Crystal had made by lying to Conn O'Brien and robbing him of his land. The enormity of the lie would always hold her prisoner. She'd bought her mother's freedom at the cost of her own.

There was no way a mother could ever repay such a debt.

And poor Royce, with his bruised and broken face. He wouldn't take his injury well. He seemed the strongest of the Bradens, the source of Edgar's pride and joy.

But Edgar was wrong, as he was in other things. Royce was the weakest of them all. In all the twenty-six years she had tried to love him, something held her back. It was as if a basic part of him was missing. Or maybe it was missing in her.

Her greatest pride came from knowing her first-born didn't know how she felt.

With a sigh, Annabelle ran a brush through her long hair, her thoughts returning to herself. Once as black as the night, the waist-length locks were streaked with gray now. Her complexion was much too pale, but then, she seldom went outside these days. She couldn't seem to work up the strength, and why should she? There was nothing out there she wanted to see.

Her eyes, dull brown and sunken, worried her the most. She could see well enough, at least at a distance, and she had her spectacles when she wanted to read or to sew.

It was the spark in them that she missed, the spark that had been there when she was a young girl and full of life. She had loved to ride across the Virginia countryside. Papa and Mama had worried, but she hadn't cared. She'd been spirited and foolhardy, the way she feared Judge was turning out. And she'd fallen in love too soon.

She'd been far too inexperienced for such a powerful emotion, but he was handsome and dashing, the worst kind of man to turn a young girl's head. She hadn't really known what he was like. But she'd learned—oh, how she had learned.

Footsteps sounded in the hall outside her room.

"Helga?" she called.

The door flew open, and her husband stepped inside.

She dropped the hairbrush and her hand flew to her throat. "Edgar."

His eyes met hers in the mirror. Cold eyes, judging eyes that shredded her new-found peace. He stood straight and square and strong, not a tall man but still more vital than she could ever hope to be. She understood why. He had twin tonics of hate and obsession that nurtured him, while she fed upon lost hope and a thousand memories.

The memories were beginning to fade. She couldn't remember him wearing anything but fine black suits similar to the one he was wearing now. Even at this pre-dawn hour, his hair was carefully groomed, his moustache neatly trimmed. When he strode closer to the dresser, she could barely detect his limp.

"What are you doing here?" she asked.

"I own this place. Or have you decided it's yours?"

She shook her head. "I thought—"

"That I wouldn't bother you again?"

She looked at her unmade bed.

"Don't worry," he snarled "I'm not demanding my rights, although, by God, I ought to."

He often made such threats, but he never acted on them. He hadn't touched her in such a way for the past fourteen years. During the first part of their marriage, he'd been passionate, and so had she. But passion between them, the loving kind between a man and woman, was a long time gone.

"Then what do you want?" She asked the question with uncharacteristic courage. "It's long before dawn."

"I wanted you to get an early start."

"I don't understand. Start at what?"

"Moving home."

Her hands shook. She clutched them in her lap. "This is my home."

"Not anymore. You wanted to be at the Bushwhack often enough when Daniel O'Brien was alive. You'll live there now with me."

The breath rushed out of her. She should have known. She should have been prepared.

"You promised Crystal that Judge and I would live here," she said, her voice dull and flat. But she had to speak; she had to let him know he was doing wrong.

"Don't mention her name. I never want to hear it again."

"She did what you ordered her to do."

"She humiliated me in town."

"Yesterday? You saw her there?"

For a moment his thoughts turned inward. She felt his anger like a blast of heat. Crystal usually came between them when he showed signs of getting so distressed. Crystal the peacemaker, who could hold off his show of anger, if not his hate. But Crystal was not there.

"Whatever she said or did," Annabelle said, "I'm sure she didn't mean it."

"No more," Edgar roared, and the walls shook under the power of his rage. "Right now she's probably spreading her legs for that bastard she married." He was standing close, staring down at her as though he'd never seen her before. For the first time in all their years together, she saw true madness in his eyes, and she felt a new kind of fear.

He grabbed her hair, his fingers wound tightly in the long strands. "Just like her mother. She's nothing but a whore."

Annabelle fought back tears, but she could not fight the trembling that started inside her, for herself and for her daughter as well.

"He's her husband, Edgar. She thought she was doing what you asked."

He yanked hard and she cried out at the pain. Throwing up his hands, he backed away. "You never could take things rough, could you?"

In shame, she stared at her lap, and she held her silence. Against the malevolence of her husband, silence was the only weapon she had. She should have remembered it the moment he walked into the room. He seldom hurt her, not physically, and he rarely raised his voice, but that was because she didn't try to explain herself or argue with him or in any way talk back.

He was a gentleman, after all.

Until today, when she had dared to protest his ugly words. Today he was a man she did not know.

"Pack your things," he said, more calmly, once more the man who was in charge. "There are men and wagons below to help you. I want all of you out of here by dawn. If you're not, I'll come back and burn this place to the ground."

And then he was gone, leaving her to stare once again into the mirror. She pressed a shaky hand to her lips, but she had no time to give in to frailty. He'd given her until dawn, which could be no more than an hour away. She knew he meant what he said.

She fumbled at twisting her hair into an untidy bun. What difference did it make what she looked like? Her life was done. This past week without him had been the happiest she could remember since long before they'd moved to Texas. But it was over. The sooner she put it from her mind, the better she could endure the coming days and years.

Poor Crystal. Her sacrifice had been for nothing. She mustn't find out, not right away, not until the madness passed from her father's eyes.

When that might be, Annabelle had no idea.

Killing was too good for Conn O'Brien. Royce needed to think of something more appropriate, something that involved permanent pain.

He stared out the door of the Bushwhack kitchen and watched the beginnings of daylight over a far hill. His face hurt; he couldn't sleep; he couldn't much breathe. At first, each breath had been like sticking a knife up his nostrils. It was better now. Better but a long way from good. The only thing he could do really well was pace and think about getting revenge.

Permanent pain. He liked the sound of it. Oh yes, Conn O'Brien would pay in ways he couldn't imagine.

But care would be needed. O'Brien would be watching for him. And O'Brien wasn't a fool.

Royce stopped himself. O'Brien not a fool? Hadn't he been tricked by a woman with yellow hair and big, brown, innocent eyes? Hadn't he kicked that same woman out of his bed, all noble like and proud, then taken her back the first chance he got?

Baby sister must have her bridegroom under her pretty little thumb. Of course she did. She was Royce Braden's sister, wasn't she? She ought to be good for something.

Royce would have smiled except for the pain. Crystal was definitely the answer. If she could be made to cooperate. She had before, against her will. Given the right motivation, she would again.

He would give the situation some thought, but later, when he didn't hurt so much.

He heard footsteps behind him and turned to see the servant Graciela enter the kitchen. She was carrying a lamp, and she didn't know he was there. He hadn't been with her since moving to the ranch house, hadn't been with any woman for more than a week. Not since that night here at the Bushwhack when Daniel O'Brien had gone to the promised land.

He brushed the details from his mind. And he had been with a woman. He'd forgotten the whore in San Antonio, the one who liked to be hurt. All women did. They needed only to be convinced.

Graceless needed new lessons from time to time. Standing in the shadows away from the door, he watched the way her full breasts moved beneath her blouse. His gaze slid to her thick lips, and he thought about her skill with them and with her tongue. Her eyes were deep and dark and turned inward, but he knew ways to light them up.

Too, he knew ways to make her beg.

She was wearing her thick black hair long and loose, the way he liked it. She must have been thinking of him. And if she wasn't, she would be. When he got around to her.

He stepped into the light. "Good morning, Graceless."

She stared at him in the doorway. "*Madre de Dios.*"

Suddenly remembering what he looked like, with his face smashed and bruised and swollen, he turned his back to her.

"You need the cool cloth on your face," she said. "I left it at your door last night."

"It'll be wrapped around your neck if you don't leave me alone. I won't have a woman telling me what to do."

Because of the swelling, his voice sounded strange, as if he couldn't get the words out right.

"Whatever you say, *escarcho.* I try only to help."

Damn her and her sweet talk. The woman could

be a pain in the butt. She'd been getting uppity lately, not lowering her eyes when his father was around, not waiting on him the way she ought, avoiding him when he was alone. She needed to be put in her place.

She bustled around the kitchen behind him. Every noise she made sent more pain shooting through his head. Pressure built. He couldn't think. He was about to order her to get the hell out of the room when she laughed.

He was on her in an instant, grabbing her wrist, twisting it until she bent almost to the ground.

"What's so funny?"

She shook her head. "*Nada.*"

He twisted harder. He wanted her to cry, to beg, to plead for him to let her go.

But Graciela was not so easily broken. With a toss of her hair, she stared up at him.

"I laugh because Señor O'Brien has made you look like a raccoon."

Dropping her wrist, he slapped her hard, and she fell onto the floor. Like a crab, she scurried sideways toward the hallway. He stepped on the hem of her skirt, stopping her, and began to unfasten his trousers. He knew how to deal with the likes of her.

"No!" She threw the word at him as she might a Mexican blade. "You will not. I know too much." A smile of triumph lit her face. "You will not hurt me again."

"I will kill you if I want."

Fear flared in her eyes, and then the fear turned

to scorn as she watched him lower his pants.

"Not with that pitiful thing."

He stared down at his flaccid manhood. He ought to be stiff, hard, ready. Never had this happened to him. She dared to laugh again. Rage raced through him. He raised a fist to hit her. Only the sound of arriving horses and wagon stopped him.

"What the hell—"

Hiking up his trousers, he peered out into the early morning. Damned if it wasn't his mother sitting high in the wagon beside one of the ranch hands, her belongings piled in the wagon bed. After just a week, she was moving back where she belonged.

It figured. He hadn't expected his father to honor the promise for long. Edgar Braden was a man who did what he wanted. Or thought he did. He could be manipulated. Royce did it all the time.

His mother had never figured out the way of it. Instead of flattering him and saying what he wanted to hear, she stayed out of his way. She was loving enough to her children, but like all women she was weak.

Helga was with her in the wagon, and Judge rode one of the horses to the rear. It was a damned parade, that's what it was. He covered his face with his hand. He was not in a greeting mood this morning, not in a mood to show himself.

"Get up," he ordered Graciela as he stepped past her.

She rubbed at her face.

"Up!"

She scrambled to her feet, but she held back, cringing, out of harm's reach. The sight of her made him hard. Too late, with the voices getting louder outside.

He put his face close to hers. Let her see the ugliness, let her feel the hate. The fear returned to her eyes. Satisfied, he left and made quickly for the solitude of his room. She'd distracted him too much, as would his returning family. Damn. He would just as soon never see them again.

He must not let anything or anyone get in the way of his revenge on Conn O'Brien. He'd hole up as long as it took until he came up with a plan.

Chapter Fourteen

On Saturday, the first day of May, 1869, two days after she moved into Conn's bed, Crystal marked the two-week anniversary of their marriage. Conn didn't mention the fact. Neither did she.

She did, however, with Stoke's help, bake her first pie. When the effort was completed, she came to a definite conclusion: she'd rather shoe a mean mule.

Riding the range with her husband was more to her liking, and this was how the following days passed. Except for remembering her family in her prayers, she blocked out the rest of the world. Her conscience barely bothered her. The Bradens would no doubt return to her life soon enough.

Conn made such blocking easy. With him so close, he was all she could think about. He always sat tall in the saddle, his broad-brimmed hat pulled low on his forehead, his sky-blue eyes picking out details that most men overlooked—the smallest signs of straying stock or wildcat predators, a curious cloud pattern over a distant hill, a buzzard riding the valley breeze.

He wore a bandanna tied at his throat, workshirt and gloves, a fringed vest, and leather chaps. Everything about him was masculine, practical, and, in her admittedly biased opinion, gorgeous. She especially liked the chaps; they outlined his front and rear in ways she'd never noticed on any other man. She fed on the sight, like a beggar thrown a scrap of bread.

Most of all, she liked watching the way he handled horses, training some for herding cattle, others for more menial tasks like wagon-pulling, a few for racing, though he claimed none would beat the slowest plug back in Saratoga.

She had always been good at working the stock, but he was better. She'd never seen anything like him. Most of the animals gave him no trouble, but every now and then he came upon a challenge, a horse that declared with a snort or the toss of a proud head, or any other of a dozen horse-talk ways that he was a creature who wouldn't be dominated.

These were the times her husband was lost to her. It was as if he and the animal existed only for each other. He never pushed the confrontation, showing his target who was boss in the manner of other ranch hands she'd seen—a manner that almost always failed, or if it didn't, broke the horse's spirit beyond repair.

Instead, Conn would come up slowly, straight-on and easily seen, stroke the horse's neck and get nuzzled in return, and he'd talk where no one but the animal could hear.

After a while of talking and stroking and nuzzling, he could get the horse to do just about anything he asked, with no loss of spirit or pride or courage on either side. Often the two of them worked up a heavy sweat, but even after the session was done, Crystal always felt they could have gone on for hours without rest.

In several ways it was similar to their lovemaking, to the harmony and enthusiasm on both sides. The difference was that after the work on the range or in the corral, Conn seemed more at peace than he ever did in bed. Perhaps not as satisfied, although she could easily be rationalizing about that, but definitely more at peace.

She would have been jealous except that during these times he lost all signs of tension. He had purpose. He had success. She loved him so much that she could do nothing but push aside her bittersweet observations and, for him, rejoice.

A week following the silently observed anniversary, having sold off a dozen cow ponies to a rancher in Mason County, he decided he needed new stock and he left for a buying tour. After a two-day absence, one of the loneliest periods of Crystal's life, he returned with twenty horses to add to their range, and with news that another twenty were on the way.

Stoke told her he'd bought up animals from a few of the ranchers who'd come upon hard times.

"Most didn't hanker to sell," he elaborated while peeling potatoes the evening of Conn's return, "but they're practical men and Conn offered a fair price. Through the banker, of course. He don't go on all the ranches just yet."

"What's he going to do with the horses after he gets them trained? He said himself he was lucky to find a buyer for the cow ponies."

The spittoon pinged. "Breed some of 'em, sell others to the government, take a few down to San Antonio. Mostly, I think he's just moving back in, letting a few folks understand he's here to stay. Word'll spread soon enough."

"Of course he's here to stay," she said, a little too quickly, pushing aside any worry that he might choose to leave. "This is his home," she said, and then more softly, "or at least it used to be."

Stoke pitched a potato into the pan and got to work on another. "Ain't no business of mine, understand, but he's putting money out on more than horses."

He spoke offhandedly, but Crystal detected an edge of unease in his voice.

Another woman was her immediate thought, but only because she was so insecure. If there was one thing she knew for sure, it was that she left him too exhausted to sleep with anyone else.

"He didn't mention any other expenses," she said.

"I ain't surprised. He never was a man to spill his business."

She stood at the sink, her back to Stoke, and stared out the window over the sink. "So what is he buying?"

"Land, most of it going for taxes. Everything around the old place he can get his hands on. Again he's working through the bank. He pays more than a fair price, but then, he never was a real practical sort."

He fell silent, and she knew the talking was done. Conn's business was not brought up again, not that night nor any time in the following days. Not by Stoke and certainly not by her husband.

He never was a real practical sort.

Crystal choked up every time she remembered Stoke's words. He hadn't told her more about her husband's character than she already knew. Of course Conn wasn't practical. Look at the way he'd chosen a wife.

Look especially hard at how little he'd gained, and how much he had lost since they'd met. More than once she'd seen him gazing toward the Bushwhack with a special kind of longing she didn't read in his eyes when he looked at her.

He never called her *love* anymore; he never teased or talked about fate bringing them together.

But he talked about how much he liked her body. When they were making love, he didn't hold back. And they made love often, especially after the buying tour, every night and sometimes during the day.

It seemed he couldn't get enough of her. For sure, she couldn't get enough of him.

Stoke managed to disappear when Conn got the look in his eye. And Crystal always responded. Eagerly, frantically, whenever he wanted her, she wanted him.

Usually it was in bed, but one night, when it was just the two of them in the house, he took her in front of the fire. If "took her" was the right phrase. She rather thought she'd taken him, since it was the only time she had ended up on top.

The wildest time came two days later, and for Crystal it marked a change in their relationship. Like most of the other changes between them, this one wasn't for the better.

They'd been searching for a mare and colt that had escaped the corral; they found them in a stand of trees near the creek. She and Conn dismounted, the breeze cool in the high branches, the water barely making a ripple of sound. At their feet, the grass grew soft and thick.

Their eyes met. Crystal's body hummed like a guitar.

"It's daylight," she said, as if he couldn't see the sunbeams streaming through the trees.

He tossed his hat aside. "Yep."

Her heart drummed its way to her throat. "We're outside."

His vest joined the hat. "Yep."

"This is wrong, Conn."

"Why?"

"It's not natural."

"It feels natural to me."

She licked her lips. "We could be seen."

"I don't think the horses'll mind."

He eased from his chaps like a dancer and began unfastening his trousers.

She felt like a bird trapped by a snake.

Except it wasn't a snake he was getting ready to show her.

And, she admitted, she wasn't trapped in the least. He would let her go if she insisted. Uneasy though she was, leaving was the last thing on her mind.

She stripped down to her waist. The breeze felt good on her bare skin. Her nipples grew pebble-hard, but everything else about her felt soft and warm and wet.

He just stood there staring at her, the cad.

"Don't you ever get tired of looking?" she asked, not being so sure of herself she didn't like to coax a compliment out of him.

"Nope."

Not very flowery, but from the way his trousers were taking on a different shape, she knew he liked what he saw. Her fumbling fingers unbraided her hair. The long pale locks were crimped, and she thought they looked silly, but he liked them loose. Whatever he liked was fine with her.

Cupping her breasts, she offered them to him.

He was on her in an instant, taking off the rest of her clothes, lowering her to the grass, kneeling between her thighs, dropping his trousers just low enough to allow him the freedom he needed.

The grass tickled. She laughed.

"You think I look funny?" He rubbed between her legs with his sex.

The laughter died. "I think you're beautiful."

"Nobody's ever called me beautiful before." His blue eyes seemed to catch the sun. "Sounds almost womanly."

"Oh, Conn," she said, moving herself against him, "womanly is far from my mind."

She wrapped herself around him, and he took her fast, but then she wasn't in a mood to slow him down. He made her feel so good, she wanted to shout with joy. And so she did.

The mare and the colt took off. "We'll have to find them again," he said.

"I'm sorry," she said, suddenly feeling foolish. "I couldn't help myself."

"Neither could I," he said, kissing her, running his fingers through her hair. He had a way of touching her that for a while could keep her doubts at bay.

Hiking up his trousers, he wrapped her in his arms and lay with his back to the ground, letting her rest on top.

His hands started exploring.

"Are you cold?" he asked when she started to shiver.

"Nope."

He squeezed her backside. "Would you like to lie here a while?"

"Please."

"We're outside."

"Are we? I hadn't noticed."

He chuckled. She snuggled against him and nestled her face against the crook of his shoulder. It was all so glorious, so exciting, so sweetly thrilling. She was every kind of fool she could think of not to feel content.

Yet she didn't. As sweet as it was, making love in this clandestine way seemed somehow wrong, too, as if they weren't really married. When he'd started taking off his chaps, she'd brushed aside her initial doubts. In truth, she hadn't been thinking at all. But she was thinking now.

He took her the way horses mated, not front to back, but still wild and sudden, not private in the least, the thick trees notwithstanding. Would he have done such a thing to a woman he really loved and respected?

Worse, would any other woman in the county have behaved so shamelessly? She was just as bad, just as wild as he. She couldn't imagine the good widow Jennie Weathers ever offering her breasts the way she would a cup of milk. Crystal's cheeks burned from the memory, and yet she knew she would do the same thing again under similar circumstances. If Conn treated her more like a mistress than a wife, she must be glad he treated her any way at all.

Maybe if he loved her, she could look at all of

this differently. But she couldn't stop thinking that the high-minded man who wouldn't take her to bed until they were wed was now taking her on the floor and in the woods.

His hands stopped their roving, and his breathing grew regular, and in a minute she heard the familiar sound of his low snore. The sound was soothing when they were in bed, but it bothered her out here. Even with him close by, it sounded so distant, so impersonal. She tried to tell herself it meant he felt comfortable around her.

But a man could be too comfortable with a woman, she was discovering. She eased from his arms and dressed, braided her hair, and slapped her hat back on her head. He snorted once but otherwise just kept on sleeping and snoring.

He looked so helpless and, yes, she dared to admit it, he looked at peace. She noticed for the first time the dark circles under his eyes, and she was ashamed she hadn't seen them before. He was working hard, sleeping little, pushing himself as though demons spurred him on.

If she were any kind of decent person, she would tell him no more lovemaking until he got some rest. But she wasn't decent. Just look at what she'd done this afternoon.

The best she could do was let him sleep now and later, when they settled down for the night, pretend she was too tired to make love again.

She blew him a kiss. "I love you," she whispered, and then she left to find the mare and her colt.

* * *

The next day, in a stiff breeze that portended rain, Conn watched as Crystal gave her first thorough inspection to the new stock.

"Prime," she said with a smile when she rode up to him at the edge of the pasture. Her cheeks were flushed from her efforts and tendrils of hair whipped about her face. She looked good. She always did.

And she sat a saddle as well as any woman he'd ever seen. She knew horses, too. He took the *prime* as more than empty praise.

The memory of yesterday afternoon came to him. Why couldn't he keep his hands off her? It was doubtful that the way she rode a horse had much to do with it. The only answer he could come up with was that in this land where he'd been a lusty kid, he'd become a lusty man.

And she was a temptation the likes of which he'd never before seen.

He forced himself to study the grazing horses. "Still not a racer in the lot."

"Is that what you're really after?"

"Racing is exciting, Crystal. It's what I know."

"In a few months, after the summer heat has passed, they'll have races outside of Kerrville."

"Good ones, as I remember. Stoke says they still are."

"I wouldn't know. Father wouldn't let me go to them."

He heard the catch in her voice. Much as he preferred to forget her family, he wondered whether she missed them. As far as he knew, she'd received no word of the Bradens since Judge's visit more than a week ago. Did she suffer the same aching sense of loss that refused to leave him?

There were times when he wanted to talk to her about those feelings, like after supper when he sat before the fire. The trouble was that talking was never easy between them when it wasn't about horses or sex.

And so he turned the conversation to the horses, discussing what he had in mind for each, listening to her comments, asking for suggestions, passing the time as any rancher ought.

When a horse and rider came over one of the hills, he stopped, and the two of them watched as the man approached. It didn't take long to recognize him.

"Hamilton Gates," Conn said with a broad grin when his old friend had reined to a halt beside them.

Ham returned the grin. "I thought I'd catch you out here." When he glanced at Crystal, the smile died. "But I figured you'd be alone."

Conn caught the wounded look in his wife's eyes.

"Ham, this is my wife."

Ham tipped his hat. "Hello, ma'am."

"Please, call me Crystal. I've heard Conn mention you."

"I've heard him mention you, too. Ma'am."

If it wasn't an outright insult, it came close. As much as Conn liked his long-time friend, he wished Ham hadn't been the one to tell him the truth back in San Antonio.

He was still pondering how to handle the delicate matter when Crystal spoke up.

"I need to get back and start supper. You'll stay and eat with us, won't you, Mr. Gates? I'm not much of a cook, but Stoke kindly steps in to cover my mistakes."

Polite, direct, without being overly friendly, Crystal was setting the tone. Ham mumbled an acceptance, and she rode off. Conn watched her until she disappeared over the crest of a hill. When he looked back at Ham, he saw questions in his eyes—questions he didn't want to answer because it wasn't any of Ham's business what was going on between him and his wife. More importantly, he didn't know what to say.

"I thought you were headed for New Mexico," he said.

"I tried it on for size."

"It's been less than a month since you left. You couldn't have tried very hard."

"I got to the edge of the Territory and saw right away it wasn't Texas. It just didn't fit."

"Lots of good folk live there, I'm told."

"So are you pulling up stakes and leaving for the Territory anytime soon?" Ham asked.

"No."

"Over the past month, I decided I didn't want to do that, either. Not that I have the stakes you do, but I've got druthers. There's good folk here, too." He paused a moment. "Good and bad."

Ham looked in the direction of Stoke's cabin,

and Conn could see what he was getting at.

"And there's more grass," Conn said, redirecting him to the pasture. He began talking about the new stock and the plans he had and before long he was offering his old friend work.

"I've taken on too much for just me and Stoke. You always were good with horses."

"That's a real compliment coming from you."

The two worked out the particulars, with Ham swearing he wouldn't mind sleeping under the stars, and saying the money Conn offered was more than he'd been expecting, more than he'd ever made before the war, and before long they were inspecting the stock up close and forgetting all about what had happened in San Antonio.

But Conn saw all too clearly over the next few days that Ham hadn't forgotten the way things had begun with Crystal. His new wrangler was polite, but he didn't do much talking when she was around. As a result, she stayed away, not riding the range anymore, busying herself indoors the way she had the first few days after moving in.

Conn stayed busy, too, and not only with the stock. He had plans for doubling the size of the cabin. Through Stoke, he found down-on-their-luck workers who were looking for something to do and the building was scheduled for the following week.

Stoke objected at first.

"I don't mind sleeping in the barn. Kinda like being close to my old mare, truth t' tell."

"Then I'll build quarters for you, too. It's your

place, Stoke. You may not be bothered by that, but I am."

Stoke shrugged but put up no further argument, and Conn added another project to his building plans.

Busy as he was, with a thousand ideas roiling around in his head, when he fell into bed each night he was ready for his wife. She came to him with an urgency he didn't remember, too intent for talk but not for a wild inventiveness that drove him crazy.

Once he caught her by the fire and tried to make love on the hearth-side rug.

"No," she said. "It's not decent."

"Decent?" He'd never heard her use that word before.

"That's what I said."

"We did it before. I don't recall decency getting in the way."

"It's in the way now."

With her long hair rustling against the back of her gown, she took him by the hand and led him to the bed and proceeded to show him that while she wouldn't frolic in front of the fire, she could do just about everything he wanted in bed, from letting him be in control to binding his hands to the headboard and driving him wild with her lips.

Later, when they had both cooled down, he tried to tell her some of the things he'd particularly liked, thinking in his foolish manly way that she wanted to hear such praise.

She shushed him.

"I got carried away," she said with such finality, he gave up on the compliments.

The next morning she was up before him. He found her in the kitchen in one of her prim dresses, hair braided, her attention directed to rolling out biscuits. He was walking a little unsteady at the time, but except for the shadows under her eyes, she seemed as strong as ever.

He came up on her with plans to nuzzle her neck, but she shrugged him away and held up her floured hands. Domesticity, it seemed, was hampering his style. Another *d* word, like decency. He got the feeling that the two of them would never again make love by the creek.

And he could give up completely on getting tied to the bed.

On the evening of the fourth day of Ham's appearance, after a particularly tense supper during which Crystal excused herself and sat on the porch while the men ate, Conn decided he'd had enough.

As Crystal cleaned the kitchen, he sought out Ham and found him in the barn brushing down his horse.

"You want me to leave," said Ham without looking at him.

"No, I don't, at least not permanently. That's up to you. But a few things have to change."

"Concerning Crystal Braden."

"Crystal's my wife."

"Why? You're not forgetting she cheated you out of the Bushwhack, are you?"

"I'm not forgetting. But I made vows. We've made our peace."

Which wasn't exactly the truth, but it was close enough so that he could say it to Ham without telling a lie.

"You don't owe her a damned thing, Conn. I know how you felt about that ranch. I know you went through hell when you decided to leave."

"Times change us. I'm not the sentimental young man you knew."

"The hell you aren't. Leastways you were when I saw you in that bar, sipping expensive liquor to celebrate."

"Look, Ham, I'm uncomfortable talking about Crystal."

"You'd have to be dead not to be. I was there when you found out the truth. Told you myself, as you recall, though I would have sooner ripped out my tongue. I would've sworn you'd go upstairs and kill her."

Conn wanted to protest, but he knew Ham remembered right. That night had been the worst of his life, tearing at him more than leaving his family had done because in those long-ago days he'd held hope of seeing them again.

With Crystal, he'd lost something that could never be regained. And he wasn't thinking solely of the Bushwhack Ranch.

And yet they'd made their peace, uneasy and incomplete though it was. He couldn't imagine life without her now.

If sometimes he felt like crying—and he'd never

cried since he was a tad, not even when his mother died—he decided it was from working so hard during the day and staying busy half the night.

"A lot's happened. I'm not denying it. But I've learned that there are no easy solutions in life," he said. It was the best he could do in explaining things, to both Ham and himself.

Ham set the horse brush on a shelf at the back of the stall. "I always figured you were the smartest one of us all. But Stormy Weathers did better in picking a wife."

"You mean Jennie."

"Right. Jennie." Ham said the name with softness, and Conn wondered if maybe he hadn't wanted her for himself.

"I can't argue with you there. The widow is a fine woman. She's one of the few people who'll speak to me when I go into town."

Jennie Weathers was pretty, too, as well as courageous, and amiable and probably pliable most of the time.

But he couldn't see her offering herself beside the creek.

It was a comparison that Conn was not prepared to make, at least not out loud.

And so, as he usually did in his talks with Ham, he shifted the subject away from Crystal. "I've got something I want you to do. If you've no objection to travel."

"As long as it ain't to New Mexico."

"How about New York?"

Ham let out a cuss word.

"There's a horse up there that I need to transport back to Texas. I've got the details worked out, but I need someone to oversee the trip."

With Ham listening and nodding and asking a question here and there, Conn went on to explain exactly what he had planned.

Crystal stepped away from the barn door, barely hearing the New York talk. Mama always said one never overheard anything good while eavesdropping. Mama was right.

She hadn't meant to listen in. She'd come down to the creek for a quick bath, but the voices in the barn had attracted her in the same manner a dog was drawn to a bone. She'd known the men were talking, and she'd known they were talking about her.

She cheated you out of the Bushwhack, Ham had said.

I'm not forgetting, Conn replied.

I would've sworn you'd go upstairs and kill her.

Conn hadn't put up a single protest. Instead, he'd listened to the praise of Jennie Weathers. *A fine woman,* he'd called her, which was far more than he'd said about his wife.

She hugged herself, fighting the way everything inside her had turned cold. Conn hadn't killed her on their wedding night, but he'd come close to doing it on this spring evening. Life being filled with irony the way it was, it just happened to be the first month's anniversary of their marriage.

He'd wounded her without laying on a hand. He'd done it with words.

So he'd learned there were no easy solutions in life, had he? Crystal had known that all of her life.

She hurried toward the cabin. A dark figure in the shadows took her by surprise. He stepped into the moonlight. She saw it was Stoke. So he, too, had heard.

She could read the pity on his face. Or maybe it wasn't pity but sympathy. She couldn't take either one, not right now, or she would collapse and never get up again.

And so she waved to him as if nothing were wrong and went inside to steel herself against this latest hurt. In her opinion, she managed very well. Except for the lovemaking, which ceased when her monthly flow began, life proceeded pretty much the way it had before.

The calm didn't last. A few days later, while Conn was in San Antonio with Ham making arrangements for the New York journey, someone raided the stock and took a dozen of the finest horses. Stoke was laid up with a fever, and so she didn't tell him what had happened. But the thief had left behind a clue as to his identity, a gold Masonic ring Papa Stewart had given his first grandson at his birth.

Royce had never become a Mason, and neither had Edgar. But he'd kept the ring. And he'd dropped it to let her know what he'd done.

She knew, too, where he'd taken the horses.

Here was something she could do for Conn beyond cooking barely edible meals. She could find every one of those animals. She could return them to their rightful range.

Chapter Fifteen

Early the next morning, with Stoke sleeping peacefully in the bed, his fever down, Crystal left him a pot of oatmeal porridge and some coffee on the back of the stove and headed out for the horses.

For the better part of an hour, she rode straight and true, tracking them down to where she'd known they would be: in a narrow, limestone-walled box canyon at the edge of Shingle Camp Ranch far from the creek. It was as good a hiding place as any she knew. Royce used to find her there when she was in a mood to be by herself.

He never could leave her alone for long. It seemed he hadn't changed.

She spied him right away, sitting close to the mouth of the canyon in the shade of a scrub oak, leaning back on his elbows, chewing on a weed.

He was staring into the canyon, to where the horses milled restlessly, not turning until she rode close.

She couldn't stop a quick intake of breath. It had been weeks since Conn had hit him, but there were still faint signs of bruising around his eyes. His nose, always so straight and well proportioned for his face, had become a misshapen hump.

In truth, she thought it gave him a touch of character he had lacked before. The hardness in his eyes said he didn't agree.

He braced himself against the trunk of the oak and looked her over. "You got any bruises that don't show? Has he broken anything on that pretty body of yours?"

"Is that your way of saying hello and asking if I'm all right? Well, I am. Conn treats me fine."

He stroked his nose. "Then you haven't riled him."

"We both know that's not so." She looked beyond him to her husband's horses. "Why did you take them?"

"We needed to talk. In private."

Crystal shook her head in disgust. "That's what I figured. You're usually not so careless." She tossed the Masonic ring into the dirt by his side. He picked it up and slipped it on his right hand.

"So start talking," she said.

"Have you heard about Mama and Judge?"

Her stomach tightened. "What about them?"

"Tsk, tsk. I thought you were the loving one in the family, and here you've kept yourself in ignorance. Seems like you found a more earthy kind of love, if you know what I'm getting at."

"What about them?" she repeated. "You've gone to a lot of trouble to tell me, so do it."

He grinned. The broken nose made his mouth look twisted, taking away the charm of the smile, making it look mean.

"They've moved to the Bushwhack. If you're thinking it was their idea, think again."

It took a moment for her to assimilate the news. "But Father promised—"

"Yeah, he did, didn't he? The rascal."

"Why did he go back on his word?"

"You're kinda simpleminded, aren't you, baby sister? You insulted him in town. You and that bastard you married."

"He insulted us," she said, her voice rising in a protest she knew was useless. "Conn and I were just talking when he came up waving a gun." She shivered as she recalled the scene. "He said some terrible things to us both. I thought he was going to shoot."

Again Royce stroked the ridge of his broken nose. "Edgar was protecting his only son and favorite child, seeking retribution for the violence that had been done to him."

"He's got two sons, Royce. You're not the only one."

"I should have said the only son he knows is his."

The argument was old, but never had it been brought up in such terrible circumstances. She sat back in the saddle and fought the turmoil inside. "How could Father—" she began but broke off. The real question was how she could have believed he would do otherwise.

Royce and Edgar were so different in so many ways, yet they were alike, too. They seemed . . . evil. She didn't want to put such a harsh name to it, but nothing else could describe thc way they made the rest of the family suffer.

"Does he know you're telling me what's going on?" she asked.

"Hell, no. When he's not out riding around playing lord of the manor, he stays in that room he calls his library, though why I don't know. He's never read a book in his life."

"Then the horse stealing was your idea. Why? What do you want?"

He shrugged in innocence. "I'm letting you know the way things are."

She shook her head. "Not good enough. I know you too well. At least I'm beginning to."

"You have a suspicious mind. I thought you'd want to hear about your dear sweet Mama and precious Judge, and maybe, if you still care, what you could do to change things. Our ambitious father is not making life pleasant for them. Every night he orders them to supper, then all the time they're trying to eat he takes tiny little pinches out of their hides with complaints."

"He always did that."

"Not the way he does now. Nothing seems to please him. My guess is owning the Bushwhack isn't as wonderful as he thought it would be."

He shook his head as if in sorrow. "Judge takes it, but I don't know for how long. We surely do need you, baby sister, back where you belong."

His gentleness caught her unawares, and she almost believed his concern. But then she saw the calculating way he was watching for her reaction.

"Cut the bullshit, Royce."

"My, my, you've become vulgar since you left home."

"I didn't leave home. I found it." She sat tall in the saddle and spoke from her heart. "Conn O'Brien is the best thing that ever happened to me."

Royce almost came off the ground. She could see the flash of rage in his face. His hands shook as if they would hurt something or someone, and then, just as suddenly, he settled back to his relaxed sprawl.

He seemed like two people, one composed and the other out of control. Both frightened her to her bones.

"Leave him," he said. "Make a fool of him. Let everyone know he wasn't good enough for you. Edgar will be so glad, he'll probably decide to keep his word and set Mama up wherever she wants."

"Never." Her answer was quick, instinctive, heartfelt.

Royce just grinned. "Never's a long time," he said, drawling out his words.

"He wouldn't let me go." She spoke what she saw as the truth. If she left, Conn would come after her, not because he loved her but because he couldn't let the Bradens win.

If she and her husband ever separated, and such was always a possibility, it would be his choice and not hers.

"What if something happened to him?" Royce asked.

Crystal's heart stood still. "What do you mean?"

"I'm just saying what if, you understand, but what if he met with an accident? Or maybe not an accident. He rides after you, gets a little rough, and your loving family protects you by shooting him down. I can see it happening."

Crystal shivered. She could see it, too.

Royce did not let up. "You'd inherit everything he owned, wouldn't you? Edgar would get control, you being his distraught widowed daughter and all. That'd make him real happy. About as happy as taking over the Bushwhack."

"If you do anything to hurt him, I'll kill you."

"Your own brother? Why, baby sister, that sounds almost Biblical."

"I'm not lying."

"And I'm only saying what if. There's lots of things can go wrong. Indians, for one. They're in the area. I heard they burned down a farm over in the next county. Renegade Comanches. They're the worst kind."

He snapped his fingers as if a thought had just occurred to him. "Isn't O'Brien out on the road now? Be a shame if he came across them. Wouldn't stand a chance. And I'd be innocent.

Even you would see that."

He stood and whistled for his horse. Crystal watched him brush the dirt from the seat of his pants and pull himself into the saddle. But she really wasn't seeing the details. She couldn't think clearly, not with fear tearing her apart.

With another horse close by, Trouble stirred restlessly.

"Are you telling me the truth about the Indians?" she asked.

"I swear it on our grandmother's grave. Think about what I've been saying. You want to protect O'Brien, the best thing you can do is leave. Maybe he wouldn't come after you. Maybe we wouldn't have to shoot him down."

Anger and despair warred within her, and underneath it all a sense of hopelessness. She felt as if the blood had drained from her, taking with it the last of her strength.

"How can you do this to me?"

"I'm doing it *for* you, baby sister. You've changed. In the past I could make you see reason. Not anymore."

He put his whip to the horse's flanks and left her in a cloud of dust. Staring into nothingness, she listened to the sound of the receding hooves pounding the hard ground. For the first time in her life, she simply couldn't think. In the silence after he'd gone, she just sat there on Trouble, letting the sun climb higher in the sky, her mind trying to take in all that her brother had said, all that he'd threatened.

With each memory, her heart died a little more. Royce truly was evil. It tainted them all.

The day was hot, promising an uncomfortable summer to come. A pair of hawks rode the heat waves over the limestone walls. She took off her hat and rubbed a sleeve against her forehead.

Mama, Judge, Conn—each was her responsibility. The burden weighed too much. She was one person. And not a very smart one at that.

At last she forced herself to move, to herd the horses together and, roping them in a single line, take them back to their home range. It was close to noon by the time she got back to the cabin. She found Stoke tossing on the bed. His fever had returned. Her heart went out to him, even as she thought that here at least awaited a problem she could deal with.

After much protesting, he let her bathe his forehead with a cool cloth and change the sweat-soaked sheets. She couldn't get him into sleepwear, however. While she made the bed, he stood in the corner naked, but only after she promised not to look at him.

"Ain't no woman but my ma ever seen me in the altogether, and that was in ought-seven." He said it like a brag.

Without comment, she waited, back turned, as he settled under the clean sheet. "Will you be all right alone for a little longer?" she asked as she helped him drink a cup of water.

He choked, but he swallowed. "You run along. I don't need no babying."

After she'd settled him down, she went to the barn for a fresh horse. The men Conn had employed were already working on the bunkhouse for Ham and two more hands he planned to hire. Next, they would move to doubling the size of the cabin.

"I'm going into town to see if I can find the doctor. Would one of you check on Stoke from time to time?"

"You sure riding out alone is smart?" one of them asked. "Heard tell there's Injuns about."

"They don't usually come into this part of the county," she said. "I'll be all right."

And she was, taking the ride fast, thinking that if something really did happen to her, Conn's problems would be at an end. Unfortunately for him, she wasn't prepared to shoot herself just yet; she still had Mama and Judge to worry about.

She found the doctor in his office close to the bank. After she'd described Stoke's symptoms, he prescribed a tonic she could get at the general store.

"Let me know if that doesn't work, and I'll come out to take a look at him."

"Have you heard anything about renegade Comanches in the area?" she asked as she prepared to leave.

"They burned out a family over in Kendall County a few days ago."

Crystal steadied herself. Kendall lay between Kerrville and San Antonio, on the route Conn would have to use to get home. Royce hadn't lied.

Comanches were close by.

"Maybe you better take some of that tonic, little lady," the doctor said. "You're looking a little peaked yourself."

She paid him for his time and hurried to Ochse's store, hitching Trouble close to the door. It was her bad luck to run into Jennifer Weathers and her mother-in-law coming in at the same time. Jennie looked freshly groomed, as if she'd just stepped from her bath, her black gown starched and clean, a white lace collar at her throat, a pert bonnet framing her delicate face.

Crystal not only looked peaked, her buckskins carried a pound of trail dirt and her rumpled felt hat should have sat between the ears of a plow mule.

But she wasn't in a mood to worry about vanity or even about courtesy. Slipping past them with barely a nod, she bought the tonic and hurried out to start the ride back to Stoke's Place.

"Well, I never—" she heard Dora Weathers say behind her.

The two women were standing in the doorway, watching her as she approached her horse, judging and condemning. Because she was brusque? Because she'd tricked her husband into a disastrous marriage? Because of who her husband was?

It didn't matter. The absurdity of the situation got to her. Conn on a dangerous road, his life threatened by her brother, Mama and Judge forced to live in misery—these were terrible situations, unthinkable, unsolvable. Yet it was the rudeness of Dora Weathers, something she had experienced more than once, that got to her. She wanted to laugh and cry and scream and stomp and throw things, all at the same time. Mostly she wanted to sit on the ground and cry.

She needed a friend.

Jennifer Weathers came up behind her. "Are you all right? Can I help?"

She didn't need consolation from a woman her husband admired. Especially one so ladylike and pretty and available.

She shook her head. And then she saw a familiar figure down the street. She blinked once, twice, and then again. It couldn't be. But it was.

Tucking the tonic into the saddlebag, she patted the horse in reassurance and started down the walkway.

The woman saw her coming, stopped, and smiled.

Around her, she could feel the whole town watching. Like Dora Weathers, they were displeased. What she was doing was truly disgraceful, something no decent woman would even think of.

Crystal didn't care.

"Mrs. Truehart," she said, almost throwing herself in the madam's arms. "I don't know what brought you here, but you are the most welcome sight I've seen since I left San Antonio."

* * *

Conn returned late that evening to find Stoke propped up in the bed complaining about no tobacco and no dogs, and about life in general, with particular attention to how the body could let a man down.

"I take it you've been sick," Conn said.

"Ain't no more. Tell that stubborn woman you married to let a man get some peace. She keeps fussing over me, poking poison down my throat."

Conn spied the bottle of tonic on the bedside table. He felt Stoke's forehead. "You feel a little warm to me."

"She put you up to saying that?"

"I haven't seen her. I used the front door, thinking to catch her by surprise."

Stoke smirked. "And looky who you found in your bed." He started to cackle, but it turned into a cough. Conn settled him down with a swallow of water and abandoned him to his complaining, there being little to do for him that his wife hadn't already done.

His old friend had good color in his cheeks and more than adequate cussing on his lips. He would be all right.

Conn heard Crystal slamming pots around in the kitchen. Supper must not be going well. He tiptoed to the door separating the kitchen from the parlor, but he shouldn't have bothered being quiet. She couldn't have heard a gunshot with the noise she was making.

She was wearing a dress, the green one with the tiny little tucks over her breasts, and her hair, freshly washed, fell loose against her shoulders and down her back. After four days away from her, he was stunned at the impact the sight of her made on him. He seldom caught her when she wasn't on guard. Her slender arms and tiny waist, the way she kept blowing a recalcitrant curl out of her eyes, the graceful hands, the way she twisted and turned as she moved from the table to the sink to the stove—he could have watched it all for hours.

She wasn't especially pleased at what she was doing, but she was working hard. Warm feelings stirred inside him, feelings that involved more than undressing her and taking her on the table. Although the undressing occurred to him, too.

Mostly, he wanted to tell her she didn't have to try so hard to please. She pleased him just by being near. He never told her anything gentle, except when they were making love, and then it was mostly about how he liked the way she made him feel and how he liked making her feel the same.

Saints above, he ought to be spanked. Maybe she could try that, too.

Before he could speak, she grabbed up a cloth and pulled a pan of fresh bread from the oven. Turning toward the table, she saw him for the first time, yelped, and dropped the bread. The pan clattered on the floor.

"Conn," she said, as if he were the last person on earth she expected to see.

She stood there staring. He took the cloth from her hand and picked up the pan. The bread fell, sinking in the pan in little waves as if it were alive, putting out a sigh, and then it lay still and brown, changing from something that might have been edible to a rock-hard mass that would break a tooth.

"Sorry," he said, trying to apologize as he set the pan on the table.

"You're back."

She lifted a hand as if she would touch him to make sure he really was there. Instead, she turned from him. He was sure he saw tears in her eyes.

He stepped close and took her by the shoulders, liking the feel of her, enjoying the smell of her hair. Shaking him off, she moved away.

"You're supposed to be glad to see me," he said.

"It's been a long day."

"For me, too."

He could have elaborated with details about how he'd started out late yesterday, riding harder than he ever had, going all night, spurred on by the feeling something at home was wrong, something that only he could handle. She would say he'd sensed that Stoke wasn't well, but Conn knew that wasn't the way it had been. His worry had been for her.

"Supper will be a little late," she said, keeping her back to him.

"I'm not worried."

"I just wanted you to know."

"What's wrong, Crystal? Something's troubling you."

"I dropped the bread."

"Forget the bread. Something's different. Something's changed."

"I don't know what you're talking about except that Stoke's back in the bed where he belongs."

"Damn it, that's not what I meant. Do you think that when I see you I immediately think of sex?"

She turned to stare at him. He didn't like the look in her eye.

"Maybe I do," he said with a shrug, "but it isn't all I think of."

He saw right away it was the wrong thing to say. She'd be remembering the circumstances of their marriage, thinking the same memory had hit him. That wasn't what he was referring to at all. He cursed under his breath. Always and forever those circumstances stood between them, like a wall that neither could breach. The way she stood there keeping herself from him, holding him off with nothing but a warning glint in her eye, made him think the wall was higher and thicker than ever.

Worry ate at her, that much was clear, but she seemed disinclined to tell him what that worry was.

She looked away. "Give me a little while, and I'll get you and Stoke some food."

"What happened while I was gone?"

"The men started work by the barn."

"That's not what I meant."

"I rode into town to get Stoke's medicine."

"Anything happen there?"

She hesitated. "I met an old friend."

"Maybe I know him. What's his name?"

Conn could hear the jealousy in his voice, but she didn't seem to notice.

"It wasn't a *he*. And *old* was the wrong word. I might as well tell you. You'll hear about it soon enough. Mrs. Truehart has moved to Kerrville."

Conn almost laughed in relief. "I'll be damned."

"She bought a place at the edge of town. That's what she called it, *a place,* but we both know what it really is. I got the impression she ran into some trouble in San Antonio and decided to move on." She lifted her chin and stared straight at him. "I spoke to her on the street. I even gave her a hug. Everybody was watching. You know how they are."

"You thought that would bother me?"

"It bothered her. She told me I shouldn't be doing such a thing, but I . . . well, I was in a mood to see a friendly face."

Conn wanted more than ever to take her in his arms, but the warning glint had not gone from her eyes.

"It's not easy for you, is it? Going into town, I mean. You married a traitor. What's that old expression? You're tarred by the same brush."

"They'll forgive you faster than they'll forgive me. Everybody knows I tricked you into marriage. Everybody but Mrs. Truehart. At least, if she does, she's not letting it bother her. I guess she's seen worse—"

"Crystal, stop."

"Stop what?"

"Stop beating yourself. What happened is behind us."

"It can never be behind us."

He ran a hand through his hair. "You are the most exasperating woman I have ever met."

"I wish that's all I was." The smile she gave him didn't cover the despair in her voice. "Now please, leave me to put together something to eat."

Conn cursed some more. He had no choice but to do what she asked. Later, when his horse had been rubbed down, and the dogs fed, and the chickens fed, and Stoke fed, and he had pushed his food around his plate, he took her by the hand and guided her away from the kitchen sink and onto the back porch.

"You didn't eat much," she said.

"I wasn't hungry. Come with me to the barn."

She tried to pull away; he held on tight.

"It's not so bad out there," he said. "We'll have blankets and a pile of straw in the loft." He ran his fingers across her palm. "We've never made love on straw."

He thought he had her for a minute, from the way she swayed toward him and bit at her lower lip.

But Crystal was not an easy woman to read.

"I can't," she said in little more than a whisper.

"Why not?"

"It's not . . . you wouldn't take . . ."

Her voice trailed off, and she left him waiting for her to finish.

"You'll have to be more specific. Otherwise I'll

just throw you over my shoulder and—"

"Jennifer Weathers!"

"What?"

"You wouldn't take her to the barn."

"Damned right. I don't want to. And what has she got to do with this?"

"Nothing. Forget I mentioned her name."

Conn knew he walked on eggs. How he had gotten into that position was beyond him, but then, he was a mere male and lacked a devious turn of mind.

"Look," he said, standing with his arms at his sides, "if I've done something wrong, why don't you just punch me in the mouth. It worked before."

She stifled a cry. "I don't want to hit you."

"Then what *do* you want to do? Have you decided you don't like sleeping with me?"

"That's not the problem. I'm still a Braden. Why would you want me?" She spoke with a despair he'd never heard. It shook him hard, and made him angry, too.

"That's the stupidest thing I've ever heard." And then a calmer sense took over. "Something did happen, didn't it?"

"I had time to think."

Conn shook his head in exasperation. Thinking time was always a danger where a woman was concerned. But Crystal wasn't like other women. She never had been. One of her problems was that she didn't know he was glad about it.

He tried to tell her. She wouldn't listen.

"I'll sleep on the sofa so I can be close if Stoke needs me."

It was a good excuse, but that was all it was. Stoke was snoring so loudly that the timber posts on the porch shook. But she stood her ground. By the time Conn had settled down in the barn, leaving her without so much as a goodnight kiss, he was more puzzled than ever. Greeting the town's latest madam on the street wasn't something that should bother her so much.

And what was that business about Jennifer Weathers? Worse was the talk about being a Braden, as if he needed reminding. If he could overlook it—and he was finding it easier every day to do just that—then she ought to do the same.

The next day and the next she rode with him on the range. She kept her distance, but she never let him out of her sight. Except when he went to the barn to sleep. She kept insisting Stoke stay in the bedroom. For his part, Stoke put up a protest, but it was clear he knew something was wrong between the O'Briens and, like Conn, he did what she said.

All the while, frustration built inside him. He didn't sleep, he didn't eat—even when Stoke took over the cooking—and in general he was so tight and tense, he feared if she ever touched him, he'd embarrass himself before he could ever get her undressed.

When Nat Zink, one of the workers, told him about a herd of wild mustangs supposedly roaming the hills to the west, he decided to go check them out. Nat was a mustanger from the early days, and an Indian fighter, too. He'd know what he was talking about.

"You can't," Crystal protested. She seemed genuinely fearful for him. He assured her he'd handled wild horses before.

"That's not what I'm worried about."

He waited for her to go on, but he wasn't surprised when she didn't.

"You don't want me here, you don't want me gone. Would you like to explain that little inconsistency?"

She shook her head, and so, with Nat riding at his side, he left early the next morning without saying good-bye. Whatever was going on between them, he would settle matters when he returned.

Crystal was awake when she heard him getting ready to ride, though dawn was just a streak of pale blue over the trees. She stood in her nightgown on the dark porch and watched him leave. Worrying about him all the time was stupid. Royce wouldn't track him down and shoot him, not because he wouldn't want to but because, being a bad shot, he would miss and get hurt himself.

He'd done what he wanted. He'd stirred her up, started her thinking, brought unrest to the already unsettled O'Brien home.

Yes, worrying was stupid, but wanting her husband wasn't stupid at all. She'd tried to explain to him why she couldn't sleep with him. She was a

Braden; she didn't deserve the happiness she found in his arms. He hadn't been much impressed.

She should have told him how she really felt. She came from evil stock. After her talk with Royce, she saw it more clearly than ever. Any man with sense would know she was unlovable, certainly in the husband-and-wife kind of way. A cancerous sore, that's what she was. And that's what she should have said.

But the words wouldn't come. And now he was gone.

Somehow she had to break away. And he had to let her go. Making him restless, irritated, and finally bored was not the most brilliant plan she'd ever come up with, but it was something to try.

Helping Mama and Judge was something else. An impossible task. Unfair. But help them she must, though she doubted that her eventual, inevitable return to the Bushwhack would bring peace to anyone.

She started to enter the back door and sensed someone coming up behind her. The dogs stirred restlessly, then settled back down by the rocker. Worthless hounds.

Slowly she turned, wishing she had the rifle that was stored beside the parlor hearth. She made out a woman on foot, a shawl pulled over her head and shoulders.

"Señora O'Brien." The voice was soft and low and urgent in the cool morning air.

"Graciela?"

"Sí."

"What's wrong?"

The woman didn't speak. Crystal gestured for her to follow her inside.

By the dim light of the kitchen lamp, she watched as Graciela entered the cabin. The woman moved slowly, cautiously, with none of her usual grace.

"What's wrong?" she repeated.

Graciela lowered the shawl to reveal a battered face. Her lip was cut and swollen, her eyes blackened, and there were dark bruises on her throat.

"Oh," Crystal cried in sympathy. "I'm so sorry," and then, "Was it Royce?" She knew the answer before the woman's nod.

"He thinks I like it," Graciela said, and then spat out, "*escarcho.*" She winced at the effort and touched her lip.

"Cockroach?"

"He thinks it is a loving term. He is a fool."

"Sit down, please," said Crystal, pulling out one of the chairs. From the careful way Graciela lowered herself, it was clear she had bruises other than the ones that showed.

Crystal got her a drink of water and dampened a cloth. "Let me tend your wounds."

"First I must speak."

Crystal held herself very still.

"Your mother cries and the boy runs wild. The German tries to help, but she has been ordered to leave." She took a small sip of water, then met

Crystal's eyes. "Your father drinks. He has become a man I do not know."

Graciela looked as if she would say more, but something stopped her. Crystal did not urge her on. Already she had been told too much.

Her father's jealousy and greed had created a hell for them all, beyond anything her presence could heal. A momentary panic took control. What was she to do? What was right and what was wrong? The difference had been simple once. Before Conn. Nothing was simple now, certainly not the course of action that suggested itself. Could she really do it? No. It was too much.

And yet, she saw no other way out.

Her hands shook as she searched for an ointment to treat Graciela's cuts. Stoke would help. She must talk to him, and then, with the good Lord helping her, she would do what she must do.

Her eyes misted. If the cost was her husband, she told herself, he had never truly been hers.

Chapter Sixteen

When Conn topped the rise and got a look at the green valley before him, he broke into a big smile. His Irish luck—the good kind—had finally returned.

"Purty," Nat Zink said as he reined his horse beside him.

From Nat, that was high praise indeed, and well deserved. Here at last was the *manada* of wild mustangs the two men had been tracking. They'd been four days on the trail, the first three riding hard, cutting back and forth through the hills, knowing they were close to their quarry but not quite close enough. Yesterday, with Nat's senses "a-quiver," as he'd said, they'd stopped to build a mustang pen.

And here were the animals to go inside, a hundred of them grazing in the deep grass that grew beside a meandering creek. Conn didn't want them all, just those best fit for breeding and up to two dozen others that would do as cow ponies.

Let the rest run wild and free and multiply.

"They look fed and watered to me," he said.

"Yep."

"And lazy." Impatience ate at Conn's belly. "Let's go get 'em."

Nat held up a hand. His pale blue eyes squinted at the sun and he chewed at his moustache, a grandiose growth not much smaller than his horse's tail. Except for the streaks of grey in his hair, he was nut-brown from head to foot, small and compact and solid, a *mesteñero*, a mustanger most of his life, until the war brought hard times to the hill country.

He'd learned the trade from Tejano vaqueros, which meant he'd learned from the best. Conn put his age somewhere between his own thirty-five and Stoke's sixty, tending to peg the number at the upper end.

"Ain't hot enough," Nat said.

A May mid-morning seemed hot enough to Conn, but he took the mustanger's word. After four days of riding hard and sweating and four nights of pulling out thorns by the campfire, they could wait a few more hours.

Which they did, spending the time scouting the area. For their purposes, the mustangs were well situated. Beyond the creek to the west, a limestone bluff cut off any avenue of escape. To the north a dead-end canyon lay a mile ahead in their path, to the south the waiting pen, which they'd built at the edge of a cedar brake. That left the horses only the east, and Conn and Nat.

When the sun had reached its zenith and was spilling heat onto the valley, the two men rode slowly down the rock-studded grassy slope, heading into a stiff breeze that was blowing their scent away from the *manada*. Conn's heart pounded. The horses weren't handsome by Saratoga standards, being small and wiry and shaggy, but they were tough and fast and they had a dignity that came with surviving on their own in the wild.

The lead stallion, a magnificent black, reared his head, his ebony mane and tail caught in the wind as he spied the two men. His dark eyes caught the sun and fixed on Conn. It was as if the two communicated.

I'll take your mares and a few of the stallions, but I'll leave you alone, Conn tried to tell him.

Like hell you will take a single one of us.

That's what the stallion would say if mustangs could curse. This one looked as though he might color the whole county blue.

The stallion would know the area better than he or Nat. Mustangs were territorial animals. In a single year the wildest of the horses might not roam past a twenty-square-mile area, if that area provided sufficient water and grass.

This was one of the facts Conn had gleaned from the *mesteñero* during the evenings of thorn-pulling and stretching out stiff joints.

They'd discussed ways two men could capture a

herd of wily mustangs. During the wait for the heat to build, Nat had, in what was a burst of conversation for him, suggested the one they would use.

"We'll walk 'em down."

Conn could see the wisdom in the choice, though he'd have preferred chasing them back to the pen and corralling as many as possible inside. Four days gone, and he was ready to get back to Stoke's Place and find out what was going on with his wife.

The last time he'd seen her, she'd been spouting malarkey about not wanting to sleep with him in the barn, somehow getting Jennifer Weathers and the rest of the Bradens into her excuse. But Crystal was a passionate woman. It could be she would be the one to drag him to the hayloft, and not the other way around.

At least it was something to contemplate during the long, moonless nights.

Walking the horses down would take at least another week, but if that's the way Nat thought best, that's the way it would be. Bringing along the packhorse they'd staked on the far side of the hill, they headed north behind the herd, slowly and steadily moving them out of the valley. Nat and the packhorse stayed at the rear, Conn more to the east, their destination the box canyon. The stallion took the lead, but on occasion he twisted his proud head to stare at Conn.

They walked and then walked some more. At first the men stayed upwind, but gradually they edged close so that, when the time seemed right, they could mingle with their quarry. Neither Conn nor Nat had bathed since heading out; they wouldn't bathe again until they returned, not wanting to give the horses new scents that might cause alarm.

They were ripe, and they were going to get riper. If Crystal were ever to get near him again, he'd have to scrub himself with lye.

They walked the rest of the day and well into the night, turning the mustangs at the mouth of the canyon late the next day and heading back toward the valley and on to the pen.

Another fact Nat had imparted was that mustangs needed sleep. They didn't get it. Neither did the men, except for periodic dozes in the saddle. By the time they arrived at the hastily built corral, six days after they'd first been spotted, the horses followed the men inside as if they'd done so every night. When the gate closed behind them, only the black stallion lifted his head.

Under a half moon, men and animals slept, and in the morning Conn began selecting the horses he wished to keep. The first thing he did was keep his word and let the stallion go. There were other stud mustangs in the herd that would serve his purposes, and some fine mares, and more potential cow ponies than he'd expected.

Among the mares were three who were close to foaling. He suspected the stallion's bloodline would live on in at least one.

They ended up keeping thirty of the original one

hundred. The capture hadn't been dramatic, but it made up for the deficiency by tiring both men down to their bones.

They rested another day, milling with the horses, gaining their trust, taking them down to the creek for water and for grazing in the rich grass along the bank, hobbling them at night, letting them roam the pen during the day.

The night before they were to head out for home, they both jumped naked into the creek and afterward made a ceremony of burning their clothes, which Nat said was a waste but Conn insisted was essential.

Nat also thought dirtying up the creek was wrong. It had been less than a month since his last bath.

"You're the expert in mustanging," Conn told him, "but sometimes a boss has got to be boss. We brought clean clothes. We're wearing them. I'm not staying upwind of you the whole ride home."

"You sure picked up weird habits whilst you was gone."

It was the longest sentence Conn had ever got out of Nat.

They were a day's ride from Stoke's Place when they came upon a band of ten of the county's ranchers, and double that number of their cowhands. Conn recognized most of the ranchers as friends of his father, and one-time friends of his. The hands were young and strangers to him.

Dalworth Weathers, Stormy's dad, rode at the head.

Even out here in the middle of nowhere, Conn expected Weathers to ride on past him—either that or start looking for a tree stalwart enough to take a hanging rope; instead he motioned for the men to stop and wait for Conn and his entourage to draw near. Nat held back with the herd of mustangs, leaving Conn to face them alone. The men acknowledged one another with a nod and a few tipped their hats and mumbled a greeting.

Conn called a few by name. They looked embarrassed that he remembered who they were.

Weathers dismounted and set his horse to graze; the others followed his lead. The cowhands stayed to the rear, watching the mounts.

Pulling a charred pipe from his pocket, Weathers tamped down some tobacco. Conn offered him a match. He hesitated, then took it and drew fire. Conn studied the ranchers. They were all cut from the same cloth, more alike than different—big, weathered, and middle-aged with signs of a paunch, but still strong and tough.

"We're tracking Comanches," Weathers said at last.

"We've been riding from the north. I didn't see any signs of them."

Weathers stared at him with the squint that came from looking too long into the sun. "Maybe you forgot what to look for."

"There are some things a man never forgets."

Weathers grunted and puffed at his pipe.

Conn wanted to tell him how sorry he was about Stormy, but he didn't think his words of sympathy would be taken well.

"Are you tracking the ones that burned out the people in Kendall County?"

"Don't know for sure. I'm looking for the ones that hit my place three nights ago." He held up a hand. "And don't be looking like you're ready to take off. We checked around. Far as we can tell, the Double D is the only ranch they got to. Stoke's Place is safe."

"Is your family all right?"

Weathers nodded, his mouth tight. Conn knew he was thinking of his son.

"It was the first real moonlight we'd had in a spell. They were sneaking around the corral, ready to take the whole damned remuda, and me sleeping away like a fool. And then the shooting started. Wasn't any of my men. Someone else spooked 'em. Couldn't have been just one, neither. The shots seemed to come from everywhere. The cow ponies scattered, but when we rounded 'em up, only two were missing."

"You were lucky."

Weathers stared at him hard, a long time, and again Conn wanted to bring up Stormy, but again he held his tongue. The rancher had lost his only child in a war fought far away. He wouldn't think he had anything approaching good luck.

Conn had learned from bitter experience that when something terrible happened to a man, it never strayed far from his mind.

The rancher puffed at his pipe. "We've got some bad sorts moving into these parts. If you talk to someone wondering about us"—Conn knew Weathers was thinking of Dora and his daughter-in-law—"tell 'em we've headed toward the South Fork of the Guadalupe."

He remembered the area from the escapades of his youth. It was still uninhabited country, wild, rocky, and mountainous, with caves good for retreat, and wild grasses and water and plenty of game. Both Indians and outlaws could hole up there for a long while. In times past, Comanches didn't run to ground that way, but these were renegades, separated from their brethren on the reservations. That made them unpredictable.

"I'll see that anyone interested gets the word," Conn said with a nod. "I'll be on the lookout for renegades, too."

He turned to get his horse.

"O'Brien."

He turned back to see Will Buchanan, one of the ranchers, holding out his hand. They shook, but Buchanan didn't look him straight in the eye.

"I wanted to thank you for buying those horses from me. You paid more'n I was asking."

"They were good stock, Mr. Buchanan. I sold most of them for a profit."

"Not much, I'm betting. You could've had them for less. There's more than one of us here owe you."

Several of the men murmured their assent, but Dal Weathers wasn't one of them.

"How did you find out I was the buyer?"

"Ain't nobody else around here got the money."

"I'm not apologizing for it."

"Nor should you. You're returning it to the county, buying places from folks that are desperate to sell and move on. Don't see how you can make a profit on everything."

"I know what you're doing." This time it was another of the ranchers who spoke up, Jeff Quinlan by name. Quinlan didn't appear quite so friendly as Will.

"You're buying up everything around the Bushwhack," the rancher said. "Fencing Edgar Braden in."

"Not on purpose. It's just working out that way."

Quinlan shifted a chaw of tobacco from cheek to cheek and spat. "We heard about how you lost the ranch—"

"Look," Conn said, "whatever you heard is probably an exaggeration of the truth. I'm back and glad of it, I'm married, and the two of us are settling in with an old friend. Texas is my home. Anything I do is for the state and its people, but it's also for me and mine."

He looked straight at Dal Weathers. "The Bushwhack was a dream, but sometimes dreams don't work out. I've got a lot of regrets to live with, but leaving and then coming home don't number among them. I just wish I hadn't waited so long to get back."

* * *

That night, after a meal of beans and hardtack, he and Nat side-lined the horses, tying a front leg to a rear one, and settled down for some needed sleep. But he was restless. He had a lot to think about.

Will Buchanan's friendliness had been welcome, and the others had eventually been almost as cordial, even Jeff Quinlan, putting aside their differences and looking forward instead of into the past.

Not Dal Weathers. And it was Weathers's opinion he valued above the others, mostly because they'd both lost a great deal in the war.

Somehow his thoughts skittered from the rancher to Crystal, which wasn't surprising. He thought about her much of the time. He'd lost much, true, but he hadn't lost everything, though he'd spent a few bad weeks thinking he had. Land was land and people were people. He'd left the land because he hadn't wanted to see its people suffer during a senseless war.

People had meant the most to him ten years ago. They meant the most to him now.

One person in particular. He hadn't forgotten what she'd done, but the anger was getting blurred by simply having her around.

A long time ago his mother had wished that both her sons would find wives to bring them joy and peace.

"Much joy, lads, to be sure, but not so much peace. A man can get too settled in his ways when there's no one to oppose him. In faith, I mean for his own good."

He'd been just a tad and too young to appreciate her wishes. He was beginning to appreciate them now. Crystal brought him joy, but peace kept eluding him.

She'd accused him of not taking Jennie Weathers to the barn, which was about the strangest accusation a wife could make. Women. Before Crystal, he'd thought he knew them as well as he knew horses.

For understanding, he'd take a wild mustang any day.

He shifted on the hard ground. Tomorrow night he would be sleeping on soft hay, naked instead of bound by clothes, and if he hadn't completely lost his persuasive abilities, he wouldn't be sleeping alone.

He was Irish, after all, and still had the gift of gab. And his wife had complimented him more than once on the way he used his hands.

Picturing Crystal curled against him in the loft, flesh to flesh, her hair spread out on the straw, he was about to fall asleep when the horses stirred. Immediately his senses became alert. It couldn't be much that bothered them, probably a prowling animal. The noise hadn't awakened the snoring Nat. But he couldn't settle down. Animals could mean danger. Pulling on his boots and strapping the holster at his waist, he went to check out the pen.

He circled the fence, but he could see nothing

amiss. Even in the moonlight, the surrounding cedar brake looked like nothing but an impenetrable wall, and he could detect no sign of life, man or beast. He walked quickly back to the campsite and, on impulse, moved beyond, down to the small stream they'd used for watering the herd. Kneeling, he scooped up a handful of water.

He sensed more than saw someone watching from the opposite bank. Holding still, nerves tight, he looked slowly up at the boots, the long line of trousers, the empty holster, the pistol pointed straight at him.

He eased to a stand, keeping his gun hand well away from his pistol. The man was tall and lean, and he wore a white man's clothes, but the bones of his face were more sharply hewn than any white man's Conn had ever met, and his hair was long and straight and black.

Black, too, were the eyes staring across at him. Even in the moonlight, they reminded him of the wild stallion he'd set free.

Indian or white, Conn couldn't be sure. He also wasn't sure that the man was alone, though he seemed to be.

The only certainty was the gun.

"You stirred the remuda," Conn said, breaking the silence, while he wondered if the intruder could understand.

"I'm usually quieter," the man declared. "And you have a good ear."

Not only did he speak English, but he sounded like an educated man, his voice deep and rich, each word carefully enunciated. Considering the circumstances of their meeting, Conn was surprised.

"So you're white," Conn said. "I couldn't tell."

"Does my ancestry matter? I would think you'd ask about the gun."

"You've got a point there. It doesn't matter who does the shooting, a man will be dead just the same."

"You don't sound afraid."

"I'm irritated at being caught so flat-footed. My father, rest his soul, must be turning in his grave."

"Irritated?" In the moonlight Conn could have sworn he saw a hint of a smile cross the intruder's lips. "You're supposed to be soiling your trousers."

"I haven't heard the word *soiled* since I left New York. You seem an unlikely thief."

"I wasn't after your herd, Mr. O'Brien. If that were the case, they'd be gone."

"How do you know my name?"

"I roam, and I watch, and I listen."

"You have the advantage of me, Mr.—"

"Great Britain Iron Hand. I am not, as you suspected, all white. My mother was a Comanche, and my father—well, I suppose you can guess his nationality."

"Great Britain Iron Hand, is it?"

"G. B. I. Hand at school. It made life simpler. Those whom I call friend know me as Brit, though they are few in number."

Conn wondered if maybe he wasn't dreaming,

but the glint on the metal the man was holding seemed all too real.

"So you're British and Indian both, are you? That makes us enemies on two counts. I'm Irish and white."

"Born enemies."

"So why don't you shoot me?"

"You have enough troubles without adding a bullet to the heart. But you have a wife to be cherished, despite her betrayal."

The harmony of the scene ended for Conn.

"It seems to me you listen and watch too much."

"Others have said the same. I come to say but two things, and then I will leave. Beware of Royce Braden. He has become crazed with anger and hate."

"He never was too sane. Why warn me?"

"He shames my white blood. At the end of the war and afterward he dealt guns and ammunition to the comancheros while he pretended to serve as a soldier on the frontier. For this he made money, which he shared with his father. It did not make him a good son. It disgraced them both."

"Stoke suspected something like that."

"And the second is to report that the Comanches have left the county. Your ranches and your people are safe. How do I know? I am Indian, as well."

"It's my guess you had something to do with their leaving. Did you run them off from the Double D?"

But Conn might as well have asked the trees. G. B. I. Hand was gone before he finished speaking, disappearing in the shadows as suddenly as he had appeared.

Conn stood staring into the dark. He'd seen some strange things in his thirty-five years, but tonight topped the list. An educated half-breed with a social conscience and a steady pistol hand. He was also cursed with the strangest name Conn had ever heard.

At the campsite he found Nat sitting upright, a shotgun at the ready, once again the Indian fighter of his youth.

"He's gone," said Conn, and to the question in Nat's eyes, he added, "a half-breed telling us the Comanches had left the county."

"Should'a shot 'im."

"He didn't threaten me. Besides, he was the one with the gun."

Conn would have told him more, but, taking a cue from Nat's natural reticence, he decided enough had been said. Brit Iron Hand had warned him of Royce and praised Crystal. He felt a rising impatience to get back home and hold her tight.

More than impatience, he felt a clawing, vital need.

They rode out early the next morning, and by late afternoon they had reached Stoke's Place. Nat and the workers helped him put the mustangs in the corral and take care of their mounts. He took a minute to look over the work that had been accomplished while he was gone.

He shook his head in amazement. In little over

a week, they'd gone from rock base to split-log walls and a shingle roof. The bunkhouse was done. They'd even added a separate room behind the barn next to the stall that held Stoke's mare.

A stack of cut lumber rested beside the cabin, ready to be added to the already laid foundation of the planned new rooms. Amazing. He must be paying them more than he realized.

No one was working now; they'd scattered after helping with the stock. And no one came out of the cabin to greet him with a warm, loving hug.

He caught sight of one of the men peering out from the barn door. "Where's everyone?" he asked.

"Stoke's gone hunting." The worker shook his head. "We don't see much of him no more." Without further explanation, he eased back into the shadows, leaving Conn to scratch his head.

Something was going on, but it wasn't anything that couldn't be seen to after he'd kissed his wife. He wouldn't stop at kissing. He wanted her so much, walking proved tricky. So she didn't like the barn, did she? With Stoke away, the bed would be free.

He headed for the back porch. He missed the dogs, who'd normally be lying beside the rocker this time of day. They must be with Stoke.

Their absence wasn't the only thing different. The window looking onto the back was sparkling clean.

Hard as she worked, Crystal had never done windows. Somehow he doubted she was turning more domestic, even to pass the time in his absence. More likely, she would ride the range.

She came through the door. Her hair was down, soft and golden the way he'd remembered it, and she was wearing the blue dress. She was the most beautiful sight he had ever seen.

Wishing he had the patience to clean up, he started for her.

She held up a hand. "Conn."

She said his name softly, but she didn't take a step in his direction.

"At least you remember who I am."

"I remember." Her voice was breathy. It was almost his undoing. He started for her again.

"Wait," she said.

"Wait for what?" he asked.

Before she could respond, a horse came pounding around the cabin, kicking up dirt, barely missing Conn as it thundered on past him into the woods.

He stared after the thin figure hunched over the saddle. "Was that Judge?"

Crystal nodded.

"What's he doing here? And why the hell is he riding so fast?"

She twisted her hands at her waist. "You're angry."

He took off his hat and wiped a sleeve across his brow. "I don't mean to be. If you get down here to me with the right hello, I can get un-angry fast."

"Oh, Conn," she said, her voice breathy again, her eyes holding all the promise he could want.

She made it to the steps before the back door

opened. A gaunt woman of middle age, dressed in black, her dark hair streaked with gray, walked outside. Conn recognized her as Crystal's mother. He'd seen her once before, sitting at the table in what used to be the O'Brien dining room.

Close behind was Helga Werner, as tall and formidable and stern-faced as he remembered her. They stood like a phalanx barring his way to the house.

He looked at Crystal for an explanation, but a sinking feeling in his gut said he already knew what she would say.

"They moved in soon after you left, Conn." She tried to smile, but it was a weak effort. "I had no choice but to bring them here. We'll leave if that's what you want."

Chapter Seventeen

Crystal's heart ceased to beat. Conn was home, trail-weary and wonderful—and watchful, too, as he had every right to be.

She should have told him in private what she'd done, breaking the news to him gradually, but of course the opportunity hadn't been hers. If the fate Conn believed in so much really existed, it was a fate determined to ruin her happiness.

We'll leave, she had told him. She didn't add that if she did, she would truly die.

To Crystal's surprise, her mother was the first to speak.

"We do not wish to be a burden, Mr. O'Brien. My family has done enough to you as it is."

Mama, hush, Crystal thought. Of course the Bradens were a burden. They would be until Conn's dying day.

Conn stared at them all, and then his eyes settled on her, their expression unreadable. He gestured toward the creek. She followed, thinking she would go with him to the most distant horizon if that's where he wanted to go.

He led her to the water's edge, moving on farther away from the cabin and the barn, the late-day sun warm against their backs. His hair had grown longer, past his collar, and he seemed leaner than before, but his spine was just as straight, his stride just as long. She had to sprint in order to keep up.

He didn't halt until they were deep into the woods that lined the bank. They stood on a carpet of grass, with only the water and the wind to hear what they said.

The creek was wide here, more than a stone's throw across to the far bank and slow moving; she stared at the ripples on the surface, turned opaque gold by the sunlight. Conn stood so near she could hear each breath he took, could feel his warmth, could feel his gaze upon her. All she had to do was reach out to touch him. All he had to do was reach out to touch her.

But he did not, and neither did she.

"What's this about, Crystal?" he asked just when she thought she might scream. "Do you really want to leave? You started pushing for it long before I left."

Her heart caught in her throat. *No,* she wanted to cry out, but she shook her head, not trusting herself to speak.

"That's not much of an answer."

He was right. He deserved more. She forced herself to look at him, at his solemn visage and probing eyes and at the lines of his face that were carved upon her heart. Love and regret surged like storms inside her. She dug her fingernails into her palms and told him about Graciela's visit the morning he rode off with Nat. The brutality of her brother, the cruelty of her father—she told it all. Conn scarcely blinked as she spoke; he seemed sculpted out of stone.

"I took her to Mrs. Truehart in town. And then I talked to Stoke. He said—" She blinked back tears. "He's a good man. That's why they're here."

"If I'm not so good, you leave?"

His voice was harsh, cutting.

She drew a sharp breath. "That's not what I meant."

He acted as if he didn't hear. "Braden just let them leave with you?"

"He was gone when I got there."

"You didn't think he'd come after them?"

"I had to take the chance. He's not as strong as he used to be."

"He's strong enough."

He's sitting on O'Brien land. She could almost hear Conn saying the words.

"Oh, Conn," she said, closer than ever to breaking, "everything I do hurts you."

They stared at one another, and the earth stood still.

"Not everything." He gripped her arms and

pulled her to him. "Not this."

He kissed her. Not gently, not lovingly, but closer to a punishment, as if he wanted only to prove a point.

He took possession of her, his hands tight on her arms, his mouth hard against hers, and just when she sensed he was warming to her and she could curl her body against him and hold on tight, he thrust her away.

She swayed, her mind reeling, and she drew in ragged breaths.

"Why do I always feel a distance between us?" he asked. "It's there even when we're in bed."

He spoke the truth, the hurtful truth. She started to speak.

"Don't give me that nonsense about your being a Braden. The world is made up of Bradens. I'm talking about you and me."

The tears came; she brushed them from her cheeks.

"I don't know. I don't want it that way. Maybe it's because we don't really talk."

"So talk." He threw it out as a challenge.

I love you. He'd think she was buying time for her family. He had the right to think the worst.

She loved him with a passion that frightened her. *He* frightened her, more than he had ever done, more than that terrible moment in a San Antonio hotel when she'd learned he knew the depth of her lies. He frightened her because he could so easily be lost to her, not for just a week but forever.

How tough he looked, standing there with his black hair thick and mussed and his eyes shimmering hot and his face brown and lean and bristled. Everything about him looked hard and strong. He still wore his gun and his leather chaps and vest. She wondered if his heart was as hard as his eyes.

She would have liked to touch his chest to feel the beat. Was it a pounding force as hers was? It couldn't be. His heart was not consumed by love.

And that was what frightened her the most. Even if they stayed together, he could never again feel for her what she felt for him.

He wanted talk? She had nothing to say that he wanted to hear.

"You're right, Conn. This isn't working. We'll leave."

"Don't be a fool. Where would you go?"

"Mrs. Truehart—"

"You'd take your mother to a whorehouse?"

"After my father, Mrs. Truehart will seem like a saint."

"And Helga? And your brother?"

She shook her head in helplessness. "There's a whole army of us, isn't there?"

"That's how it looked to me."

"You didn't get much of a welcome home."

"Not the one I had planned."

For a moment his eyes softened, his expression the one that melted her bones.

"Don't look at me like that," he said. "Unless you

have a bed waiting for us somewhere I don't know about."

If only she did.

She caught him staring at the grass at their feet. She'd told him never again. Such lovemaking wasn't decent, she'd said. She really was a fool.

He gave her no chance to tell him so.

"Of course you can stay," he said with a shrug of resignation, and the promise of passion between them was gone.

"Oh, Conn," she said, wanting to throw herself into his arms, but he'd think she was acting out of gratitude when the truth was she just wanted to hold him and let the world go away.

They started back along the creek toward the cabin. When he mentioned checking out the bunkhouse, she wanted to say they could bolt the door and check it out together, but all she did was nod.

They parted without so much as a touch of their hands. Walking alone onto the porch, knowing her mother would be lying down awaiting word about what he'd said, hearing Helga at work in the kitchen, wondering where Judge might have gone, she decided to do something she should have done long ago.

She would confront the eldest Braden and tell him matters had to change.

She rode out early the next morning, hoping to catch her father sober. According to Helga, who was the only one to know her destination, morning was the best time to find him that way.

With Conn sleeping somewhere out on the range—"I'd like to keep an eye on the new stock," he'd said over a tense evening meal—she saddled Trouble quickly and walked him away from the cabin.

Her mother wouldn't want her to go. If Judge found out, he would ride along. This was something she had to do alone.

Once in the saddle she rode all out, going quickly from Stoke's Place onto the land that should belong to Conn. All was quiet on the Bushwhack. In the morning light, dimmed by an overcast sky, even the main house looked deserted, except for a light in the room Royce had said their father used as a library—and as his private drinking room.

She walked in the back door. The house had a musty smell to it, as if no one lived there and hadn't in a long, long while. The lack of warmth, the lack of love had changed its very air.

She found her father in his private lair, slumped in a chair before a cold hearth, his suit wrinkled, the collar of his white shirt stained. An empty glass lay overturned at his feet. Gray bristles covered his lax face. He seemed paler, thinner. He'd aged a dozen years in the few weeks since she'd seen him in town.

He looked . . . helpless. She'd never seen him in such a state.

Her heart twisted unexpectedly. She wanted to love him; she wanted to comfort him. He was her father, after all. But in all her twenty-four years, he had never let her show the least sentiment toward him, not even when she was a very little girl, and he'd never shown it to her. Over and over again he'd proven himself incapable of giving or accepting love. He'd missed out on the best of life, and she ached for what should have been.

She looked away, unable to stand the pain of remembrance. Nightly she prayed for Conn to forget the past. She ought to do the same.

During her brief stay at the Bushwhack, before she'd forced herself on Conn, she'd not entered this room. It truly was a cloister, with dusty bookshelves lining the walls and dark draperies closed against the day. Except for the desk and a couple of chairs, there was little furniture. The air was close and rank with the smell of whiskey. She moved past her father to draw the draperies and open a window, desperate for light and a cool breeze.

He stirred and she turned to face him. He blinked once, then sat up straight, the old wariness, the distrust, the belligerence glinting in his eyes. He came from his sleep that way, his natural state.

"What are you doing here?" he snapped.

It was the kind of greeting she should have expected, and she felt a sense of loss for them both. Conn was right. Edgar Braden still was strong.

So was she. She got it from him. Taking off her hat and gloves, she tossed them on the desk and smoothed back her hair. "It's so quiet here. Are you alone?"

"I've got men working. Both sides of the creek, if it's any of your concern. There ought to be someone around the barn."

"And what about in the house?"

"You pretty much emptied it." He spoke with such contempt, she shivered.

"And Royce?"

"The boy keeps to himself."

"He's a man, Father. Or at least he's supposed to be. Did you know he beat Graciela?"

"Don't come telling tales. She probably deserved it."

A thousand replies sprang to Crystal's lips, but she needed to save her arguing for matters closer to her heart than her brother's meanness. She'd already protected Graciela all that she could. Others needed her now.

"We need to talk, Father."

The sentiment echoed what she'd said to Conn a few hours past, but she hadn't handled the talking very well. She had to do better today.

"Why did you break your promise?" she asked.

"Is that why you rode over here? To ask me that?"

"You swore Mama and Judge could live at Shingle Camp if I got you the Bushwhack. You've got it. Why bring them back?"

He half rose from his chair, then settled back down. "Listen here, girl, I don't have to answer to you."

"You must. We had an arrangement. Are you saying I shouldn't trust your word?"

He looked around him, his watery blue eyes squinting under thick gray brows, and for a moment he seemed lost to her, the change in him as startling as it was incomprehensible.

"This place. It's not what I thought it would be."

"What did you expect?"

He blinked, and once again she sensed the vulnerability that had rested upon him in his sleep.

"I don't know. Something. All my life I fought for everything I got. And now . . ." His voice trailed off, and he was truly trapped in his thoughts.

This was not the man who'd snapped at her only a minute before, not this lonely, bewildered soul who stared around him as if he didn't know where he was. He seemed like two people, his former tyrannical self, and someone far weaker, someone she did not know.

He frightened her, not in the way Conn did, not at all for herself, but for him.

She touched his arm. "Papa," she whispered.

He jerked away. "What the devil are you doing? Why are you really here? Did that bastard husband send you?"

Crystal shuddered and gave up. Here was the real Edgar Braden, suspicious, condemning, cold, worse than before because he'd become erratic; she couldn't predict what he might do. Any sign of gentleness, of confusion, of needing someone was just a momentary aberration. In the end, as far as his family was concerned, he would keep himself apart.

She had hoped to find solutions this morning;

instead, she'd only added to her grief.

"I wanted to ask if there was any chance you could treat Mama better. She and Judge ought to be here, but they can't return as long as you're like this."

"I'm the way I've always been."

Not quite, she thought, no matter how straight he sat in the chair, no matter how firmly he spoke.

But close enough.

From somewhere in the distance came the sound of gunshots.

She started. "What's that?"

He listened a moment, and then he smiled. "That'll be Royce, taking target practice. Tell Conn-the-Bastard O'Brien he'd better watch out. That boy of mine'll put him in his place." He laughed. "Six feet under. Beside his wife-stealing pa."

Crystal felt as if the bullets were slamming into her. With shaking hands, she reached for her hat and gloves.

"Get cleaned up, Father. I'll cook you breakfast before I leave. And get someone to help you here. Someone to cook and clean."

"I don't need help. I started out life taking care of myself and I can end it the same way."

The gunshots ceased for a minute, then started up again.

"You were poor then. You've got the money now. Hire someone. A man would be best, big and brawny. Someone Royce will leave alone."

She left him and went to the kitchen. By the

time she had a full breakfast on the dining room table, he had not yet made an appearance. She left his plate under a napkin embroidered with a scrolled letter *B.* It was one of Mama's works, delicate and pretty like her.

She stared at the table. It all seemed like too little to do for him, but she knew it was the most he would accept. She straightened the kitchen, checked the larder, and forced herself to leave, wondering what pain would accompany their next meeting while at the same time she wondered whether she would see him again.

The gunshots had ended by the time she rode away. All her thoughts were on Conn. She could never offer him fancy things like handworked napkins. But she could offer him something she hoped he liked far more.

If he still wanted her, she would offer him herself.

Conn rode under a noonday sun back toward the ranch. He hadn't seen Crystal since dinner the night before, and he hadn't talked to her in private since their conversation by the creek, when she'd tried to explain what she had done.

He was hungry, he was weary, and he was dirty. And he was a little more than furious with just about everybody he could name. Even Stoke, who'd complained all evening and all morning about "that damned German" until Conn had finally said, "You let her in and you can kick her out. You own the place."

But Stoke had gone on complaining, leaving the impression that maybe he liked cursing the woman's character and ancestry, and Conn had let him be.

Stoke was the least of his worries, along with Royce and Edgar Braden. Both were rotten, no-good skunks, that was a given. It was also an insult to skunks to make the comparison. Getting angry at them was like getting mad at a Texas tornado. They did what they did, tearing up everything in their path because that was their nature.

Turning his anger on Crystal was about as useless. Her mission in life seemed to be saving the world. She had a long list of specific people to work on. He knew whose name was at the bottom.

His.

So the fury ended up self-directed. He could have taken her yesterday, right there on the grass. He'd seen it in her eyes; he'd felt it in her kiss. He should have. He wouldn't have made matters any worse between them, and he for sure would have had a better night.

Hammering filled the air as he walked in the back door of the cabin. Helga thrust a note into his hand.

Remember the mare and the colt. It was signed with the letter *C.*

He fingered the paper. He remembered very well. What was she up to now? Whatever it was, she had already heated his blood.

He claimed his horse before one of the hands could take him to the barn, and he lit out through the woods, riding fast and maddeningly slow, getting hotter and harder with each widening stride as he neared the isolated spot where they'd found the strays. He was probably torturing himself for no reason. Considering the way his life was going lately, he wouldn't have been surprised to find a church choir practicing in the private bower he considered his and his wife's.

Instead, he rode up to a blanket spread on the grass in the small clearing, a basket of food to the side, and a corked bottle of wine bobbing at the edge of the creek. He rode up to his wife.

Her clothes lay on the bank, but like the wine, she was in the water. Her hair was damp against bare shoulders, and droplets of creek water caught in her thick lashes. Her lips were parted, but not in a smile. She seemed to be waiting for him to respond.

If she looked him over closely enough, she'd see well enough. His boots went one way, hat the other, and he dropped his gun holster.

"Have you ever worn chaps without trousers?" she asked.

"Can't say that I have."

Her eyes flared. "It calls up an interesting picture."

"There are those who would call it indecent."

"Not anymore. At least no one nearby."

Conn loosened the chaps. "Underside's a little rough. They might rub."

She cleared her throat, and he suspected she was more nervous than she appeared.

"Speaking of rubbing," she said, "I've got an itch I need you to work on."

"Then come here where I can get to it."

"You come here."

Conn knew when to give in. Leather and Levis littered the bank as he dived into the creek and came up beside her. The chill, chest-high water lapped against him, but did little to cool him off.

He raked his hair back from his face. "Now where's that itch?"

The smile she gave him was small, but it was enough to put a dimple in her cheek. He saw it so seldom, he'd forgotten she had only the one.

She fought for balance on the mud-and-pebble creek bottom. "Have you ever needed scratching all over?"

"Only when I'm with you."

"No one else?" she asked.

"No one else."

The heat that passed between them should have set the water boiling.

His provocative water nymph looked down, then lifted her lashes to stare at him once again, no longer saucy, no longer teasing, no longer welcoming him with her smile.

"This isn't any kind of penance, Conn, or payment for what I've done."

"You don't have to explain."

"Maybe not for you," she said, "but for me."

Conn's heart and soul went out to her and he saw the truth. It hit him hard. He loved her as much as he had the first time he saw her in the saloon. No, he loved her more. Then he'd seen only surface perfection. Now he loved her for everything she was.

The realization settled the unrest that had torn at him for weeks. He loved her. How could he do otherwise?

"Crystal—" he began, wanting to tell her.

She covered his lips with her fingers. "Don't say anything more. Whatever passes between us is for the here and the now because we both want it to happen. I want you to do to me every indecent thing you can think of, and I'll do the same to you."

She rose high enough out of the water to expose the tips of her breasts. "In case you're wondering where you should start—"

But Conn had his own priorities. He kissed her, wrapping his arms around her slippery-wet body and holding her close, and then he led her to the bank and out of the water, her hand in his.

They stood face to face and he kissed her again. Her hands slid over his chest and into his damp hair. He fingered her spine and cupped her buttocks against his thighs, against his sex. Wet satin, that's how she felt in his arms, a yearning softness that was everything he could desire.

Wanting her made him weak and made him strong. They lay down on the blanket and he took her into his arms.

"Indecent, you say?" He kissed her eyes, her throat, the tips of her breasts, and returned to kiss her lips. "Nothing is indecent between a man and wife."

She grinned, and he saw a hint of the nymph who had invited him into the water.

"Please, let me believe what I want. In all my life I've never sought forbidden pleasures. I'd like them now."

He moved a thigh between her legs and rubbed back and forth.

"Is that indecent? Have I found an itch to scratch?"

"Oh, yes to both," she said, her voice little more than a sigh.

He stroked her body until her skin was as dry and smooth as silk, and all the while he loved her more than he had ever realized. His lips roamed, and when he parted her thighs she let him kiss her in the most intimate of ways.

With the wind soughing in the trees surrounding the clearing, their bodies joined and he did not know where she began and he ended, they were so much a part of a whole. The love was sweet, the passion sweeter, and when the earth tilted for them both, he went out of his mind.

She clung to him for a long, long time. Such sweet spiraling down he had never known. His wife. He liked the sound of it. She came with fetters, with problems, with more complications than the ordinary man could comprehend.

But she made him something beyond the ordinary. She made him the best he could be.

He thought that maybe he'd found the definition of a wife.

But she'd made no declaration of her own. And

she didn't want him to speak. Each time he tried to do so, she found a way to distract him.

She was very good at distractions.

They put on their shirts while they ate. Conn spent more time staring than chewing. She had good legs, long and gracefully curved and strong from the years of riding. Good calves, good thighs, good . . .

He stopped himself. He'd better concentrate on less dangerous territory. The problem was, everything about her was dangerous.

She offered him wine in a cup; he did the same for her. But he needed no alcohol to grow dizzy; her presence was enough.

When the meal was done, they lay side by side, staring up through the trees at the clouds moving overhead. In the peace of the afternoon, he was prepared to doze with her for a while, and then, when her defenses were down, to talk whether she wanted him to or not, and when he was done talking, to make passionate love to her again.

"I went to the Bushwhack today."

Peace fled. She might as well have hit him in the gut. Instinctively he pulled away. So that was behind this little scene, and here he'd been thinking her wanting him was more than she could control. She'd said the lovemaking was no penance, no show of gratitude, but maybe she had lied, not just to him but to herself as well.

"I tried to talk to Father about Mama and Judge, but he wouldn't listen. He's changed, Conn. He's the same as ever one moment and then he's different. He frightened me."

The tremor in her voice tore at him. He felt like a cad, looking at her problems through his own eyes. He took her in his arms. She kissed his chest and wrapped an arm around his waist.

"I told you I didn't mind if they're here," he said.

"But it's not good for them or for you or for me. It's no real solution and we both know it."

She was right. Telling her otherwise would come out the lie that it was.

"Royce wasn't there, but I heard him. He was practicing his shooting somewhere in the hills."

"Do you think he'll get any better?"

"I don't know. He might."

"I saw him in action once. He's a coward. He can't practice enough to get over that."

She fell silent, and for a moment he thought she'd fallen asleep. But her breathing was too ragged, and he could feel the tension in her body as she held herself close to him.

She needed something to think about besides her family. *He* was her family, too. Let her concentrate on him.

Peace might be gone, but not his loving her and his wanting her. Whatever else she felt, he knew she liked making love.

"You once told me you were a woman of your word. Something like that."

She looked up at him. "I am. I haven't lied since—" She bit her lip. "Why do I always let that come between us?"

"Because you're who you are. Now about your promise—"

Her eyes grew wide with worry. "What promise?"

"The one about letting me do anything I wanted to you and you would do the same to me."

The worry turned to a glint. "*That* promise. I thought you had forgotten."

"Not likely. So get to it."

She sat beside him and took off her shirt. Her breasts were full and high and already hard-tipped.

"Get naked," she ordered.

He did.

Pushing him back to the blanket, she reached for a half-empty cup of wine. "I stole this from the larder at the Bushwhack. I don't know whether it belonged to your family or mine, but it's ours now."

She dribbled the dark liquid from his abdomen down to his thighs.

He jerked involuntarily at the cold wetness.

"What are you doing?" he asked.

She shrugged. "I don't know. I saw the cup and I saw you and I remembered the things you did to me." She blinked in mock innocence. "I'm going on pure instinct here. Tell me if I do anything wrong."

She licked the wine from below his navel, sat back and licked her lips. "Not bad."

"Not bad at all," said Conn, his voice two octaves below its normal pitch. His body sprang to the ready.

And she proved she could be as decadent as he.

Chapter Eighteen

As things turned out over the next couple of weeks, construction around the place, ranch business, and a dozen family upsets kept them from experimenting with either decadence or decorum.

Abstinence became the order of the day. Conn wasn't much good at abstinence, and from the looks his wife gave him, he knew that neither was she.

The worst part of the situation was that in the day-to-day details of living, she seemed to grow farther away from him, as if she thought they had something valuable between them only when they were making love.

If that were so, and he didn't believe it for a minute, they would just have to make love all the time.

Helga, a woman of many talents, took to overseeing the construction work, pointing out flaws, imperfections, and boards that didn't line up. How she became an architect and overseer he didn't know, but she certainly knew how to bark orders in English and German both. If she said something had to be redone, redone it was. The work expanded from one bedroom to two, then a separate dining room and a hall, a wraparound porch, extended overhang, three fireplaces, and an enlarged pantry as well.

They could paint the thing white and President Grant would feel at home.

Not that inviting him to call would be smart, given the general antipathy toward anything Yankee. As far as ranch matters were concerned, Conn was generally accepted by the men he dealt with. But none of their wives came to call on Crystal or her mother, and no one extended an invitation for them to call in return.

Crystal didn't seem to notice, but he knew her mother did, from the questions she asked each time he returned from town. Most of the time she took to her bed—the lone bed—leaving Crystal to sleep on a makeshift cot by the front bedroom window.

From the first, Helga had taken over the couch and, during the few hours he hung around, Judge slept in the barn. Conn bunked down with the workers in the overcrowded bunkhouse, when he didn't sleep out on the range, and Stoke moved his belongings to the new room close to his mare Alice's private stall.

Conn wasn't sure anyone was satisfied, except

maybe Stoke, who said at least he had a place where he could keep his cuspidor.

Conn didn't pay much attention to Judge at first, barely aware of the boy's presence, knowing only that he wasn't around much except for the evening meal. A time or two he'd walked in on a conversation between brother and sister, but they always hushed when they saw him. He knew they'd been arguing, but he didn't know what about.

And he wasn't in a position to interfere. The boy equated him with the other men in his life: he didn't trust Conn and he didn't like him.

So be it. The two left each other alone.

Until the early morning when Judge pushed Crystal to the ground.

She was in her buckskins, walking toward the barn to saddle Trouble. Conn was up on the roof of the almost completed addition studying the newly laid shingles before riding out to the range. Mostly he was studying his wife. Unaware of his proximity, she had hurried down the porch steps, pulling on her gloves, settling her hat in place. She had a nice sway to her walk, and in the morning light the leather across her backside looked almost like bare flesh.

He was counting the days since he'd actually seen that particular flesh when the back door of the cabin slammed shut and Judge came out at a run.

She called his name, but he hurried past her. She followed him into the barn. Conn heard loud voices, and in a minute brother and sister were out again, the boy leading his saddled mount, Crystal hurrying after.

"Don't go, Judge," she said. "They're up to no good."

"You can't tell me what to do," he snapped. "You're not Mama."

He put one foot in the stirrup. She grabbed him by the shirt, and that was when he shoved. She stumbled backward and fell.

Judge went for her, as if he would help her to her feet, then held back. "I told you not to stop me, Crystal. Leave me alone."

He mounted and started to ride around the cabin. Without thinking, Conn jumped, knocking the boy to the ground, startling the horse and Judge both, and himself as well. The horse took off, man and boy rolled on the ground, and Crystal came at a run.

She went to Judge first, which brought little joy to her husband. He stood and gingerly brushed himself off, thinking he was too old for such shenanigans.

Judge remained on the ground glaring up at him. Crystal stood and stared in disbelief at Conn. "I can't believe you did that."

"Neither can I."

"You could have hurt yourself."

He wasn't sure that he hadn't. He knew he'd picked up a new bruise or two.

He looked past her to the boy. "You touch her again and you'll answer to me."

"I didn't mean it," the boy mumbled. "Damn."

"You ever had your mouth washed out with soap?"

Conn realized he sounded like his own father, who'd said much the same thing to him once when he'd cursed around his mother. But he'd been trying the words on for size, seeing how they rolled around on his tongue.

Judge Braden was angry and surly and belligerent. Neither James nor he had ever been surly in their lives. He didn't know how to deal with the boy, except maybe take him to the woodshed for a paddling.

But that wouldn't work. Whatever else had influenced the boy, he'd already known too much violence in his life.

Conn looked at Crystal. Behind her, the men had gathered at the side of the cabin, trying not to look as if they were watching, but not trying too hard.

"He really didn't mean it," she said. "I shouldn't have tried to stop him."

"You had the right. He's a child."

Judge leapt to his feet. "I'm man enough to take care of myself."

Maybe he would have looked it a little more if his arms and legs weren't so gangly, and if his trousers didn't hit him about midway on his boots. He'd grown too far up and not enough out to call himself a man, at least in the physical sense. Conn didn't know enough about him to determine if he was close to manhood by way of character.

"Where were you going in such a rush?"

Judge rolled his eyes. It was a trait Conn could grow tired of fast.

"He's taken up with some ruffians," Crystal said. "I don't know what they do, but he stays with them for hours at a time. They're trouble, Conn. I know it."

"Hell—" the boy began, then caught sight of Conn out of the corner of his eye. "Heck, all we do is ride and horse around."

"You're good at riding, aren't you? I've watched you. You're a natural."

For a moment the boy stood straighter and pride flashed in his eyes. "I'm the best."

"Not quite."

That was when the idea came to him.

"But you could be. You ever done any racing?"

"No," Crystal put in fast, as if she were defending him against another assault. "It's too dangerous."

Again the boy's eyes rolled.

Conn's hands itched to take him by the collar and give a good shake. But that would be as wrong as paddling him on the butt.

He wasn't sure he ever wanted to be a father if any son of his turned out like this. Fourteen, he saw, was not the most cooperative age.

He held his temper. "She's right, Judge. Racing can be dangerous, if you do it wrong."

Judge hitched at his trousers. "All you got to do is give the horse his lead and beat the devil out of him."

"If I ever see you taking a whip to one of my

horses, it'll be the last time you ride around here."

Judge started to come back with something, then looked straight at Conn and closed his mouth. It was the first smart thing he'd done since he ran out of the house.

"You'll be with me today, out on the range."

The boy's eyes widened as if in pleasure, but then he eased away with a shrug. "I got things to do."

"You eat here, you sleep here, then you work here. Besides, I could use another hand. Did you get breakfast?"

Judge shook his head.

"Get back in and tell Helga I said to fill you up."

"Don't nobody tell Helga what to do."

"Nobody tells Helga," Crystal corrected, but both boy and man looked at her with such an expression that she fell silent.

"Go on," said Conn with a nod of his head.

"My horse—"

"He'll be back by the time you're done. And don't take all day. I've got a mustang I want you to put through his paces. Or teach him a few. He's a little wild."

The boy hesitated, unsure of what to do, but he managed to assume an air of self-importance as he moved toward the house.

Husband and wife looked at one another.

"He'll be all right," Conn said.

To his surprise, Crystal threw herself into his arms and with every cowhand on the place looking on, she gave him a great big kiss.

"Thank you," she whispered, tears in her eyes.

Saints above but she felt good in his arms.

"You're playing with fire, Mrs. O'Brien."

"I like the heat."

"Maybe we need some wine to douse it."

"There's no maybe about it. Next time you're licking it off of me."

She spoke low and soft, whispering in his ear. Easing from his arms, she left him standing there in full arousal. One of the men whistled. Conn shrugged and grinned. Some things were useless to deny. At the top of the list was how he felt about his wife.

Bringing Judge around to more civilized behavior didn't prove as easy as Conn had hoped. The boy had an impatient way about him that bordered on the wild. He wanted to ride hard and ride often, but in the area of training a horse to specific chores, he had a difficult time seeing to the details of repetition and drill.

But Stoke worked with him, and then so did Nat Fink, and the wildness in the boy gave way to his natural affinity for horses, and better still, their affinity for him. The animals and he communicated in a language no one else could hear. That was the best way Conn could put it. He'd seen it before. He did a little communicating himself, and so did Crystal.

When one of the mares foaled, Conn gave Judge the new-born colt, a solid black that he suspected was sired by the stallion he'd left to run wild.

Judge named him Licorice, and while he didn't exactly thank Conn, he threw himself into his work all the harder, going so far as to sleep outside Licorice's stall every night.

Nat began teaching him the riding methods of the Comanches, and after only a week, all who wanted to watch were invited to a demonstration of his new-found skills. Annabelle Braden declined, but Crystal watched from afar as he raced across the grassy plain.

With hands hooked around the pommel of the saddle, Judge leaned forward and raised his body from its resting place. He flung one leg behind him and dropped both feet to the ground, bounded upward and swung across the saddle to land for an instant on the other side of the galloping horse, then lifted his body upward and sat astride the horse as he reined to a halt in front of his sister.

A cloud of dust rose around him as he grinned down at her. His arms and legs were longer than those of the squat Indians, but he made up for the excess with a suppleness that was beautiful to behold. Swallowing her fear for him, Crystal applauded, and the watching men cheered.

The boy dropped to the ground, clearly pleased.

"The horse," Nat said with a nod toward the slavering mustang.

With a wink at his sister, Judge led his mount toward the creek.

"I'd swear that boy has some Comanche blood in him," Stoke said.

The light that had been in Crystal's eyes died. Conn took her aside.

"What's wrong?" he asked.

"Nothing," she said with a shake of her head. "I'm being foolish."

"Crystal."

She looked up at him. "I told you it was nothing. Stoke just reminded me how Father always claimed Judge wasn't his child." She attempted a smile. "One thing I know for sure. He's not part Comanche since he was born back in Virginia." She looked at the distant hills. "Father always gets things wrong."

Not always, Conn wanted to say. *He sired you.*

"He's hired help for the house," he said instead. "I heard it in town. A woman and her husband to cook and care for the place."

"I hope the woman's eighty-five and the man is big and burly."

"That I don't know. I also overheard some of the men talking about how Royce has taken up with a band of hoodlums. When Judge found out, he decided the gang he had been riding with no longer had anything to offer him."

"He doesn't want to be like either his father or his brother." She had a lost look about her as she stared at the ground. "Sad, isn't it?"

"Not so much," said Conn. "It shows he's smart. Did you also hear Royce tried to get into Mrs. Truehart's place and she threw him out?"

Conn had meant the story to cheer his wife. Instead, she turned away.

"I'd better get back to the cabin. Mama wants to talk with me about the furniture needed for the new rooms. It's not my place, I tried to tell her, but she wouldn't listen."

"It is your place, Crystal. As much as mine."

She looked over her shoulder at him. "Is it?"

Whistling for Trouble, she mounted and rode away. Conn stared after her until she dropped over the hill.

The next day Ham returned with Oro, the champion thoroughbred stallion he'd brought for Conn from Saratoga. The horse was a chestnut, with a rare golden mane and tail, hence the Spanish name for gold. Mounted on a gray gelding, Ham led Oro to the back of the cabin. Work stopped as everyone appeared to view the magnificent animal. He stood seventeen hands, his neck long and arched, shoulders sloped, chest deep, his back strong and short.

The power of him lay in his muscular hindquarters and hard legs, and in the proud look in his eye. Stoke, Nat, the other men, Helga, even Annabelle Braden came out to watch Ham hand over the reins to Conn.

Crystal stood to the side.

Conn stroked Oro's neck, but his eyes were on his wife. "What do you think?"

Her whole face glowed with a light he hadn't seen since she last picked up a cup of wine, and that had been almost a month ago. Conn was almost jealous.

"I think that is the single most beautiful animal

I have ever seen," she said.

"Wait'll you see him run. There's a county race a month from now. He'll be entered."

"Don't think you'll get many to run against him," said Stoke.

"I'll handicap him. And I won't keep him a secret. Anyone interested in racing can watch him all they like."

Stoke snorted. "Everyone around here's interested in racing."

"*Nein,*" Helga put in. "Not everyone."

Stoke sent a stream of tobacco juice in an arc over the dogs lying in the shade, the pair of them the only living, breathing creatures in the vicinity not impressed by the thoroughbred. "I'll make a side bet right here and now that you'll get that way by racing time. If you're honest enough to admit the truth."

Helga's bosom quivered with indignation. She stood half a head taller than Stoke and outweighed him by fifty pounds. She was not a woman to be challenged lightly. "I am an honest woman, Herr Price. Five dollars."

Stoke did not back down. "Done." He turned to Conn. "How you planning on handicapping a beauty like this?"

"Extra weight. Within reason, of course. And there's the jockey, too."

He looked past Oro to the corner of the cabin, where Judge stood watching. "The race is yours to win or lose, Judge."

The boy took a step forward. "What are you talking about?"

"I'm talking about you being in the saddle when Oro crosses the finish line. First, of course. That goes without saying."

"No," Crystal and her mother said at once.

Conn ignored them. "You'll have to work hard."

"I've been working hard."

"You'll have to work harder."

Judge walked slowly toward the horse. Oro watched with rounded eyes.

"Of course the horse will have to take to you."

"What if I don't take to him?"

Always the defensive answer, Conn thought, but from the way horse and youth were sidling up to one another, he didn't much doubt they would eventually share a mutual regard and respect.

As to whether Judge could actually ride Oro to victory, that depended on a number of factors. Judge had proven himself with the mustangs, but Oro was a handful of horse for any rider. The boy had to have faith in himself if he were to win and, more important, if he weren't to be seriously hurt.

Faith was something Bradens didn't have in oversupply. He glanced at Crystal, who was staring at her brother. She seemed lost in the tangle of her family. He wondered if she would ever truly be free.

Chapter Nineteen

"That's as fine a breast as—"

Conn stopped at the look on Stoke's face. "I said something wrong, didn't I?"

Stoke shifted a tobacco plug from one cheek to another. "It ain't my place to have an opinion about such things, one way or t'other."

Conn thought a minute. "A fine beast," he said, adding a few frustrated mutterings under his breath.

Stoke fought a grin. "Yep. Fine as I've ever seen."

The two men were riding the range, Crystal on Trouble to the right, Oro cropping grass in the shade a dozen yards beyond her.

With his golden mane catching a shaft of sunlight, Oro did indeed look splendid. So did Crystal. That was the trouble. In the August heat, she'd taken off her buckskin vest. Her sweat-dampened yellow shirt clung to every place Conn wanted it to cling. Every place he wanted to touch. Every place he wanted to . . .

Saints above, he was horny. Cranky, too. Stoke had said so more than once, and even Nat had twitched his moustache in irritation at something he said. The twitch was as much as a harangue from anyone else.

Six weeks had passed since the creek-side tryst with his wife. He was six weeks overdue for some more loving.

But ranch work brought on by the excessive heat and a series of steamy summer storms had kept him from his wife. Worst of all had been a long and potentially dangerous sinking spell by his mother-in-law. Annabelle had recovered, but not he.

He was like a man covered in ant bites, kept apart from the only woman who knew where to scratch.

The lack of a bed didn't help his dilemma either. Construction on the cabin was finished, but a craftsman in Kerrville was still working on the furniture.

To make matters worse, the race had been postponed until mid-September, dragging out the time all the more. He shouldn't complain. The extra time could be spent training Judge to handle the thoroughbred. From things Crystal said and the worry in her eyes, he knew she didn't think the boy could handle the task put to him. Recovered from her illness, Annabelle vocally and frequently expressed her fear that Judge would be hurt. Ham wasn't much in agreement with the decision, either, but then, he wasn't inclined to view any Braden with sympathy.

His friend had come up with so many disparaging remarks, Conn gave him time off in thanks for the long journey to bring Oro to his new home. Ham had readily accepted; he hadn't been seen much the past two weeks.

Conn remained Judge's lone champion, a fact that was as much a surprise to him as to anyone. He had to give the boy credit for not complaining at the daily work of putting Oro through his paces, of holding him back, of learning his moods.

Despite his confidence, Conn was the one who carped and complained, the one who said stupid things like *breast* instead of *beast*. He hoped Stoke didn't repeat this latest blunder when they joined the other men.

Thunder rumbled in the distance. It matched his mood.

Mumbling something about checking the stock, Stoke rode off, and Conn eased his horse over to join his wife.

"Storm's coming," he said.

"Hmmm."

She took off her hat and wiped her brow with her sleeve. Damp tendrils of wheat-colored hair framed her face and the back of her neck—her long, slender neck with the tiny mole at its base. The mole hardly showed. He'd discovered it one night with his lips.

A single thick braid lay against her sweaty back; good as it looked, Conn was more interested in her sweaty front.

"We could strip and let the rain cool us," he said.

"Hmmm," she said, then shot him a quick look. "What did you say?"

"I was just making sure you were listening."

"For a second I thought you were serious about stripping. But you couldn't have been."

She shrugged, as if it didn't matter. Important parts shifted beneath her shirt. Conn cleared his throat.

"Crystal, I'm serious about anything concerning you."

She started to say something, her eyes so wide and shadow-deep that he could drown in them. Then she looked past him to Oro. "You ought to be thinking about the race. That's what I was doing."

"What's set is set. The time for thinking is past."

She sighed. "I know. But it's drawing so much interest that I can't get it out of my mind. Some men from Fort Worth came down yesterday to take a look at Oro, while you were in town. They said there would be some fast horses running against him. Are you sure you're doing right?"

Half listening, Conn watched the lines of worry between her brows. He would give the horse beneath him to smooth them with his tongue.

"The only thing I'm sure of is that I want to strip both of us and roll in the mud. They've got some fancy places back East that give what they call mud baths. They charge a fortune. I'd give you one for free."

A pair of very kissable lips twitched into a smile. "You're a generous man."

"What I am is close to exploding."

She settled her hat back on her head and peered at him from beneath the low brim. "I'll tell you the truth, Conn O'Brien. You're not the only one."

Conn was guiding his horse closer when a sudden gust of wind struck. Lightning and thunder came almost simultaneously, shaking the ground. Oro bolted. With a curse, Conn took after him, Crystal close behind, and, like all the other sexy talk between them lately, the subject of mud baths was lost.

Conn thought about the baths over the next few weeks when he wasn't working the land and the stock, working Judge, taking care of details concerning the race. Two days before the big event, almost everyone from Stoke's Place rode into town, everybody but Helga and a few of the men who stayed behind to watch over things. He didn't expect any trouble, not having heard much about Royce or Edgar Braden lately, but that didn't mean they weren't planning something.

Especially Royce. As best he could tell, the smash he'd given Royce had broken more than his nose. He was still riding with a wild bunch, the rumor went, seldom showing up at either the Bushwhack or Shingle Camp.

Because people were coming into Kerrville from across Central Texas, Houston, Fort Worth, even New Orleans, hotel accommodations were almost an impossibility. Crystal and her mother were sharing the only room he could find. He and the men, including Stoke and Judge, would camp by the Guadalupe with Oro staked close by.

He wasn't surprised at the crowd. Texans liked horses, liked racing them, liked gambling, and liked having a good time. They'd been down so long, what with the war and a poor economy, that as things began to look up they were ready to cut loose and roar.

More was offered than just the race, primarily a barbecue and dance the night before, a demonstration of trick riding and roping, a greased pig race, a pickles-and-pie contest for the women, a pair of preliminary races for the men.

The first races scheduled were short. A stayer, not a sprinter, Oro was taking no part in them. The big race, over a two-mile course east of town, was for him.

Betting was high. Conn hadn't put any money down, but he planned to. He would match the big-spenders and the small who were foolish enough to bet against the thoroughbred.

The first day in town went smoothly, with everyone settling in, but on the second day, with less than twenty-four hours until the main event, Judge disappeared. Conn told himself not to worry. When the boy finally showed up at camp close to evening, keeping to himself, Conn let him be.

Nerves, he told himself. He was suffering from

them himself. When he got word that Edgar Braden wanted to see him behind the hotel, they jangled a little more.

But he went, against Stoke's warning that it was some kind of trap. They met in the dim light from the fading sun. Braden wore a black suit and white shirt that hung loosely on what used to be a solid frame. He was cleanshaven, except for the moustache, his gray hair slicked back, his cheeks and eyes sunken.

In most ways he looked like the Edgar Braden Conn had seen before, and yet he seemed different, too, as if more than just the weight had been sucked out of him. But his eyes blazed with the old fire as Conn walked up.

Braden didn't bother with amenities or with questions about his wife and children, though he hadn't seen them in weeks.

"I hear talk about your horse. I hear he's fast and strong."

"You hear right."

"Must have cost you a pretty penny."

"He was worth every cent."

Braden's eyes narrowed. "I guess he means more to you than almost anything except the Bushwhack."

"Does that anything include your daughter?"

"Leave her out of this."

Conn looked up at the back of the two-story hotel and wondered if she had any idea her father and husband were close by. He hoped not. Whatever Edgar Braden was up to, it could bring her only pain.

Then he remembered he was supposed to meet her at the barbecue right at dusk. Damn, he'd forgotten. He owed her an apology. He owed her more than that.

The eye he turned on his father-in-law was not a friendly one. "What do you want, Braden?"

"I want to place a bet."

"Against me."

"Right. The deed to the Bushwhack against the horse."

Conn wasn't sure he'd heard right. "Let's get this straight. Oro wins, I get the ranch. He loses, you take him and keep the deed."

Braden nodded.

"Why would you risk so much to get a loser?"

"He wouldn't be a loser once I got hold of him. I'd put a decent rider on his back."

"You don't trust your son?"

"He's not my—" Braden broke off. "Judgement's a quitter and a laggard. And you're a fool for having anything to do with him."

"You Bradens don't have much faith in one another, do you?"

"Is it a bet or not?"

As the two men stared at one another, Conn saw the truth. Braden's desire for Oro had nothing to do with the horse's value, or with any money he might make off him. He wanted the horse because he belonged to an O'Brien, just the way he had wanted the ranch.

And all because he believed his wife had betrayed him. The man was crazy. But he wasn't a fool.

"I'm going to win," Conn said. "Your boy is going to win."

Braden's answer was a smirk.

"So be it." Conn held out his hand. They shook.

"I want witnesses to this," Braden said.

"My word is good."

"Not to me."

Rather than argue, Conn took him to the office of Hugo Ridley, attorney-at-law, where they drew up papers representing the deed to the ranch and the ownership papers for the horse. Ridley didn't say a word except to promise to keep them safe and turn them over to the right party when the race was done.

Braden didn't hang around. Standing on the walkway in front of Ridley's office, Conn listened to the fiddle music from down the way and asked himself if Braden wasn't making a fool of him for the second time. Braden thought so. It had been in his eyes.

Conn would have to join Crystal later. First he must check at camp to make certain all was well. He hadn't gone more than two steps when Jennifer Weathers stopped him and wished him luck.

"Why aren't you at the dance?" she asked.

"Why aren't you?"

"I'm going. Mama Weathers and I are staying with friends here in town and she's already there with them. But I saw you and wanted to let you know I've put some money down on the thoroughbred. So has Papa Weathers."

"He bet on Oro to win?"

"It was you he was betting on, not just the horse. And it was more than a little bit. Mama Weathers doesn't know how much, but he doesn't know she bet on you, too. The whole town's rallying around you. I think it's their way of welcoming you home and thanking you for all you've done since you got back."

Conn hardly knew what to say.

"Just don't lose," she said. It was not an encouraging admonition, well meant though it was.

"I don't intend to."

But Conn knew where the best of intentions led. Straight to hell.

Pressures were mounting here, and more than ever he sensed skullduggery lurking in the shadows. He made fast for his campsite and found Judge apart from the others, standing close to the river bank away from the light of the fire. He came up to him from the rear, but the boy, lost in thought, gave no sign of recognizing his presence.

"Did you see your father this afternoon?"

The boy jumped and whirled to face him.

Conn repeated the question.

The boy's nut-brown complexion paled. "I don't know what you're talking about."

"Don't lie. You were gone a long time. Did you see him?"

Judge tried to look at him straight on but failed. "What if I did?"

"Did you make a deal with him?"

The boy rolled his eyes. He hadn't done that in a while.

"No."

Conn recognized the lie. His heart fell somewhere around his toes.

"He just bet me the Bushwhack against Oro. He seemed certain you would lose."

The boy looked momentarily taken aback, but then he rallied with a lift of his chin. "What else would you expect? He doesn't think much of me."

"He thinks you'll do what he wants. Why? Did he threaten you? Did he offer something? Land? Money?"

Conn saw he'd struck a bullseye with at least one of his guesses. It could be all were right.

Like Crystal, Judge could be susceptible to threats of harm against his mother, or even against Crystal herself. Despite the scorn Judge felt for his father, he could also want recognition as his son. To a boy long denied acceptance, such an offer might prove hard to turn down.

But throwing the race was wrong, no matter the motivation, a matter of integrity that went to the heart and soul. Conn had to trust that the boy would see it as clearly as he did. A small voice whispered that it was the integrity of a Braden he was depending upon. But Crystal was a Braden, and he would trust her with his life.

He reminded himself to tell her just that, in case she didn't already know. In the meantime he had Judge and the bet and his reputation as a racehorse expert, and he had, too, the burden of a county's faith that he was not the villain they'd once supposed.

These were heavy burdens for any man. They rested, too, on the shoulders of a boy.

"If you lose tomorrow, Judge, lose honestly. Forget about disappointing me and Crystal and everyone else. We'll get over it. But if you lose on purpose, there's one person who will suffer more than anyone. And that's you."

"They bet what?"

Crystal had the lawyer Ridley backed up against his desk.

"Just what I said, Mrs. O'Brien. The horse against the ranch."

She threw up her hands in exasperation. When Conn didn't show up at the barbecue, she'd worried that something was wrong. Feeling ill at ease around so many people she barely knew, consumed with unknown fears, she'd left without eating.

She'd gone to the hotel first. Her mother told her not to worry, but she saw the troubled look in her eyes and heard the tremor in her voice. Both feared the same thing, though they couldn't put a name to it except to say something was wrong.

When she saw Conn with her father standing outside Ridley's office, she'd known it for sure. She was standing in the shadows across the street at the time, her heart twisting a thousand times and not once from joy.

She'd been about to join them when her father had left and Jennifer Weathers appeared, looking prim and neat and as pretty as ever, and they'd had a nice little conversation that she would have given her best buckskins to hear.

Thinking she didn't look so bad herself in a new ivory gown her mother had sewn for her and with her hair worn loose the way Conn liked it, she thought about joining them. But maybe he preferred less complicated women. That would be every woman in the world.

And so she'd waited for Jennie to leave, debating whether to stalk her husband or accost his lawyer.

Ridley seemed the safer choice. Watching Conn from afar brought too much pain.

And here she'd found out only bad news. Her father was up to something, otherwise he'd never have risked losing the Bushwhack. She knew it in her bones. He had fixed the race. He had hobbled the horse. Something. She wouldn't put anything beyond him.

Leaving the lawyer sputtering, she hurried outside. Conn had to be told. She stopped herself. He already knew trouble awaited. Of course he did. The bet itself had told him. He knew what Bradens were like. She'd taught him well enough.

She felt sick inside, helpless, desperate, and very much alone. Her mother could offer no consolation, keeping to her room the way she was. Crystal understood, though her mother had not confided in her. She was terrified of seeing her husband after all the weeks they'd been apart. Several times recently she'd expressed doubt that she had done the right thing in leaving. But she'd never suggested she return to her husband's side.

Standing in that hotel room, seeing her mother's misery, wondering if she were the cause, Crystal had almost been broken. She always tried to do her best, but somehow it was never quite good enough.

More than anything else in the world, she needed to see Conn, to hold him in her arms, to tell him that no matter what he thought of her, she loved him with all her heart and would stand by him against the world if he would let her.

She wasn't much of an acquisition, and she doubted he valued her love very much, but right now it was all she had to offer.

Unsure where exactly the O'Brien camp was located, she moved toward the river and the flickering campfires. Trees were scattered sparsely along the bank where once cypress had been as thick as weeds. She passed few people, and no one who looked familiar. She was walking at the edge of a stretch where the growth of shrubs and cottonwoods precluded campsites when a tall, dark figure stepped into her path.

She jumped and stifled a scream.

"I didn't mean to startle you, Mrs. O'Brien. I mean you no harm."

In the moonlight she gave her accoster a quick perusal. He was taller than Conn and leaner. His hair was straight and as black as the night, and so were the eyes that stared at her with an unsettling intensity.

His face had the sharp-boned lines of an Indian, but except for his shoulder-length hair, everything else about him was white. A half-breed, she decided. Comanche blood flowed in his veins. If she had any sense, she would have felt menaced. But when had she shown any sense?

"Who are you?" she asked.

"You wouldn't believe me if I told you. Call me Brit. That will suffice."

Suffice? It was a strange word for a breed.

"What do you want? What are you doing here?"

"I stand guard over the thoroughbred. Your husband does not know of my presence."

"But why—"

"You have an older brother. I do not trust him."

This was getting crazier and crazier.

"Why haven't I seen you before?"

"Because I did not choose for you to see me."

"But you know Conn."

"We met briefly months ago."

"I don't understand. Why bother helping out someone you barely know?"

"Because you and your husband are the only two people I have observed whose problems are more tangled than mine. Take care. And do not approach your younger brother. He has much to think about this evening. Such thinking is best done in solitude."

Doubting him didn't occur to her, though she could never have explained why.

"It has to do with the race, doesn't it? And the bet my father made with Conn."

"Your husband is a lucky man to have you for his wife."

"Tell him."

Brit's smile softened the lines of his face. "He knows."

It was the one thing he'd said that she didn't believe. He didn't know their situation *that* well.

Then he was gone. She stared at where he had stood an instant before, and slowly, carefully, she put together all that he had said, all that he had implied. Judge was worried about the race, but not because he was unsure of his abilities. He was unsure about whether to win.

Her father had jiggled with the race all right, just as she suspected. He had somehow reached his son.

She turned cold and hugged herself. Conn would figure out the truth. The Bradens were getting to him again.

She tried to whisper his name, but it caught in her throat. Every time she sought a way out of their situation, she found only blank and solid walls. She was trapped by who she was, and so was he.

Mama and her worries, Judge and his dilemma, even the shadows of Royce's long-ago threats held no importance for her except as they affected Conn.

What could she do for him?

She could give him the one thing he wanted from her.

She could give him sex.

They needed a bed. But all were taken.

A thought occurred. The hotel wasn't the only place in town with beds. Did she dare? She did.

After all, she was still the woman who'd lassoed her not-yet spouse when he was about to get away.

She practically ran back toward town, to a two-story structure standing alone at the end of a narrow lane, to the brightly lit windows that welcomed her.

She knocked sharply at the door.

"Mrs. Truehart," she said when it opened, "we need to talk."

Chapter Twenty

"You sent word I was to come here."

Conn's voice drifted up the stairs of Mrs. Truehart's establishment and into the room with the partially opened door.

"That's right, I did."

"Look, Mrs. Truehart, I know what's going on here. There's been a mistake. I've been out of sorts lately, and with the race tomorrow, some of my men have provided me a little distraction."

"Is that what you really believe? That would be very generous of them. My rates are high, especially with so many visiting gamblers in town."

"I'll be happy to pay you any money you're out—"

"That won't be necessary. Just go up the stairs and open the first door you come to."

"I don't mean to be rude—"

"You're not. You've turned me down before, back in San Antonio, remember? Just do as I ask. Look at the woman waiting for you. If you don't want to spend some time with her, explain the situation. She might understand. She's a reasonable sort."

"She wouldn't be Graciela, would she? The one who worked for my father, I mean. My wife said she brought her here."

"Graciela Gomez has returned to her family in Mexico. Please, up the stairs."

A pause, and then his footsteps sounded on the stairs. The door creaked open. Crystal stared at him from the bed.

Goodness, she was nervous, and feeling more foolish than she'd ever felt in her life. Why hadn't she at least kept on her dress? Mama had put hours of work into the tucks. But she had seen the black hose and the red garters lying at the foot of the bed, courtesy of a smiling Mrs. Truehart, and here she was curled up on top of the covers dressed in nothing else, except for the three-foot-long band of red feathers tickling against her breasts.

"Saints above," Conn whispered as he stopped in the doorway.

Crystal hoped no saints were watching, although there was nothing wrong with what they were doing. They were, after all, man and wife, and even more important, a man and wife who'd been forced into celibacy for more than two months.

"Are you going to turn me down?" she asked.

He leaned against the door frame. He wore a black hat low over his thick brows, and his blue eyes pinned her to the bed. His black shirt was open at the throat, and he wore black trousers that could have been painted on him.

He was a tempting man.

"Turn you down?" he asked. "After you've just got me up?"

"I guess that means I don't look so foolish."

He took a long time to look her over, from her yellow hair resting against her shoulders to the red feathers across her breasts to her bent legs, the garters, the black hose.

"No, you don't look foolish."

His reassurance served only to agitate her more. She swallowed. "I couldn't find you at the barbecue. I guess you weren't hungry."

Or maybe my father made you lose your appetite.

Why did she have to think of such a thing? It was a consideration she would not entertain, not now, not ever, if she could help it. She must think of only Conn.

"I'm hungry, all right," he said. "Starved, as a matter of fact."

She let out the breath she had been holding. "Then I guess we ought to do something about it."

Kicking the door closed, he came close and tossed his hat on the bed. "Aye, that we should," he said, staring down at her.

Her breasts reacted to him so fast, they shook the feathers. Or maybe it was just her heart pounding like one of the hammers she'd been listening to for weeks.

He sat at the edge of the bed and snapped one of the garters. "It's been a long time."

Shivers raced along all the paths of her body and settled in a place not too far from his hovering hand. "Too long," she said.

"I've got one problem."

Her heart caught in her throat. "What's that?"

"Moving slow. I don't think I can manage it."

"Slow is good sometimes. But not all the time."

She rose to her knees and wrapped her arms around his neck. She kissed the corners of his mouth.

Cupping her face, he returned the kiss, sweetly, gently, and so tantalizingly, she thought she might die.

"I want this to last a long time, Crystal."

She dragged her tongue across his throat. He tasted salty and sweet at the same time, like ambrosia mixed with nuts.

"We don't have to have just the one time," she said, whispering her way to his ear.

He was unfastening his pants before she'd finished speaking.

All right, she told herself, he had set the pace. It was her task to keep up. With Conn sitting at the edge of the bed, dressed only in a shirt, she threw one leg across his lap and eased herself down on his erection.

He sucked in his breath. She ran her tongue across his lips. He moaned, and she did it again.

She didn't feel the least bit scandalous or disgraceful. She felt good.

"You know what?" she asked. "I'm glad I didn't eat tonight. You taste better than any barbecue."

He eased the strip of feathers from her breasts. "Are you sweet-talking me?"

She unbuttoned his shirt and rubbed her nipples against his chest. All the while she enjoyed the feel of his body between her tight thighs, imprisoning him right where she wanted him to be.

She shifted her hips. "I'm speaking the truth," she managed, though it didn't come out very clearly.

And then the feelings they were bringing to each other took control, and they forgot the talk. They moved in unison, a perfect team, as if they had been practicing in their minds this very moment, the bedsprings squeaking, the room whirling, the bedside lamp bathing them both in gold. He held his breath, and then he was squeezing her tight and exploding with a powerful climax, and she was doing the same.

She marveled at the sweetness and power of such a simple act, marveled while she held onto him as if she feared he would go away and she would never know such sweetness again.

They each let the shivers ripple through them, her teeth taking tiny bites against the side of his neck while his hands cupped her buttocks and pressed her firmly against him.

She couldn't bring herself to let him go. She wasn't satisfied; she wasn't complete. What they had done was slake an immediate, desperate thirst, using one another for gratification, reacquainting themselves with the heady wine of sex.

Now it was time to drink deeply of more far-reaching emotions. It was time to truly make love.

Lifting herself from him, she lay back on the bed. She was damp with the proof of his satisfaction, and hot with the desire coiling once again inside her.

Like a satisfied cat, she stretched out beside him. "We've got the bed for the night."

"Interesting." He slipped one garter down her leg and began to roll the stocking, easing it off her thigh, past her knee, and slowly down her calf. Such a simple procedure, yet he made it incredibly erotic.

"How did you manage all this?" he asked.

"I rented the room." She could barely get the words out, so intent was she on watching what he did and enjoying the touch of his hands.

He started stripping the other leg. "Rented?"

She swallowed. "I insisted. Mrs. Truehart offered it free, but she'd already helped out Graciela and that was enough. She finally agreed I was right." She shivered when he came to her foot and caressed her toes.

"Was I worth what it cost?" he asked as he tossed the second stocking aside.

"Close. But not yet."

He took off his shirt, lay beside her, and taunted a nipple with his thumb.

"You knew I needed this."

She ran a hand across the expanse of his chest, discovering once again its breadth and contours and solid strength.

"I knew *I* needed it."

"Crystal—"

He looked down at her with an intensity that set her blood to boiling.

"I felt so foolish waiting for you like this," she said. "I was afraid you'd laugh."

He kissed the tip of one breast, and then the other. "You know me better than that."

"Does one human being really know another that well?"

"Maybe not. You took me by surprise tonight."

Unbidden thoughts of the race and all the problems that tomorrow might bring crowded into her mind. Despite the vows she'd made to herself, she grew solemn.

"It's not the first time I took you by surprise," she said.

"You're right. I remember by the creek—"

"You know that's not what I'm talking about."

"I know that's the only other surprise I want to think of right now."

She saw the worry in his eyes, saw him struggle and force it to recede. She must do the same. No problems for them, only wanton pleasure. If it took a night of constant lovemaking, so be it. She didn't think Conn would object.

"All right," she said, resting her hand above his heart. "We are the only two people in the world."

"If you say so."

"I do."

He grinned down at her. "You're getting awfully bossy."

"That's the kind of wife I am."

"You're also shameless."

"It took some working on, but I think I've finally reached that point."

"Speaking of points—" He kissed the tips of her breasts.

She arched herself into his lips. "Make love to me, Conn. Go slow."

He pulled her into his arms and nuzzled her neck. "I'll do the best that I can."

Conn's best was all that she could ask and more than any woman should expect. Was it the setting itself or was it Conn who filled her world with an aura of sensuality? Conn was the answer, the answer to everything.

Over and over again he did all that she could ask. For them both, he made time stand still.

Over her protests, Conn returned her to her hotel room before dawn. She swore she didn't mind being seen coming out of the front door of a brothel, but he'd insisted. She might not worry about her reputation, but he did, not for himself but for her.

Whether she knew it or not, she needed to be a part of the county, an accepted member of the community. And that meant not shocking the women. If word got out about what she'd done, every man would be jealous and their wives would never let her forget.

As he left the hotel, he turned to the topic they'd been holding at bay. He began to think about the race. Hurrying to the campsite, he saw that all was quiet. Even Judge, huddled on top of a tangled blanket, seemed to be sleeping soundly, though his lips moved as if he were carrying on an argument in his dreams.

Conn lay down on his bedroll, but sleep wouldn't come. He and Crystal had gotten little more than an hour of sleep. He should have been exhausted; instead he felt good. Maybe he was stupid, maybe love-drugged, but he hadn't felt like this in a long, long while.

What was the worst that could happen today? Oro would lose, Braden would take possession of the thoroughbred, and Judge would begin to learn what betrayal could cost.

But Crystal would still be Mrs. Conn O'Brien, Stoke's Place would still thrive, and a number of ranchers would learn they should never gamble more than they could afford to lose.

And what was the best that could happen?

Oro would win, and Conn would take title to the Bushwhack.

And Crystal would still be his wife. Conn had his priorities. He put Crystal at the top of his list.

Not that she knew it, though he'd tried to tell her all would be well. He'd finally decided that the best way to let her know how he felt was not to tell her, but to show her. No matter what happened today, he would take her to their home and they would begin the rest of their lives.

With dawn, time for reflection was gone. The races would be held in the morning before heat built up for the day. Several of his men went to watch the trick riding and greased-pig show, and then the first events, the short runs designed for the quarterhorses.

Nat and Judge worked on Oro, with Stoke watching nearby. They were startled by the sudden appearance of Helga, who came striding up from the direction of town. She thrust a bill into Stoke's hand.

"I lose the bet," she said, but there was nothing about her that seemed sorry about the situation. "I come to see the race."

Stoke pulled a plug of tobacco from his back pocket and bit off a piece. "I was expecting you, Helga."

Conn would have sworn she almost smiled. "For such talk you will make the biscuits tonight."

He spat a ribbon of tobacco juice into the dirt. "It'll be my pleasure and a treat for us all."

Helga did not so much as flinch. Instead, she shook Stoke's hand, then whirled and headed back toward town. Conn looked at Nat. The two of them shrugged. Something was going on here. The world really was a strange place.

Much as he wanted to talk to his rider, Conn knew he made the boy edgy. Following in Helga's wake, he went to where the bets were being placed. By the time he got there, the first race was done and the second was about to start. There would be an hour-long wait before Oro could show what a champion he was.

Crystal was nowhere around, but he wasn't surprised. She'd said she would stay with her mother until time for the race. Annabelle wanted above everything to avoid seeing her husband. Conn doubted he knew she was in town.

He saw the Weathers family in the milling crowd and, to his surprise, Ham was standing close to the widow Jennifer. They looked at ease with one another, and even Dalworth Weathers and his wife were standing arm in arm. With all the mating going on, it seemed more like springtime than the beginning of fall.

Somewhere out of sight the fiddlers were still sawing away, as if they'd warmed up so much during last night's dance, they didn't know how to cool down.

The racetrack, such as it was, had been laid out in a half-mile oval around a wide field at the opposite edge of town from Mrs. Truehart's establishment. A wooden fence ran along its outer boundaries. Half-way round marked the distance for the first races. The third, the one that would test Oro and six other fine-looking mounts, called for four complete circuits, a distance of two miles.

It was Oro's favorite race. He'd proven it time and time again back in Saratoga, winning Conn a great deal of money in the process. For himself he'd already earned long years at stud.

As the second race began, Conn caught sight of

Edgar Braden talking to his son Royce. They stood apart from the crowd, and they appeared to be arguing. A wild mustang stallion couldn't have dragged him close to them.

The rest of the crowd must have felt the same way, for they gave them a wide berth.

Royce looked past his father and locked his eyes on Conn. Even from twenty yards away, with dozens of men and women drifting between them, he felt the young man's hate.

Conn turned, unwilling to get into a staring contest, and when he finally glanced back, they were gone. During the second race and in the interim time before the third, he tried to be the good citizen, accepting the greetings of the ranchers and townspeople, most of whom he knew by name.

By the time Nat and Stoke led Oro to join the other horses in the middle of the track, he'd already put his money down. Crystal and her mother were standing by the Weathers clan against the fence, Helga close behind. They exchanged waves as Conn vaulted the fence to join the men.

He moved casually, almost sauntering, but there was nothing casual in the way he asked, "Where's Judge?"

"Got a case of the nerves," Stoke said. "He'll be here."

Conn glanced at Nat, who nodded in agreement.

When the boy did show up, the last rider to mount, Conn made his comments brief.

"Do the best you can. That's all I ask. Oro will do the rest."

The boy looked him in the eye. He even managed a smile. "I will."

In that moment, with the sun breaking through the clouds and the fiddles playing in the distance and the world looking on in anticipation, Conn knew that all would be well.

He proved right. The contest wasn't even close. Oro won by six lengths in what even those who'd bet against him swore was the best-run race they'd ever seen.

Conn met horse and rider at the finish line. Judge looked like a proud prince sitting high in the saddle, a broad grin breaking across his freckled face as he reined the thoroughbred to a halt.

When he looked at Conn, *I told you so* gleamed in his eyes, and he accepted congratulations as if he earned them every day.

They were soon surrounded by well-wishers, and in the midst of cheering and back-slapping, Conn accepted his winnings, kissed his wife, and, when Hugo Ridley joined them, took possession of the ownership papers to Oro and the deed to the Bushwhack Ranch.

Edgar Braden was not around to offer congratulations, but Conn hadn't thought he would be. Ridley explained that he'd seen him ride out of town when the race was done.

He hadn't expected the moment to be so emotional. He stepped aside to be by himself a moment. He stared at the papers, especially at the deed. He thought of all it signified—his youth, the memories of his brother, his father's dreams. With it came perhaps the most valuable possession of all, the hilltop graves of the Irish couple who had long ago sailed an alien sea and, with only their strong hands and brave hearts and a pair of suckling babes to call their own, set out to tame a wild land.

The first thing he would do was visit those graves. This time he would take his wife.

Crystal watched her husband in silence. He seemed so lost to her, preferring to savor this moment by himself. She smoothed her ivory skirt and smiled at Ridley.

"Thank you for holding the papers. I know Conn trusts you very much."

"I admired his father greatly, as I'm sure he knows, and I admire him just as much." He went on for a few more minutes, but the words came to her as a senseless drone. Her thoughts were on Conn and what this day really meant. He had his family home back. His most important dream had come true.

She prayed her father would leave the Bushwhack peacefully, but, of course, she couldn't be sure he would.

Taking her mother by the arm, she went to find Judge and make arrangements for the return trip home. Helga had made the journey into town by horseback, but she willingly agreed to join Annabelle in the wagon, with the men riding alongside.

When Judge separated himself from a host of admirers, including a half dozen starry-eyed young girls, he said he would be returning later with Nat, the winning thoroughbred in tow. He was practically swaggering around in a circle as he talked, and he couldn't keep a silly grin off his face, but he'd earned the right.

Giving up on the dress, Crystal went back to the hotel to change into her buckskins. She would ride Helga's mount. When she went to find her husband, she found him in the town's lone saloon surrounded by well-wishers who were offering to buy him a drink.

She stood in the door for a while watching him accept the congratulations. Like Judge, he grinned a great deal. Like Judge, he'd earned the right.

She left without his seeing her, and she began the long ride home, taking it slow, remembering the night that had just passed, rejoicing in the day, and wondering what all of it meant for her.

She didn't go directly to the cabin. Something drew her to the Shingle Camp and then to the crossing that led onto the Bushwhack. At each place she was told by the foreman that neither her father nor Royce was around.

It was her father she thought of. What was he going through? He'd sacrificed his honor to get the Bushwhack, and now it was lost.

Sadly, the honor could never be reclaimed.

She didn't mention to either foreman that the Bushwhack had passed into the hands of a new owner. That was Conn's good news to relate.

The moment she rode near the cabin at Stoke's Place, she sensed something was wrong. Several of the men stood around the back porch, watching in solemn silence as she dismounted. The wagon stood nearby, the horses still in their traces.

At the corner of the cabin, one of the dogs rose to his haunches and began to howl. She'd never heard either hound make a sound before.

The men parted. Dismounting, she ran onto the porch just as Stoke came outside. He wore a dazed, sad look that was foreign to him.

"What's wrong?" she asked. "Is it Conn?"

"Not Conn." He shook his head. "It's a hell of a thing to happen. I'm sorry, Crystal."

She hurried past him. Helga met her at the parlor door.

"Mein liebes Kind—"

Heart in her throat, she walked past her to a scene that would forever burn itself onto her mind: her mother kneeling before the hearth, cradling her father in her arms.

Edgar Braden lay still, his body lax, and she knew right away he was dead.

For a moment she couldn't move, and then she hurried near. Annabelle looked up at her with tear-filled eyes.

"He's gone," she said, barely above a whisper. "I was going to return to him, whether he wanted me or not, and now he's gone."

"Mama," she said, dropping beside her mother. Her father was in his shirtsleeves, his coat lying crumpled on the rug. Blood stained the whiteness across his chest. Stained, too, were her mother's hands as she held him tight. Crystal tried to ease her away and take her place, but she would not let go.

"I told him the truth," she said. "He heard me. He understood."

"The truth?"

"About Royce and Judge."

"Mama, you don't have to say anything now."

"Oh, but I do." Her voice grew stronger as she talked. "Royce did this, you see. To keep from losing more of his inheritance. Edgar told me before he—"

She broke off, then took a deep breath. "Royce said he planned to blame it on Conn, but of course that was foolishness. Only my eldest boy would think of such an evil thing."

Crystal wrapped an arm around her mother, sharing her pain.

"Royce wasn't his son."

The admission came from somewhere deep inside her, and Crystal could only sit in stunned silence as she tried to understand.

"There was a man, a traveler. A handsome charmer. I could see him in Royce every day. And I was young and foolish and sadly overindulged. I thought I was in love. When he learned of my condition, he left. And there was your father, working hard to better himself, loving me, or so he said. I believe he really did. He offered me his name, and I took it. I never told him or anyone else the truth. I was a coward. I've been a coward all my life."

"No, Mama, you stayed with him and made the best life that was possible for you. You had to do it for your child and your own parents. You did the best you could."

"I tried to love him, and in a way I did, but the jealousy was hard to take. I wasn't always as ill as I said I was, but it kept us apart and I didn't have to listen to his accusations."

She looked down to stroke the lines of his face. "We were both so foolish. I loved him for saving me from disgrace, though he didn't know it. But I couldn't love him in the way he wanted. The way you love Conn."

Crystal kissed her mother's cheek. "There are all kinds of love. I love you, Mama. We don't say the words often enough."

"I love you, child. As much as I love Judge, though I doubt you've ever realized it. Judge was born of my union with your father. Edgar's true and only son. I told him just before he . . . died that never once since we married had I been unfaithful. It seemed to bring him peace."

A shadow fell across them.

"Herr O'Brien has returned," Helga said.

Reluctantly Crystal eased away from her mother, and Helga took her place. She'd gotten her father's blood on her hands; she stared at the smears as she walked onto the back porch.

Conn met her on the steps. "The men told me."

Crystal started to speak, but words wouldn't come. With a sob, she threw herself into his arms.

Chapter Twenty-one

After sending one of the men to get the sheriff, Conn grew impatient and decided to go after Edgar Braden's killer himself. He was saddling a fresh horse in the barn when Crystal came in.

Dark shadows bruised the skin beneath her eyes, and he thought she looked close to collapse.

"Are you all right?" he asked.

"I'm fine. Where are you going?"

He hesitated before answering. "The Bushwhack. Unless there's something I can do here."

She drew in a deep breath and let it out slowly. "No, nothing but wait and worry."

Tightening the cinch, he lowered the stirrup and turned to her. "You need some rest. You didn't get much last night."

The ghost of a smile flashed across her face. "Neither did you." And then all traces of softness were gone. "You're looking for him, aren't you?"

No need to identify the *him*.

"Do you think he's at the ranch?" he asked.

"No."

She spoke with such finality, he looked at her with suspicion.

"You know where he is? Did he tell your mother something I don't know about?"

She brushed a wisp of hair away from her face. She'd washed her father's blood from her hands, but she hadn't been able to remove the haunted look from her eyes.

"I've told you everything she told me. But I know my brother." She hesitated. "My half-brother," she corrected. "That will take some getting used to."

"Where is he? He's got to be brought in."

"I'm only guessing, but I've got a good idea. Forget about asking what it is. I won't tell you."

"If you're trying to protect him—"

"No, no, never. You don't understand. I won't tell you, but I'll show you."

Moving past him, she started toward the back stall that housed Trouble.

Conn shook his head in disbelief. "I should have known that's what you were up to. I will not take you with me, Crystal. He can escape to Mexico before I'll do that."

She looked over her shoulder at him. "Then we've reached an impasse."

"Which means you stay and I go." He spoke firmly, but he got little reassurance from the stubborn angle of her head.

"I'm not going to lie. After you're gone, I'll go after him myself. We Bradens have done enough to you."

Conn wasn't about to get into that argument. "Your mother needs you here."

"She's taking this better than you think. Besides, I've never offered her much consolation. I know she loves me, and maybe things can change between us now, but not today."

"It's too dangerous."

"I'm a good shot."

"You're a better target. You might get in the way."

"A number of things might happen, including your riding on and my going out alone." She stepped close, looking up at him with doe eyes that could melt a stone. But she still held the defiant tilt of her chin. "I have to do this, Conn. I have to."

He thought of the woman who had lain in his arms only hours before, the soft, sweet, submissive wife whose only demands had been ones he had already been considering himself.

"I could tie you down."

"If we were in bed, I'd let you."

"I'm stronger than you."

"I know. And you're also smarter. If you think about it, you'll see I have no choice."

She had a way about her that turned everything he said back on him. So he was smarter, was he? There she was very much wrong.

"You are the most exasperating woman."

"I have my good moments."

She stood so close, he could see the flecks of light in her eyes and the slight twitch of tension at the corner of her lips. She looked stubborn and proud, true enough, but she also looked vulnerable and so precious, she frightened him.

"Aye, wife, you have your moments indeed."

He didn't try to stop her as she went to saddle her horse. Somehow he would have to distract her when they neared this mysterious destination she was so sure of. Bushwhack Creek would freeze in July before he'd let her risk getting hurt.

As they led the horses outside, Annabelle Braden was coming down the porch stairs. She looked straighter and stronger than Conn had ever seen her, her head high, her eye steady. Tragedy did that to some people. It gave them a reason to be tough.

"You're going after him," she said, more a statement than a question. "Where?"

Crystal gave Conn a sideways glance. "The canyon—"

"The one you liked to hide in," Annabelle said, striding close to block their path.

"You knew about it?"

"I was glad you had a place. At times I wanted to join you."

"You should have."

"There were many things I should have done." Annabelle looked at Conn. "My son has committed terrible deeds, I know, and I'm not asking you to save his life. But jail for Royce would be as bad as killing him."

"Mama," said Crystal, "we can't promise what will happen."

"I know, but I can hope." She hugged her daughter and, looking past her to Conn, said, "Bring her back safely. I'm asking you to do that."

"I will," he said.

With a firm nod, she went back inside to join Stoke and Helga in the tending of her husband's body, and Conn and Crystal set out. They rode hard to the creek crossing and onto Shingle Camp Ranch. Conn had thought he knew every part of the county, but he didn't know the route she took across her home land, through thick brush and fields of rolling pasture, over hills and along a pair of shallow, fast-flowing creeks.

She didn't stop until she came to a stand of cottonwoods by one of the creeks. She reined Trouble back in the trees and gestured toward a limestone-walled canyon a hundred yards away.

The field before them was rocky, the boulders larger near the entrance to the canyon.

"He's in there," she said.

"You sound sure."

"He doesn't know he was identified as the shooter, remember. He left thinking father was dead. He's hiding just to be cautious. Once while you were gone, he stole some horses from Stoke's Place and brought them here. I got them and took them back."

She said it flatly, as if she'd said she baked biscuits in his absence. He ought to throttle her and lock her up so she wouldn't harm herself ever again. He settled for a shake of his head.

"I guess it's a little late to tell you what a damn fool thing that was to do."

"What's done is done."

"I'm telling you anyway."

"I knew you'd feel that way. That's why I didn't let you know earlier."

"Crystal, damn it—"

Trouble bobbed his head, and Crystal stroked his neck to calm him. "I don't mean to defy you, Conn. I know I don't do what you want me to do, or behave the way a wife should. But so many things go wrong. Again and again."

Her voice quavered. He thought she would break. Any other time he would have pulled her off her horse and held her close, letting strength and love pass between them. But this was not another time.

Silently he cursed the greed and insanity that had brought them here. Staring at the mouth of the canyon, he gave her something else to think about.

"Any way out of there?"

She shook her head. "It's narrow and not very deep, but the walls are too steep to climb."

Conn glanced at the sky. The sun hovered low over the far end of the canyon. Twilight would be upon them in little more than an hour, and with it lengthening shadows where anything could go wrong.

"If he's not in there, we're losing valuable time."

"He is."

"You're sure of yourself."

She smiled weakly. "You know I'm not. But Royce is a man of habit. He's not very adventurous, and he's not very smart. He wouldn't run off. He wouldn't know where to run. Besides, he thinks he owns the Shingle Camp. He'll ride out of there tomorrow and hear that his father's dead, shot down by an unknown killer, and he'll start throwing accusations in your direction. If anyone asks where he's been, he'll say he was carousing with a woman or sleeping off too much whiskey or some such excuse. At least that's what he's planning right now. No one would think he'd kill his own father."

"You know him that well?"

"I wish I didn't. I should have foreseen this—"

"Stop it, Crystal. This isn't your fault."

But the bleakness in her eyes didn't go away, and he could see she blamed herself.

Dismounting, they tethered the horses by the creek, then stood at the edge of the trees to stare at the canyon.

"Make yourself comfortable," Conn said. "I'll take the first watch to make sure he doesn't come out. When it's a little darker, I'll ride closer to see if I can spot him. You can keep watch from back here."

"Forget that plan. I'm coming with you."

"No. Not this time. If I need you, I'll let you know."

"I could serve as a distraction."

"You certainly would. For me. I need to concentrate on Royce."

They looked at one another for a moment, neither giving ground.

"You're right," she said at last. "I'll stay back here. But if I hear gunshots, all promises are off."

Touching her cheek, he turned back to the watch. Time passed slowly. Other than an occasional hawk soaring overhead, he saw no other living creature between them and the canyon.

At last he judged the shadows sufficiently deep to cover his progress, and he went to get his horse. "I'll be riding slow, in a zigzag pattern."

"He could still shoot you down."

"The light's too bad, and, remember, he's no marksman."

"He could get lucky."

"No, Crystal, his luck's run out."

He checked the rifle in its scabbard and thrust his pistol into the waistband at his back. Mounted, he was about to start the long ride across the hundred yards, planning on circling as much as he could around the far reaches of the pasture. A shadowy figure on horseback halfway across the field stopped him. It seemed to come from nowhere, but its destination was clear: the mouth of the canyon, the same as Conn's.

Before he could turn back to his wife, she was astride Trouble close to his side.

"Can you tell who it is?" he asked.

"It's not Royce, I know. He sits taller in the saddle, and besides—" She gasped. "I think it's Mama.

It couldn't be. She hasn't ridden in years."

And then Crystal was off at a run, getting the jump on Conn, and all he could do was spur his mount to stay close behind. But Annabelle had too far a lead on them, and before they could reach her, she'd disappeared into the dark mouth of the canyon.

There was no stopping Crystal, but at least Conn was able to take the lead. They reined to a halt at a scrub oak tree just inside the high walls. An eerie silence greeted them. It was darker here, as if it were already the dead of night, and they moved slowly, letting the horses find their way.

A light flickered up ahead. "Campfire," Conn whispered, and Crystal nodded.

They reached the beckoning fire to find Royce sprawled in a patch of grass close by a pair of burning logs, Annabelle standing at his feet. She was wearing a black riding skirt, her arms held rigid at her sides, her back straight, her head high.

Royce's once handsome face looked grotesque in the flickering light. More to blame than the broken nose was the ugly look in his eyes as he aimed a shotgun at his mother's heart.

Royce flicked a glance in their direction. "Ah, a gathering of the O'Briens and the Bradens. Have you come to gloat over the race?"

"You know why we've come," Conn said. "Put down the gun."

"I can't do that," said Royce. "Even I couldn't miss this close. And it's all I've got to keep you from gunning me down."

Conn dismounted, keeping his hands high to show he wasn't armed. Crystal did the same.

"You wouldn't shoot Mama," she said.

"Wouldn't I? I'm already accused of killing Papa, at least that's what I think she was starting to tell me when you unfortunately intruded. I thought she'd gone completely mad, but now here you are, my loving, traitorous sister, ready to claim the same absurd thing."

"You did it, Royce," Crystal said. "I don't know how you could, but you did."

"Then why shouldn't I shoot her? Why not shoot you all as well? I've got nothing to lose."

Crystal reached out to him. "Please give up. If you don't, you'll never know any peace. Maybe Father threatened you. Maybe it was self-defense. Tell us how it was."

Smart woman, she was buying time with her talk. Conn prayed that it worked.

Royce laughed sharply. "I wasn't threatened by that fool. I'll tell you what he said when I tracked him down. He wasn't going to lose everything to an O'Brien. He had come after his wife. And Judge, too. He wanted to punish Judge for winning the race. He hinted at maybe selling out and moving on. And where would that leave me?"

His eyes narrowed with reptilian malice as he looked at Conn. "Might as well tell it all," he said, a hint of satisfaction in his voice. "I killed Daniel O'Brien, too."

Conn started over the fire for him, but Crystal's cry stopped him.

"Holy Mother of God," Annabelle whispered.

Royce kept droning on, unmindful of anyone but himself. "The bastard refused to die, and you were on the way to claim the Bushwhack." He dared to grin. "Got away with it, too. Even Papa didn't know, not for sure."

Annabelle stepped toward him. Royce shifted the gun higher, and she paused. "I don't think you'll kill me. I'm your own flesh and blood. Edgar and Daniel were not."

"What in hell are you talking about? You never did make much sense."

"I know exactly what I'm saying." She took a deep breath, and Conn wondered how much the confession cost her. "Edgar Braden was not your father. You never knew the man who sired you. By the time Edgar and I wed, I was already in the family way and the man who was responsible had disappeared."

Royce jumped to his feet. "You're lying."

He waved the shotgun in protest, his concentration lagging an instant. Conn saw it at the same moment Crystal did. She went for her mother, tumbling her to the ground. Conn whipped out his pistol and squeezed off a shot. The bullet caught Royce in the chest, throwing him backward like a rag doll, and the shotgun fired harmlessly into the air. Echoes of the deafening blasts bounced from canyon wall to canyon wall.

For a moment no one moved. Then Crystal, holding tight to her mother, helped her to stand. Conn went for Royce, but one glance told him he would never harm anyone again.

He turned to tell the women, but he saw from the expression in their eyes that they already knew.

The sound of horses intruded. They looked to see Sheriff Rees leading his deputy and a pair of Conn's men, and behind them Judge and Stoke.

Rees rode close to the fire. "Is he dead?"

"I'd shoot him again if he weren't."

"We heard the gunfire. Got here as fast as we could. The boy showed us the way."

Crystal stepped forward to take Conn's hand. "Royce was going to kill his own mother. My husband did what he had to do." She looked past him to Judge. "Mama's all right. Conn saved her life."

Annabelle slowly drew her gaze from her fallen son to Crystal. She was white-faced, her mouth pinched, but she stood on her own without assistance.

"You married a good man. Never forget it." And to Judge. "Now come here, my boy, and give your mama a big hug. I've lost two of my men today and I'm in need of some love."

Crystal felt the same. She was in need of some love. But she kept to the shadows, apart from everyone, while Conn told the sheriff exactly how the shooting had happened. He told it all, every word that Royce had uttered, and she could hear the pain and anger in his voice when he spoke of his own father.

It was the final, terrible atrocity for a Braden to

have committed, yet it had happened before she and Conn ever met. They had been doomed from the start. She could look at matters no other way.

Stoke and the men wrapped Royce's body in a blanket and draped it over his horse. In the midst of the talking, about the only thing she listened to was Mama explaining to Judge how she used to ride all the time and decided tonight she would try again.

"I came most of the way by wagon. I asked one of the men at Shingle Camp to saddle a horse for me."

"That must have taken him by surprise."

"It did. I'll be aching for weeks, but I guess that's the least of my worries."

She was fighting off despair, Crystal knew, talking to gather her strength.

"I'm here, Mama," said Judge. "I'll take care of things."

He spoke with a new authority in his voice, a boy becoming a man.

Crystal backed farther away and looked up at a thousand stars, and at a full moon that had risen to lighten the shadows. Cicadas chirped in the brush, and a breeze was rustling in the trees. The world seemed peaceful, unaware of the ugliness that had taken place here. She didn't know how she felt . . . numb, sad, lost, and very much alone, though a crowd of people milled only a few yards away.

It could be she was projecting how she would feel the rest of her life.

She put even more distance between her and the campfire scene, all the spirit and energy drained from her. She'd lost so much, a father and a brother, yet the loss had been men who were never really hers to love and to cherish and to call her family.

That was the saddest part of all. Wasted opportunities. Wasted years.

Like the years she could have shared with her husband, if she hadn't brought him so much woe. Because of her, he'd killed a man—and on the day of his triumph, when he'd claimed the deed to his land.

Conn wasn't a killer. She remembered the way he had appeared the night she first saw him, full of worry about meeting his father and at the same time full of life and optimism that all would be well.

She had robbed him of all that. Her family had tried to rob him of everything.

A hand touched her shoulder and she jumped. Heart pounding, she turned to face Conn.

"Are you all right?" he asked.

She took a deep breath. "I'm fine."

"Liar."

"All right, I'm not so fine, but I will be."

"I know. You're strong. It's one of the things I love about you."

She barely heard him. "Conn, I have to tell you how sorry I am." She almost broke into tears. "He killed both our fathers. And I—"

He stopped her with a kiss. She didn't try to

struggle or free herself. He tasted too good, he felt too solid, and she needed him too much. He held her close for a moment, then eased back to stare solemnly into her eyes.

"Yes, he killed them both. It's something we're both going to have to live with."

"I don't know if I can."

"Yes, you can. I told you, love, you're strong."

Suddenly she really heard all that he said. She shook her head. "What did you call me?"

"Love."

The numbness that had taken over gave way to a beginning tingle she thought might be hope.

"You haven't done that since—"

"You can say it. Since San Antonio. That's because I'm a thick-headed Irishman. A Texas Irishman, the worst kind. I should have told you long ago I love you. I never really stopped. And don't start talking about what Bradens have done to me. I did some of it myself. Be assured, lass, I'm growing fond of Judge, and your mother showed real spirit and courage tonight, but you're the one I love."

"I don't see how you can."

He shrugged, and beneath the sadness in his eyes she could see the familiar glint that caused her heart to soar.

"It's fate," he said. "Neither of us can fight it. The moment I first saw you, I said to myself you were the woman of my dreams. And you are."

"Oh, Conn, I love you so much." Once the words were out, she couldn't stop declaring herself. "I owe you my allegiance and my life and I swear to bring you as little trouble as I possibly can."

"Don't promise more than you can deliver."

He said it decidedly, but the glint grew stronger, a miracle glint considering what they had both been through.

"You doubt me, do you? I'll show you what I can deliver."

She kissed him, and responding to the enthusiasm he showed her, even with the horses moving past them, she went on kissing him. And after they had joined the others and made the long journey back to Stoke's Place, she kissed him again.

Tomorrow they would take care of the sad arrangements that must be made, but she knew that with Conn at her side she could meet whatever challenges came along.

Epilogue

Bushwhack Ranch
April 17, 1871

Crystal studied the dining room table. Everything was in place, from the pair of candelabras to the O'Brien family china and silver to the linen tablecloth and napkins embroidered with the scrolled letter *O* in the corner.

Not all the letters were even, but they'd been done by her own hand, with advice from Mama and Helga, and she was as proud of them as anything she'd ever done.

Well, almost anything.

Today was her second wedding anniversary, but it was the first one she'd had the energy to celebrate. A year ago at this time she'd weighed a thousand pounds.

It was a miracle she and Conn had survived together so long, considering the way their marriage had begun.

She barely thought about those first months now. Too many other considerations crowded her mind. The linens were her anniversary gift to him. When he got a good look at them, knowing her undomestic ways, he would understand the hours of labor that had gone into their creation.

And if he didn't, she would tell him. Just as he told her about things she didn't understand. That was the way they were together, honest and forthright. They had learned the pain of being otherwise.

Leaving the dining room, she paused at the parlor door to look once again at Conn's gift to her: a portrait of Annabelle to hang beside that of his mother Bridget. He'd teased about buying her diamonds—a tiara, a necklace, or maybe a ring. She'd said they wouldn't go with her buckskins, which she still wore from time to time.

But Conn was proud of how well things were going for them—the horse ranch, the cattle drives they were helping to finance, the friends they'd made among the ranching families—and she'd worried that he might buy something frivolous.

He hadn't. The portrait, he'd told her last night when he presented it, was the first of many family possessions they would collect through the years.

With a smile of pleasure lighting her face, she

hurried to the kitchen. A crowd was expected: Hamilton Gates and his wife Jennie, riding over from the Double D; Mama and Judge from the Shingle Camp; the lawyer Hugo Ridley; and Stoke, of course, who should be arriving any minute.

Mama was already here, and Helga, too, helping out with the meal, but this wasn't her home. After Crystal had moved with Conn to the Bushwhack, and Mama and Judge were back on the Shingle Camp, she'd elected to remain with Stoke.

"Herr Price cannot manage alone," she'd declared when both Crystal and her Mama asked that she live with them. "He needs a woman."

They had never married, and Crystal wasn't sure what the sleeping arrangements were in the fine cabin that had been built in the midst of The Troubles, as she and Conn called them now. One of the new rooms had been designated Stoke's "spitting room," and that was where he kept his cuspidor, a rocking chair, and a big round rag rug for the hounds to stretch out on when the weather was too bad for the back porch.

They were a strange couple, Helga and Stoke, but no stranger than Mr. and Mrs. Conn O'Brien, when she got to thinking about it.

Life was strange, but more important, life was good, despite all that could pass.

She stood at the kitchen door, but only her own housekeeper, the one her father had hired so long ago, was working. She heard a cry from upstairs and then another. She smiled. She knew where everyone was.

She hurried up the stairs and into the large bedroom once occupied by Daniel O'Brien and his wife and now converted to a nursery for their twins.

Mama held one squirming baby, James Daniel, and Helga held the other, Bridget Annabelle. Conn grinned at her sheepishly from beside one of the cribs.

Her heart turned a dozen somersaults, as it always did when she came upon him unexpectedly. He was as handsome and charming and wonderful as he had been that first day when he'd rescued her from a saloon brawl, and she loved him more each day.

"I woke them," he said with a shrug and a sly smile.

"You did it on purpose," she said.

"*Ja,*" said Helga, "that he did."

"I'm glad," Annabelle said. "I couldn't keep my hands off them for another minute."

Crystal pulled her eyes from Conn and looked at the babes. Eleven months old they were, with their father's blue eyes and dark hair, but he swore they had their mother's devilment in their ways.

Alike as they were in their coloring, they were different in other ways. James was the strong one, the twin who had started walking first, unsteady though his fat legs were. Bridget was more agile. She saw no need for walking since she could crawl across a floor faster than the eye could follow, and she could climb onto almost anything.

Both of them could say *Mama* and *Daddy* and

bird and *dog,* and they also chattered a thousand comments to each other that no one else could understand. Conn said they would always be in a conspiracy, and Crystal had long ago decided he was right.

She went to her husband's side and put an arm around his waist. He kissed her on the nose. "Happy anniversary."

"The same to you."

"Judge will be over shortly," Annabelle said. "I can't get the boy to ease up on his work."

"He's a man, Mama," Crystal said.

"He's only seventeen."

"He grew up fast."

For a moment Annabelle grew solemn, and then she smiled. "He didn't grow up bitter. I've got Conn to thank for that."

The Bradens had a lot for which to thank Conn. Crystal most of all.

She looked at him. Should she tell him she was expecting another child? He would be pleased. He wanted a large family.

She heartily concurred.

Family. The word had such a wonderful sound now. After the pair of funerals almost two years ago, she had wondered if such could ever be the case.

But it was, and ever would be.

She went to the open window to watch as a wagon approached, and behind it Judge astride Licorice, the black mustang that Conn had given him a few weeks before his big race. Judge hadn't raced again, and after one more triumph, with few horsemen willing to challenge the thoroughbred, Oro had retired to start the line of racehorses that would one day become a Texas legend.

Or so Conn claimed, and there was no one in the county who doubted him.

"Our guests are starting to arrive," Crystal announced. She reached for James, who readily came from his grandmother's arms to hers, then wiggled to be set down. She took his hand to help him manage the stairs.

Bridget went to her father. She always did.

With Annabelle and Helga leading the way, Crystal and Conn locked arms and took their beloved offspring downstairs for their celebration of life and love.

AUTHOR'S NOTE

With few exceptions, the places named in *Betrayal* are real. Bushwhack Creek exists. I came upon it while driving the back roads of Kerr County in preparation for writing the book. Research failed to turn up the origin of the name, but with Comanches and outlaws once roaming the area and feuds not uncommon, we can imagine the kinds of incidents that occurred on its banks.

In the early days cypress tree's grew thick along the streams and rivers of the Texas hill country, but they were soon cut down to be used in construction. Settlements along these waterways became known as "shingle camps," hence the name of the Braden ranch.

I hope you enjoyed the story of Crystal and Conn. My next book will be Brit Iron Hand's story. In *Betrayal*, he seems very much in control. Wait until he meets a tall, leggy redhead known as Temper, who proves to be his most difficult adversary of all—a tempting woman with a mind of her own.

Evelyn Rogers
8039 Callaghan Road, Suite 102
San Antonio, TX 78230
http://www.romcom.com/rogers/

LOVE
FOREVERMORE
MADELINE
BAKER